Table of Contents

CHAPTER 1	2
CHAPTER 2	13
CHAPTER 3	21
CHAPTER 4	34
CHAPTER 5	44
CHAPTER 6	54
CHAPTER 7	59
CHAPTER 8	64
CHAPTER 9	74
CHAPTER 10	81
CHAPTER 11	85
CHAPTER 12	90
CHAPTER 13	105
CHAPTER 14	117
CHAPTER 15	124
CHAPTER 16	131
CHAPTER 17	143

AF102286

Chapter 1

The house was empty apart from my mum Marge, who was baking in the kitchen. The smell of freshly baked apple pie filled the air. It was one of the family favourites and it was a way of filling a hard-working family up fairly cheaply. She had her back to the open plan stairs that ran alongside the wall of the kitchen diner. It was 11.30 in the morning on a bright sunny day and all seemed right with the world, that is until the sounds of heavy footsteps began slowly reverberating from the bedroom above. It was as if someone was slowly stomping up and down the bedroom floor, Marge looked up at the ceiling.

Fear shattered the easy-going day as the footsteps slowly made their way to the landing at the top of the stairs. There was a pause, Mum was rooted to the spot. She stopped what she was doing and focussed on the sounds. The footsteps started slowly descending the stairs and the hairs on the back of her neck began to stand up. She could feel a sudden drop in temperature, she so desperately wanted to turn around to see who or what was there but at the same time was paralysed by the fear of seeing something she hoped didn't exist. This was madness, there was nobody else in the house, she didn't believe in the paranormal. Everything had a logical explanation she was desperately trying to rationalise what she was experiencing.

The stairs creaked with each downward step, there was little point in shouting out as mum knew nobody else was with her in the house. Maybe this was a burglar, that would at least be logical – she grabbed hold of a nearby kitchen knife – more out of bravado than self-protection. She mustered all her fortitude and slowly began to look behind her towards the stairs. The noise of the footsteps had stopped but that could mean those steps were now on the solid kitchen tiled floor heading towards her as they would make no sound on that surface. She hadn't realised but she was holding her breath. As she was finally able to see across the kitchen to the stairs, she let out a gasp of air - there was nothing to be seen. She still felt anchored, in terror, to where she stood but as she scanned the space that was the kitchen, she could see nothing out of place, nothing that shouldn't be there. A shiver went down her spine even though it was a warm day.

The sound of a neighbour's dog barking punctuated the air. It gave her a start but at least it was a normal almost reassuring noise. Of course, that was until Marge began to wonder what had set the dog off barking. It's said that dogs and cats can see or sense spirits. Is that what the dog was barking at? Her mind was racing and she needed to calm down. She would be scared of her own shadow at this rate. She could feel goose pimples on her arms and see her breath in front of her face.

Marge plucked up the courage to walk across the kitchen to the bottom of the stairs. She looked up to the landing, again nothing to see. She very slowly ascended the stairs with part of her body pressed up against the wall. Marge carried on until she could see the bedroom entrance on the left and that the door was open. She shouted, "Hello?" there was no reply but the door quickly and loudly slammed shut. She rushed to the bedroom door and tried turning the handle but it wouldn't budge. Marge decided not to hang around and quickly went down the stairs back to the kitchen. Her heart was thumping in her chest. She told herself it was a coincidence and it must have been the wind catching the door, even though she hadn't opened the window and it looked calm outside.

It's amazing sometimes what you can convince yourself of if you need some reassurance. After that she decided to do some gardening to calm her down. She knew if she needed to, she could always make a quick exit out of the back gate and she would be able to see anyone entering the kitchen through the windows. Of course, if it was the wind, there would be nothing to see! That sounded positive right now and it was just what she needed to get the day back on track and to help her calm down.

Some garden time would be therapeutic, she somehow got a great sense of satisfaction out of pulling up weeds with their roots still intact. She knew that way they wouldn't come back and she liked using the small hand trowel to dig around the border soil and deal with any bugs she came across the old-fashioned way, no need for any chemicals. She passed the time of day with a neighbour and continued her battle with the weeds. The day was turning back to normal just as something caught the corner of her eye.

Marge hesitated but then looked up at the bedroom window above the kitchen, she was shocked to see a young boy staring right at her. She was even more shocked to see a large male figure appear behind the boy and put his hand over the boy's face and pull him backwards. The boy was struggling but couldn't get free. That was enough for Marge, she charged back into the house and up the stairs. She almost ran into the bedroom pushing the door open with all the urgency she could muster. The room was empty, the only thing strange she could detect was a fusty smell that pervaded the air.

She could sense there was something wrong in that room. How could she have seen not one but two people in a room she knew to be empty and also the fact she hadn't got a clue about who either of the people were? She heard the built-in wardrobe doors rattle and she could see them moving back and forth slightly but quickly. Then the curtains blew inwards and she wondered if someone was stood there. She pushed the curtains to one side quickly but all that was to be seen was the small top part of the window open and some breeze was coming through as it was strangely now quite windy outside. Where had the sudden breeze come from? It wasn't windy when she was outside. She closed the window, which she knew she hadn't opened and figured that was what was also causing the wardrobe doors to rattle.

She looked at the back garden and there appeared to be a mini tornado swirling around, taking up some of the loose surface soil. This was crazy, a moment ago Marge had been outside and it was a bright calm day. Now there was a localised storm seemingly centred on her garden. She had never seen anything like this before and after a short while it died down just as quickly as it had started. Some of the neighbours had seen it and one was even trying to capture it on camera.

There was an old clock on the wall, one that had loud chimes and a pendulum. When Marge looked at the time, she thought it must need some attention as it was still showing the time at 11.35. She knew more than five minutes must have passed since she was in the kitchen bringing the pie out of the oven. Presumably the clock was losing time and maybe needed winding. This was an original Victorian time piece that had been bought at auction and despite the fact it would have been an expensive purchase when first made, it had been very cheap at the auction as very few people wanted these large clocks on the wall anymore, not to mention the loud chimes.

Her mind returned to why she had gone up to the bedroom. She knew what she had seen from the garden, even though it would sound ludicrous to most people, she was adamant she wasn't seeing things. If that was true, where had they gone? Her thoughts returned to the wardrobe doors especially as they had started rattling again and this time, she knew there was no draft after closing the window. She pulled the doors towards her quickly. She hadn't figured what to do if she then saw two people standing there in front of her. Fortunately, there was nothing to be seen but clothes. She moved a few of them to check and again with a sigh of relief there was nothing out of place.

She searched the entire house just to satisfy herself. There was nobody but her present. Now she began to calm down and think for a minute, she was quite chuffed with herself that she had gone back into the house and searched. She was still mystified by what she had seen and she knew if she told anybody later that she wouldn't be believed. After all, could you blame them? Two unknown people showing up at random in a bedroom, while Marge was in the house on her own with the front door locked. How would they have been able to get passed the locks and evade being seen, make it upstairs and then look out of the window! What would be the point in that? She could see how ridiculous it would sound and so she decided to keep it to herself at least for now – time for a cup of tea she thought, as she went to the cupboard looking for the Yorkshire Gold, that would help clear her mind and think more rationally.

As Marge turned on the kettle she noticed the time on the oven, it was just gone 11.35, so there must be something wrong with this clock too, but then she thought, it matches the one in the bedroom. She turned on the radio and shortly after got a time check announcing it was 11.40 precisely. Marge was stunned, in her mind at least fifteen to twenty minutes had passed yet the clocks said five minutes. She finished making a pot of tea for herself but still remained troubled by the discrepancy. She also couldn't forget seeing the two people in the bedroom when she was in the garden. It was on her mind but she had done all she could for now at least.

Marge hadn't really had a chance to read the newspaper yet so she sat in a comfy chair in the living room and decided she could spare the time to have a read while she enjoyed her tea. Marge then turned to ice as she noticed the little boy she had seen earlier had returned and was looking at her. He looked sad and dishevelled. She should have wondered where he had come from and what he was doing in her house, especially as she thought she had thoroughly searched and found no one. Instead, she felt sorry for him and wanted him to come closer.

She asked his name and he said it was, "Peter." He was wearing old fashioned looking clothes, that didn't fit him well and looked like they were older than he was. He looked very thin and troubled but still managed a smile for her. She held out her hand to try and get him to come closer, her motherly instincts meant she wanted to give him a hug. He started moving slowly closer, very cautiously but before he could reach her, the man she had also seen earlier, suddenly appeared. He abruptly pushed the boy aside and marched towards Marge. She pulled back her hand, and shouted for him to leave Peter alone.

Marge realised this man wasn't going to stop and was ignoring her protestations. She stood up quickly and was going to run out of the room but as she tried, she found herself rooted to the spot. She looked down at her feet and it was as if they were glued to the floor. She made more of an effort and managed to free her feet one at a time but they felt so heavy. For now, the man had disappeared but she knew he must still be around so that made her feel worse, she knew she was panicking. She dragged herself towards the kitchen which seemed to be somehow getting further away. This was like one of those dream sequences where the background moves further away from you. She had never experienced this before.

She persisted and was fighting to get to the living room door which led to the kitchen. She saw the young boy who was now willing her to keep going. He was encouraging her by holding out his hand, she was holding out hers towards him trying to stretch as much as she could. Again, the door sunk further into the distance. Marge could feel her heart pounding in her chest. She was mustering every ounce of effort she could and she somehow managed to get to the door where the boy was standing. She grabbed hold of his hand and ran into the kitchen, only to find her feet sinking into the tiled floor. It was like running through thick liquid toffee. She looked towards the stairs and she could see the man stood at the top on the landing. He looked angry and menacing so she headed towards the back door and the relative safety of the garden.

Every time she lifted her feet it was as if she was pulling up part of the floor with her. The boy had managed to get to the back door no problem so why couldn't she? The man was slowly and deliberately walking down the stairs, Marge was about half way into the kitchen. No matter how hard she tried she couldn't move any faster and the man was gaining on her. She looked back and he was at the bottom of the stairs, she knew he would reach her before she could make it out of the door. She was terrified, this was an intruder in her house, chasing her through some unimaginable nightmare. The man caught up with her just as she had reached the boy and the door. She opened it quickly and told the boy to go through and as he did, he disappeared – just evaporated.

The man lunged at her and grabbed Marge by the arms. She felt his touch like an electric shock to her body and screamed out loud. She sat bolt upright in her chair, the newspaper was on the floor and the radio was playing a loud song, as she thought about what had just happened, she realised she had fallen asleep. She was gasping for breath as if she had been for a run. Only a few minutes had passed but she was relieved she could put the whole incident down to a lack of sleep and maybe her overdoing it a bit. Is this what had happened in the garden, was it just a trick of the mind and had she simply allowed things to get on top of her? If that was the case, why did she now have a deep red hand print on her arm? This was very troubling, if it was a dream what had caused the mark on her arm?

Marge later went back to preparing the day's main meal and a little more time in the garden. At least when she was busy, it took her mind off other things she thought.

Thankfully from her point of view there were no more incidents that day and soon the house was comfortably full of familiar people again.

The house was a large family home, nothing special in itself, or so people thought. The five bedrooms were all upstairs along with a bathroom and toilet. One of the bedrooms had a walk-in wardrobe with latched doors on the front and a hatch to provide access to the loft or attic on the inside. The hatch had a thick heavy metal bar running along its length as additional space for clothes to be hung. It's an important point to make that this loft hatch was heavy to lift. The house was only about ten years old and was part of a modern housing estate. Previously the land had been part of Bluewater Farm which had long since ceased to provide food and was now to add to the housing stock of the growing city. There were lots of young families on the estate that would gradually get to know each other in this fairly new but friendly community.

Each house had a modest but well looked after front and back garden and people took a pride in where they lived. The children all went to the same local schools and the parents tended to be employed in decent paid jobs. There was nothing posh about the people or the estate just hard-working families raising their children to the best of their abilities.

In our house there were four brothers, mum and dad. My sister (Anne) left home to be with her new husband (Will) when I was six. Anne and I always got on well. She was a lovely person who was very thoughtful when it came to others. Her and Will had been dating for some time before they decided to get married and buy a place of their own. Will was a hard worker and was very familiar to the family as he had often been coming to the house to see Anne and was always invited for Sunday lunch.

We were strung out age wise with me being the youngest at three and a half years old when we first moved in. The oldest was then nineteen (Philip) who, the siblings thought, was a bit of a strange character. He didn't get on with them and was a loner and bully to them. My sister was second oldest with only a year between her and Philip. Then came three brothers in descending age of fourteen (Bernard), nine (Charlie) and of course me (Steve).

It was rather an open secret that there was nothing planned about the ages of the children. At least it meant the eldest two were working so helping support the youngest three. Money was tight but my parents did well by us and we never felt we were poor or lacking anything. We all had strong characters which we inherited off our parents – something I would point out later when told I was being stubborn or strong willed. Of course, the retort from my mother would come back, "You have too much to say for yourself young man!"

I shared a bedroom with the next youngest brother, much to his disgust and annoyance. We had a lovely friendly ginger cat called Shandy who loved to come on my bed and suck the cover to the bed clothes which was heavily embroidered – one of these old fashioned candlewick type. It didn't take much to make him purr and he would spend hours on that cover either asleep or pretending to be as cats tend to do.

The one thing I disliked about that house was the position of the stairs and the fact they were open to the kitchen and dining area. Remember I'm still a youngster at this point.

There was a power socket at the far end of the kitchen with a red light to show it was working. When I went to bed, I had to use the stairs and all I could see with the landing light on was a very dark kitchen area with a red light looking at me as I ascended the stairs. That light always seemed to manifest a face somehow to me and I would go upstairs with my back firmly against the wall. I would get so far and then run the last part and dart in to bed. Diving under the covers was always more reassuring than it should have been. If anything had been there, I'm not sure what protection the bed covers would have provided.

The master bedroom was above an archway that allowed a footpath to pass underneath. It seems strange now when I write this but it was common on the estate. The warmest room in the house was the downstairs living room as it had underfloor heating which was fantastic to walk on in winter in bare feet when finishing getting dressed ready for school. The house had large windows especially at the back and some of them could even turn fully inside out to aid cleaning. They were floor to ceiling at the back of the house which was seen as very modern and great for allowing lots of light in. Not so great however to a youngster who sees something untoward in the garden.

Mum and dad (Henry), liked to take a two-week holiday in the summer and they would take the two youngest children with them. It wasn't cool for the older ones to come along. We weren't very sophisticated – these were the day's before there were affordable computers at home and mobile phones didn't exist yet.

The holiday destination was frequently the same as we all knew the area and enjoyed the delights of a typical seaside town with amusements, a good sandy beach and lots of doughnut and hot drink stands. I could watch those little marvels being made for ages. It was quite mesmerising watching the machine drop the hoop shaped batter in the hot oil and seeing the part cooked doughnuts travel along this hot river then get automatically flipped over and finally pulled out by a moving chain mechanism on to a bed of sugar. All ready to be put into a bag and sold piping hot, I can smell them now!

Dad was a very hard working, down to earth guy who did his best to provide for his family and he loved his garden – that was his hobby, in particular growing tomatoes in the greenhouse and Dahlias in the garden. Each day he would come home and check on his tomato plants to see if the green fruit had turned red. It was the first thing he did when he came home from work. He would then water them and come back into the house.

I remember this year one of my siblings having the nerve to attach one of mum's red tomatoes, she had bought from the shop, to one of dad's plants with some green cotton. They were very careful to make it look authentic. Dad came home and first of all we could tell he was very happy until he tried picking the ripe tomato off his plant and saw it was attached with some cotton. He pulled it off and came back into the kitchen asking who was the joker? Nobody dared say anything. Mum couldn't help but laugh quite loudly and dad scowled. She told him to stop being such a grouch and that they were only having a bit of fun and that it served him right for being so obsessed about his greenhouse.

The rest of us were quite relieved that mum had diffused the situation and we all had smiles on our faces. I never was totally sure who had dared place that tomato but I admired their bravery.

Nothing different was expected to happen this summer as I was approaching my tenth birthday, that August. We would stay self-catering in a holiday apartment which gave us the freedom we liked to come and go as we pleased. Nothing different indeed, for us but not what can be said for the house we called home that year. Little did mum know but Anne, Will and Bernard along with a few of their friends were planning to hold a party at the house with the highlight being a séance using a Ouija board. What could possibly go wrong?

I guess I should say at this point that the oldest sibling, Philip, was not a popular member of the family. He was deeply religious, (nothing wrong about that of course), but very secretive about his comings and goings. He had two very separate lives – the one he showed us that was of a bully and thoroughly nasty character and the one he showed people outside the home – a very obliging and likeable individual who was a church goer, he was also a member of some secret group.

Needless to say, Philip wasn't invited to the party being planned and everyone just assumed he would keep out of the way.

They had planned the party for the following weekend. That would give them plenty of time to plan and to clean up afterwards as it was the middle of the holiday. They invited lots of friends over and bought plenty of beers, spirits and snacks. They wanted to get a group together to conduct a séance but they wanted to try it out first so they knew what they were doing – if only! So, the day before, they had a practice session. It wouldn't be long before they would regret their actions.

They had researched what a Ouija board should look like and then made one from pieces of card and positioned them on the kitchen table. Bernard and his girlfriend had made everything that was needed and also got some large pillar candles. Everyone was getting quite excited about the Ouija session and were thinking of questions they wanted to ask.

In the practise session was Anne and Will with Bernard and Jenny. The house was quiet and they decided to wait until around 10.00 pm as this would make sure it was dark. They had all been drinking beer to get themselves in the mood, or was that to pluck up the necessary courage? They had borrowed a book from a local library about Victorian seances and they used this to learn the sort of things to say and do supposedly to have a successful session.

They laid out the table with lots of candles around the room, the letters and symbols around the outside of the table in a circular pattern. They also had "Yes" and "No" on different cards. They had a small drinking glass to use as a planchette. The four sat evenly spaced around the table and double checked in the book what they were to do. They would hold hands to start with to see if they could summon any spirits, then they would ask questions.

They were all getting a little nervous but decided to go ahead. They lit the candles, turned off the lights and held hands. Anne had volunteered to lead the séance so she started by inviting spirits to enter the room and to make their presence known. She repeated the invitation and asked for the spirits help in answering questions. Everything was very quiet to start off with. Jenny asked if they were doing it right. They put their hands on the table this time with their fingers spread out and made sure they were still touching each other.

Anne tried again to invite spirits into the room. Again, nothing happened, no response, no noise or anything. So rather disappointedly they decided to try asking questions. They all placed one finger on the upside-down glass and Anne asked if anyone was present to answer questions. No movement. Jenny asked if Bernard and her would get married. The glass began to move to the yes rather quickly. You didn't have to be Sherlock Holmes to realise Jenny was pushing the glass. They all had a bit of an argument about it and Anne and Will said they were supposed to be taking this more seriously, not treating it as a game.

At that point there was a loud bang from the bedroom above the kitchen. It was the most active room in the house and the four were suddenly very quiet. Jenny asked if the others had heard the noise. They all said of course it was too loud to miss. Will said it was probably the cat knocking something over in the bedroom. Anne and Bernard knew that Shandy, the cat, didn't go into that room so it had to be something else.

BANG! Another loud noise from the bedroom followed by two loud thumps. The four of them were stunned and began frantically looking at each other as if one of them had the explanation. Will and Bernard said they would go and have a look to see if they could tell what was going on. Anne and Jenny were adamant they weren't moving from the kitchen. Will got up and told Bernard to follow him. The two slowly ascended the stairs with the landing light on. Neither of them was enthusiastic about what they were doing but they knew they couldn't just leave it. The sounds were too loud to just ignore.

The two of them got to the top of the stairs. The bedroom where the sounds had come from was on the left. They slowly approached the closed door. As Will placed his hand on the door handle there was a tremendous thump on the door from the inside. Will and Bernard both jumped back in shock. Anne and Jenny both let out a scream and shouted, "What was going on?" and "Why did you do that?" Will shouted down that it wasn't them. After plucking up every bit of courage they had, Will and Bernard approached the door a second time. Will was determined to open the door quickly so in a rush he turned the door handle and pushed the door inwards with some force all in one movement. The door opened and slammed against the door stop.

Will and Bernard both looked at each other and paused before they went into the bedroom. Slowly they entered and Bernard turned on the light. Instantly they could see the room was empty. Nothing was damaged or even appeared to be out of place. The only thing of note was the wardrobe cupboard doors were wide open and the loft cover was lifted and moved to one side. They listened for a while but they heard no sounds. The girls shouted to ask if everything was alright. Will told them about the cupboard doors and hatch cover. Suddenly the bedroom light turned off. The clock on the wall chimed for 10.30 which startled Will and Bernard who looked at each other, now in just the light that was coming from the landing.

There was a bang on the floor that made them both jump. Then there was the sound of slow heavy footsteps on the bedroom floor but nothing to see. They were coming from the cupboard and heading towards the bedroom door. Will and Bernard both froze for a few seconds, not saying anything. The bedroom door slammed shut Bernard rushed towards it and tried the handle but it wouldn't budge. Will pushed him to one side and pulled on the handle with everything he had but he couldn't open it either. Will let go of the door handle and as he did, the door slowly opened on its own with a creak coming from the hinges. The two guys weren't going to hang around. They rushed out of the bedroom to the landing then paused to catch their breath. They looked back at the bedroom and saw the shape of a dark figure appearing to look right at them.

Anne and Jenny, both presumed the footsteps they could hear was from their two guys walking around. Even when the sounds reached the landing and then slowly descended the stairs, that's what they thought. Right up to the point where they should be able to see who was coming down the stairs but there was nobody to see. Will and Bernard had composed themselves a little by now and rushed down the stairs into the kitchen. All four of them looked at the open plan stairs and still they could hear someone very slowly descending them.

They all looked at each other. The temperature had dropped so much you could now see your breath in front of you. Anne turned on the kitchen light but there was nothing to see, the footsteps stopped. There was one final sound as the bedroom door slammed shut – the one Will had desperately tried to open and then had done so on its own accord. They decided this was because the hatch cover was off and the cupboard doors were open. The two questions of course they ignored was, who had opened the doors and moved the hatch cover? The two guys thought it best not to mention the dark figure as they must have imagined it.

With no more noises, they decided to have another drink and put away the Ouija pieces and candles. They said they would forget the session the following night with the partygoers around. They would settle for drinks, snacks and someone acting as DJ.

It was Saturday evening and people started arriving for the party. A lot of people had been invited. How my siblings expected to get away with this I have no idea as this amount of people were bound to do something that would be noticeable later. I guess they thought they would just need to do a lot of cleaning up and nobody would be any the wiser.

Will was to take care of the music and if the party got too warm, they could open the large windows and even spill out into the back garden to provide extended space for drinking and dancing. There were plenty of garden chairs for anyone wanting to cool off and have a drink and chat outside.

The night went well and everyone was getting drunk and having a good time. Some people did spill outside with drinks and started smoking and even telling each other stories. Recounting short ghost stories as people seem to do when they've had too much to drink. It was getting late and a few people were leaving already when the group in the garden decided to cosy up and try scaring each other. They started off by each telling part of a ghost story they were making up as they went along. The garden was lit by the lights from the house but they thought it would be fun to get a couple of candles to help the atmosphere.

There was a group of five outside all telling their part of the story, each trying to spook the rest of them. All of a sudden, a scream came from one of the girls, Gill. Everyone was startled and one of them asked what was wrong. Gill said she had looked up at an upstairs window of the house and thought she saw a figure standing there but that she definitely saw two red eyes looking at her. At first the others thought this was Gill's attempt at scaring them but she was getting upset and insisted it was genuine. Anne had heard the scream and gone outside to see what was going on. When she looked up at the bedroom there was nothing to see but it was the bedroom above the kitchen Gill was pointing to.

Gradually the party started to wind down as more people left until the only guests still present were the five outside. They had calmed Gill down but were still quite tense about what had happened. Alcohol of course was helping them dismiss it as a reflection of some sort and they were talking about how they had all been having a good time with the music and what a great job Will had done.

Then Bernard said, "Maybe we should have that séance after all." Everybody looked at him and Anne said, "No!" She was out voted as most people just said it would be fun and the fact, they didn't take it seriously. Strange how a short while ago, Gill was taking the red eyes in the window very seriously. It's amazing what affect a few drinks can have on people's behaviour.

They decided they would hold the séance in the back garden so they could all take part. They dotted lots of candles around the garden and arranged the Ouija letters and symbols around a large outside table. The inside kitchen lights were left on. They all sat around and Anne asked them to join hands. It was like the day before when they had held a rehearsal, nothing happened to start with and everyone was telling each other how brave they were and that there was no such thing as the paranormal. Anne had everyone lower their hands to the table but to stay in physical contact with each other through their fingers.

Anne called on the spirits of the departed to join them and to make their presence known. There was a pause, they all looked at each other expectantly. Still nothing, then one of them heard some rustling in the garden, which dad had filled with huge dahlias. Anne asked if this was a spirit trying to make themselves noticed. Half the group placed their fingers on the upside-down glass they had used the day before as a planchette. Anne repeated the question. The glass moved quickly to yes. Gill gasped, Will and Bernard were looking intently at the dahlias to see if they moved. Anne was focussed on the table, concentrating intently.

The rustling got louder and they could see the large dahlia plants swaying in the far corner of the garden. Then it was like a rush with the plants being parted as if something was walking between them and pushing them to either side only quickly. Everyone was scared and focussed on the plants. Gill looked to the upstairs window and there were the red eyes again, she let out an ear splitting scream and pointed to the window. Everyone looked and saw there was the outline of a figure. The only facial feature they could make out was the two red eyes. Two large plants nearest to where they were sat snapped and they all jumped at once expecting to see something leap out at them but nothing did. There was just the evidence of damaged plants. They got back around the table and Anne asked who this was that was causing the damage. The glass moved to the letter, "M." Then, "E." Bernard said in a rather puzzled tone, "ME?" Anne asked if "ME" referred to the figure in the bedroom and the glass quickly moved to, "Yes." They all looked at each other, this was really scaring them and making them regret they had ever thought about a Ouija board session.

The lights flickered in the house. Will said they should call it a night but Anne wanted to carry on. Jenny and Bernard said they should find out what the entity wanted. With people's fingers back on the glass she asked the name of the entity. It spelled out the name, "FREDERICK." When Anne asked what Frederick wanted the glass spelled out, "SOULS." This was a chilling response. Anne asked rather shocked, why do you want souls? The answer spelled out this time was, "TO TRADE." They were all shocked at this and there were several arguments about whether or not to stop. Some of them carried on and asked for friendly spirits to show themselves. With that a gust of wind came and blew out all of the candles. There was a loud and terrible high-pitched blood curdling shriek from a corner of the garden. At that point everyone decided they wanted to finish and go inside the house rather quickly. They had made a basic mistake they hadn't closed down the Ouija session properly. They had forgotten their research in their haste to go inside. These sort of events, should be closed down properly and a blessing given to stop any unwanted spirits being able to come through. They had left the door open!

Everyone felt they needed a drink to help them calm down, soon after, the final guests left. The four of them were left with a lot of mess to clear up and they had to come up with a story to convince dad about what had happened in the garden was vandalism – they knew he would be annoyed when he saw his prised dahlias in a state.

They spent most of Sunday trying to clean up and remove all evidence that a party had ever taken place. This was easier said than done but they did their best.

Chapter 2

Our holiday was fun as usual with dad and Charlie going on a fishing boat some days with mum and me going to the cinema or playing crazy golf and such. Mum and dad would get their alone time in the evenings when they could go to the local clubs and have a drink and a dance. All was well until one evening Charlie and me were laid on sofas in the main room. We were watching television and just had some side lights on.

There was an external door directly off the main room leading to a small garden surrounded by a wooden fence. We both heard footsteps coming down the path and thought mum and dad had come back early. The trouble was there was only one set of footsteps and they didn't match those of either mum or dad. Charlie turned the volume down on the television and we both concentrated on the door which had a glass panel in the top so you could see who was there. As it was night there was a curtain that had been pulled across the door for privacy. There was some light in the garden coming from a nearby lamppost and it was enough to create a shadow from anyone approaching. The footsteps appeared to move around the garden footpath that ran alongside the house.

Through the thin curtain it looked like someone was standing by the door. It was possible to see a silhouette. We looked at each other but said nothing. We looked at the door and saw the circular handle turn as the person outside was trying to gain entrance. Charlie shouted, the door knob stopped turning and spun back. It still looked like someone was stood at the other side of the door but they made no movement. Charlie bravely approached the door and turned on the outside light by using the switch on our side of the door. He also quickly pushed the curtain to one side and starting shouting for the person outside to leave. We could both now clearly see into the garden with the light on but there was no one there. I think that was actually scarier than if we had seen someone running away. Charlie left the outside light on but pulled the curtain back over the door.

We should have heard footsteps making a swift getaway from the back door when Charlie shouted, but we hadn't. There was a shadow we could see through the curtain so someone had been there. So why had we heard them approach but not run away and how had they managed to disappear so quickly. This was quite disturbing for both of us.

Charlie did his best to reassure me and made sure the door was still locked – that helped me feel better and he reminded me the key was in the lock and on our side. We carried on watching television with no more interruptions until mum and dad came home. They knocked on the door and we had recognised their footsteps. Charlie opened the curtain and then the door and asked why they had come back early. Mum said something had made her feel that they should. At that point we both told them what had happened and they were both concerned and pleased they had returned when they did.

Thankfully the night was quiet and when we discussed what had happened over breakfast, we all put it down to someone testing doors to see if any were unlocked and that we would have to make doubly sure that they were.

The following night came a repeat of what had happened. Heavy, deliberate but slow footsteps on the garden path just outside the holiday apartment. Charlie had made sure the door was locked and that not only was the key in the lock, it was partly turned so that it couldn't be forced out by someone using a key from outside. This time you could clearly see a figure stood on the other side of the door as a silhouette through the thin door curtain. The door handle began to turn slowly. Charlie and me both looked at each other both terrified someone was trying to break in.

Charlie rushed to the door and turned on the outside light. The silhouetted figure disappeared and the door handle stopped turning. The strange thing was, there was no noise of the person running away down the path, just like the previous night. We waited and listened but everything was quiet. Charlie turned off the outside light and was about to move the curtain to one side to see what was happening but as the light went out the silhouette of the figure returned. We both shouted for the person to go away and that we would call the police. Charlie turned the light back on and tried to glimpse behind the curtain but he couldn't see anything. He pulled back the curtain and the only thing to be seen was the garden. There wasn't even any wildlife that we could have said made a noise. There was nothing!

When mum and dad came back, they asked if everything had been quiet. They could tell by our reaction that something wasn't right. We didn't want to spoil their evening so we did our best to play it down and they said the following night we would all go out as a family, which put a smile on our faces.

Later that week came a visit from Philip to the holiday apartment. It was towards the end of the second week. He announced to mum that there had been a party the previous Saturday night and that the house was in a mess. What Philip got out of this I can only speculate but it fitted his character and it couldn't have come too much of a surprise to him to find out that after this, most of the siblings wanted nothing more to do with him.

Unfortunately, the holiday ended a few days early as mum wanted to see for herself what had happened at the house and also to remonstrate with the conspirators. I was glad I had been with them in the holiday apartment so could just be a witness to events and not get told off.

It's not too relevant to go into the details of how mum dealt with the party organisers, suffice to say they were suitably regretful and that no repeat ever happened although for some strange reason they were allowed to use the Ouija board on the kitchen table every now and then.

I can't say that the happenings in the house were as a direct result of these Ouija sessions as I've already mentioned some things happened prior to them but for sure events got livelier after they started.

Everybody experienced the sound of footsteps the next floor up when the house was quiet. We would openly discuss it and dad would insist it was the floor boards expanding and contracting as a reaction to the sun and time of day. As most of us pointed out on numerous occasions, that didn't account for the noises happening in an order that made it sound like someone walking across the bedroom floor.

Dad had heard the floor walking too but wasn't a believer in anything supernatural and just thought we were all trying to scare each other into believing something was happening when there was just a mundane explanation. Dad lacked the imagination to make that leap into the unknown which made the situation quite frustrating for the rest of us. Things would go missing or be moved and dad would accuse us of playing a joke on him when in reality none of us had moved or taken anything.

Our beautiful ginger tabby cat, Shandy would sometimes scare me by staring at something that I couldn't see. He would be having a wash or something then stop and stare into the distance as if intently watching something or someone but there was nothing for me to see. Very occasionally he would growl while staring which was so unusual as he was such a friendly soul. I would stare in the same direction and even feel the hair stand up on the back of my neck but not see anything. When I told the others they just said it was a cat thing – that they do that sometimes. As for me they said I was imagining things.

I guess that's the penalty you pay for being the youngest of a stretched-out family. You're too young to be taken seriously. Just as well I had a strong enough character not to give up expressing what was happening when I was playing on my own or with friends but with no older siblings around.

The second largest bedroom had a lot of activity associated with it. This is the one with the loft access panel in the substantial built-in wardrobe. The doors to the wardrobe had their own fastening so they couldn't just open on their own. They opened outwards and to a sizeable walk-in clothes area. The ceiling to this wardrobe contained a large rectangular panel at least a yard square. Built into that reinforced wood panel was a two-inch diameter hollow brass tube that was meant as additional clothes hanging space. That panel was very heavy and sat in a recess in the ceiling to give it a draft proof seal. I guess the previous occupant had made sure no cold winds were going to come from this hatch.

The original purpose of the hatch was to provide an access point to the loft or attic. Once you moved the hatch out of the way by lifting and pushing it to one side, you could see a set of steps that could be pulled down using a special hooked metal rod. The steps would then give easy access to the loft space which had been converted to give additional storage space for the house. This was a huge open area that ran the full width and length of the house. There were two windows but most of the light came from a large central electrical fitting and some small wall lights.

Many times, whoever was sleeping in that bedroom would complain that the wardrobe doors would be open in the morning after being shut at night and that the heavy loft panel had been moved to one side. Dad would just say it was the wind lifting it from its housing. This is why I have emphasised how heavy that panel was – no wind we ever had could get into the roof space and suck that panel up, which is what would have had to have happened.

Our cat, Shandy would never go into that bedroom, if ever he thought about going in, he would always stop short and turn around although sometimes he would do that stop and stare if the door was left wide open.

I never felt like I wanted to spend any time in that bedroom and I wondered if it had anything to do with the fact that when we first moved to the house it was Philip's bedroom who was very religious and had several crucifixes in there. Religious banners were on the walls and there were lots of candles on the sideboard. He liked classical music and fancied himself as a conductor. He was certainly a very different personality to the rest of us and by being so secretive when he was heading out, he didn't exactly instil much empathy or trust from the rest of us. As it turns out we must have been good judges of character. The older siblings were convinced he was involved in some secret society. Mum and dad just said to leave him alone and that he wasn't hurting anybody. The others weren't convinced but had no evidence to support their thinking. Anyone asking Philip where he had been the previous night was met with at best stony silence and at worst a tirade of abuse. There was no doubt about it thinking back he was an outright bully. You know what they say, you can pick your friends but you can't pick your family.

Once Philip was asleep it was almost impossible to wake him. I always thought he must have been taking sleeping tablets as nobody can sleep like that normally. On a weekend I would get the job of waking him up for breakfast and I would sometimes bounce on the bed and shake Philip all to no avail. Of course, I would persist until finally he came out of his coma-like state he called sleep.

I wondered if he took something to make sure the disturbances in the loft didn't affect him or if he was somehow responsible for triggering the happenings through some sort of out of body experience like astral projection or could in some way allow his essence to leave his body and when I was trying to wake him up, I was forcing his body to come back to its normal state.

When I did manage to wake him, it was never with a start, it was always a gradual waking up which amazed me after the amount of effort I had to put in to get him to come around.

Philip was a very dark character in the house who seemed to generate a heavy atmosphere in the home. I always felt more at ease when he was absent – either at work or out on one of his secretive meetings. Nobody could ever get out of him where he had been or where he was going. He did have some insignia, rings and the like on his sideboard and some regalia in his wardrobe but he must have worn a coat over the top as I never saw him wearing any of it. I know he would come and go at some strange times during the night. Mum and dad just seemed to put up with it as he didn't bring any trouble back to the house. No bad phone calls and no unruly visitors. Come to think of it he rarely had any visitors at all.

He had a big old car he would park on the street. I occasionally got to ride in it if he was taking mum somewhere and I was dragged along to stay out of mischief. Why he had such a big car when there was just him, I had no idea but I got the feeling he wanted to be able to transport items around. He kept it very clean both inside and out just like he did with his bedroom – all very tidy and in its place. He liked a very distinctive aftershave that I wasn't keen on as it lingered long after he had left the room. He must have almost bathed in it as all his clothes and his room had its very pungent odour.

Philip worked shifts at a local factory which meant sometimes he was working during the day and others he would be working through the night. They had a 24-hour shift pattern as the business was doing well. They produced bespoke furniture for the high end of the market. Philip was a foreman and part of his role was to inspect the finished product prior to it going out to the customer. That's what gave rise to his shift patterns. Trucks would leave the factory as soon as they had a full load which helped them keep the amount of space they needed for storage to a minimum. Of course, a large amount of space was taken up with storage of raw materials and they had a large stock of expensive timber for the discerning customer to choose from when placing an order. I didn't know at the time but one of their specialties was to produce items such as desks, boxes and other furniture with hidden compartments. They produced modern looking items as well as reproduction antique looking pieces that would fit into any style of house.

The customers included the rich and powerful and discretion was their watchword. Anyone working on secret compartment pieces had to be vetted to make sure they were of honest character and they had to sign a secrecy document stating they would never discuss their work with anyone including friends or family. This was all part of the complete package sold to the customer to reassure them that their important documents or belongings were safe. Of course, all this was perfectly legal – what the customer stored in these, sometimes substantial compartments, was of no interest to the owners of the company, just that they got paid handsomely for their products.

Part of Philip's role was to check these specialist pieces over to make sure that the concealed compartments were exactly that and that to the untrained eye, there was no evidence of their presence. The obvious tell-tale sign of such compartments was the overall dimensions of a piece. If it was a chest of drawers for example, it would be pretty obvious if a drawer had a false front or was small compared to the outside measurements. The company had thought about such things and covered up very well with decoration, hollowed out legs, false panels and hidden trigger points where you would least expect them to be. In the large pieces they even fitted metal weights so that anyone trying to get a clue from the light weight would be put off the scent by it feeling very heavy and looking substantial.

All this fitted Philip's character of secrecy and his coming and going at strange hours, he could just blame on his job. Once he had satisfied himself that the object was up to standard, he would apply a red ink quality mark with the initials of the company in it. This was a triangle with BF (Bespoke Furnishings) inside. The company had been established for a very long time and were proud to announce on their marketing material that they had been trading continuously for over two hundred and fifty years.

One night when Philip was setting off supposedly for a night shift, Bernard decided to follow him on his motorbike. He was careful to keep a distance so as not to be spotted and sure enough after a while he realised, they weren't heading to the factory. Philip parked up outside a large stone building, quite an impressive looking one from the outside with large double doors. Above the entrance was a large triangle with an eye in the centre. He locked his car and went up the entrance steps, opened one of the doors and went inside. Bernard watched and wondered if he would be able to see anything. There were no windows low down and he decided to leave it at that until he noticed there was another much smaller and less ostentatious side door.

Bernard decided he was going to turn detective and try and get inside to see what was going on. He waited a while after seeing others entering – all men. He then went over to the side door and much to his surprise it was unlocked. It was a form of emergency fire door with an outside handle which was quite unusual but I guess it was so they could get back in after an alarm test and evacuation. When the building was in use, all fire doors had to be unlocked from the inside for safety reasons.

Inside the side entrance was a partition wall with another door and stained-glass panels from half way up. This opened into what looked like a main hall. Bernard carefully looked through the stained-glass and he could see a lot of men seated on chairs. There was a small number of others on what looked like a raised stage area in rather grander looking chairs and there was an organ at the far side. A figure was sat at the organ playing some classical music. It took a while but Bernard realised the figure was Philip. Everybody was dressed formally and had varying forms of regalia – sashes, waistbands and the ones on the stage appeared to be wearing gold chains and rings, presumably, to signify their rank.

There were lots of symbols around the walls and some writing above the stage in what Bernard assumed to be Latin. The triangle with the eye at the centre was in several places painted in gold. The organ stopped playing and one of the people on the stage began talking. It was very muffled and Bernard could only make out some of the words. It sounded like they were going to have some new members joining them and that their initiation would happen at the next meeting.

Bernard was about to leave but then he heard Philip being asked to address the hall about something. Voices coming from the hall were quite muffled but Bernard did his best to make out as much as possible of what was being said. Philip told them he was having trouble at home. Bernard felt the urge to interrupt but managed to stay in control as Philip carried on. He was being specific about his bedroom and explained about the attic and the open doors and loft cover. Philip went on to add that he was sensitive to certain presences from beyond this reality. He always did have a sense for the dramatic but he had his audience enthralled.

Philip went on to say he felt a strong entity was somehow attached or connected to the house or maybe items in the attic. He also said he felt the presence seemed to have a link to a secret society and the image he described was also one they used in their hall. That of the eye within a triangle. This caused a murmur in the room but as he stated, that symbol had been adopted many times and was construed to mean different things to different groupings. To them it was a watchful eye, a protective symbol that members would look out for each other. Philip asked for help from volunteers for research into this other society and the entity and if possible, to banish it and to leave the house peaceful. One of the people from the stage addressed the gathering and said they should take what had been said seriously, especially as it was possible there could be a link to their society. The last thing they wanted was any possible bad publicity but also the fact that Philip was a member asking for help and they always should take such requests as a priority.

Philip continued that there were some old objects in the attic that didn't belong to the family and that it was possible that these were somehow linked to the activity. This was looking like a long diatribe and Bernard felt he had heard enough and slipped out without anyone seeing him. He returned home and told the rest of his siblings what he had heard and seen.

None of the other's realised Philip was sensitive to paranormal activity and they wondered if it was just him building up his part, making himself sound more important. It would account for his deep sleeping if indeed he was using this time to somehow have out of body experiences in the spirit world. They were now all intrigued and wanted to know if there was any truth in what he had said. The only one of us who sort of got on with Philip was me, so the rest of them said I had to speak to him about this and see what reaction he had. I didn't fancy this one little bit as he could be quite aggressive when he wanted to be. The others however insisted, so it was either have all of them keep on at me or agree to risk speaking to Philip – this could only go one way.

The next day was Saturday and as luck would have it, I had chance to be alone with Philip and it was a day off for him. I decided to be very polite and ask permission to ask some personal questions. He stopped what he was doing and was clearly intrigued as he put down the book he was reading and told me to go ahead. I plucked up my courage and mentioned his deep sleep, no response. I asked what he thought to sleeping in his bedroom and he didn't say much – this was like getting blood out of a stone. I could tell he was doing a lot of thinking by the expression on his face. I said it was obvious he was very religious to which he just raised an eyebrow and half nodded. I then asked if he was sensitive to anything going on in the bedroom. This brought a scowl and I thought I was done for but again nothing audible, came out of his mouth. He was making this as difficult as he possibly could.

At this point I was getting ready just to ask the obvious question and get ready to run out at his response. I asked if he could leave his body in his sleep. He smiled and said we could all do that when we sleep. I said no not dreams, could he move to other places and see other things before returning to his body and waking up. He looked at me intently and asked who had put me up to these questions. I insisted it was me as I was the one who got the job of waking him up and had just wondered if this was what he was doing. He said that it was only that I was the youngest that I would have thought of this as it was sort of a child's mind at work trying to fathom things out. He said if he had mentioned this to any of the other siblings, they would have laughed but as I had been the one to ask and in a serious way, that he would tell me about it.

Philip said that he felt there was something odd about his bedroom and he wondered if it had been a reaction to his religious beliefs and crucifixes etc. He also said that he knew from a young age that he could pick up on things most of the people around him couldn't. He claimed to be able to see people who had passed on. For once he was choosing his words carefully, presumably not to scare me. He said when it first started, he had been scared but then had got used to it and if anything, as he got older this ability had become stronger. He said when he was in one of those deep sleep's I tried to wake him up from, he could hear me calling his name and get a sense of me shaking him and that he should return to his body. He said he had the ability not really to be asleep but to lie on his bed, close his eyes and after a short period of meditation, he could feel himself travel to other places. He had to think of where to go first and then he would travel there. Sometimes it would be far off places other times it would be somewhere close by, like wandering around the house.

I asked if it was him, we could hear wandering around the house. He laughed and said that when he was travelling like this, he made no sound. He said he had looked around the attic on one of his out of body walkabouts and got a shock when he had seen a young boy up there and that when he had tried to speak to him, a much more malevolent adult male spirit had shown up and had reacted quite angrily. Philip said he felt it was him that was causing the noises in the house as somehow, he could make his physical presence known unlike most other apparitions he had come across.

Philip told me he was asking people he knew to try and help deal with this entity and that they were trying to find out who it was and how they could get him to move on. He said he had looked in the attic and seen some small boxes and other bits that looked like they could have been manufactured at his factory only a long time ago. He wondered if somehow it was associated with this male presence as his clothing was very old fashioned looking and the boxes could be of a similar age. Philip said he hadn't really examined the pieces properly yet to look for hidden compartments but he felt sure there must be some. I was quite taken a back as to how pleasant Philip had been and how open he was about his out of body movements. When I asked who he had spoken to for help, he reverted to his secretive self and said that was not for me to worry about and none of my business. The brief pleasant discussion was over and I was at least relieved he had told me what he had been doing. This all made perfect sense to me at my young age whereas older minds would probably just scoff at the suggestion of someone being able to do this.

Chapter 3

Mum was very houseproud and inevitably one day she decided she wanted to check out the loft to see if it needed a good tidy. She noticed the smell of Philip's aftershave. He had never mentioned going into the loft. What was up here that could be of interest to him?

The previous occupants of the home had left a considerable number of things up there and so far, nobody had gone up to check out if anything was worth keeping or to put it all in a rubbish skip. Me being the curious type decided to help – it was an opportunity to go into the loft but not on my own and I wanted to make the most of it.

It was a bright sunny day but the two windows in the loft didn't provide enough light for such a large area so the light fittings were essential to make sense of the contents stored mostly in boxes. Not much was labelled so it would be a long job to sort out what was actually up there and then decide if it was useful.

It was quite dusty up there as you might expect. The floor of the loft had been fitted out with wood which made it easy to sweep and I guess that was the idea. The first thing to do was to have a quick sort through everything and remove unwanted objects so that the rest could be considered and put back neatly for possible future use or sale. We spent most of that day on this task and then passing things down to the bedroom below and eventually onto the front path. The house came with a storage room so items not for keeping could go in there while they were disposed of one way or another.

Most of what ended up in the storage room were old clothes, some tools that were passed their best and lots of assorted junk that should have been binned in the first place instead of finding a home in the loft. This accounted for probably half of the contents, which meant the items left had plenty of space to be stored properly so they could be labelled and recycled in some way. Some could be sent to a jumble sale and some might be used by a member of the family.

I looked at the clothes as mum was bundling them up and I was intrigued as they were very old fashioned in style. They looked like they could be used as fancy dress and mum just said they must be old costumes that had been worn to dressing up parties or maybe even come from a theatre. She could tell they were old in style but just presumed they were modern made reproductions. There was an old-style nurse's uniform and some old male dress clothes along with more manual boiler suits and even some everyday street clothes. Mum thought they would probably be quite welcome in a charity shop as they would likely sell quickly.

Among the treasure trove was a very old looking Ouija board and planchette. This had far more character than the home made one my siblings had used on occasion. The sight of it didn't make me smile. This was an item that had clearly been used many times before and had some unusual markings on it – ones that I hadn't seen before. The writing looked old fashioned in style and lots of strange symbols in addition to the usual letters. It was quite a large board that was clearly meant to be set on a large table when being used. The writing was in gold paint on very dark wood. I was sure my siblings would jump at the chance to test this board out but that filled me with a dread and I wasn't even sure why.

One thing I noticed in the loft, despite the wood floor, there wasn't much creaking during the day that dad had always used as the excuse for sounds coming from upstairs. It was a bright day that warmed up and then cooled down considerably but no great noises coming from the expansion and contraction of the wood. That was one thing to note and was another thing I didn't like thinking too much about. If dad was wrong, then that raised the question, what else made the sounds? I noticed one time when I was taking rubbish items downstairs that I could hear noises mum was making as she continued her sorting and cleaning. I could hear her footsteps and moving boxes around – the dragging along the floor.

In fact, when I tested the sounds coming from the loft in different parts of the house, I found they could be heard throughout. Some sounds were more muffled depending on which room I went in but still you could make those sounds out very clearly. They were no expansion or contraction they were easily identifiable as to where they were coming from. I even went as far as to get mum to go downstairs while I moved around so she could hear how clear the sounds were. I'm guessing it was to do with the fact the wooden floor was sort of connected to the house by the beams underneath that were part of the house structure. That and the fact that the roof space acted like a sound box for the rest of the house. The discovery that the loft space acted like this added a whole new dimension to sounds I had heard around the house – always coming from upstairs – now appeared much more menacing.

The cleaning day went mostly according to plan and some interesting objects were found – some clearly antique like a small child's wheelchair and some Victorian style wooden wall plaques with sayings on them like, "Children should be seen and not heard." I thought about the previous owners then and considered how strange it was to buy such a thing and then to keep it in the loft.

There was a collection of old black and white photos of people all looking very sombre, as they tended too then, there was even some of a cemetery and individual graves. Looking at that collection gave me a shiver down my spine and thankfully mum had decided to try and give those to a museum, she put them in a box downstairs to show people – some had names on the back.

Then there was the rectangular box with inlaid decoration. This was clearly well made and was probably antique. It was a substantial and quite heavy piece despite the fact it wasn't that big. Marge handled it carefully, not because it looked fragile but because it looked of high quality. She looked for the key among the rest of the items in the cardboard box and found it tucked in the corner. She put the key in the lock carefully so she wouldn't cause any scratches. She turned the key and the lock obligingly clicked open. When she opened the lid, the main light in the loft exploded sending pieces of glass everywhere. It made mum and me jump, she quickly closed the lid of the box again and locked it.

She decided that was enough sorting and cleaning in the loft for the day. The rest of the boxes could wait but before we could leave a very sinister figure appeared. It started out as a shadow figure and it blocked our way out of the attic. We were both terrified and held our breath. Mum asked the figure what it wanted but there was no response. Then the figure changed to that of a large man, tall and muscular with old fashioned clothes of high quality. He was an impressive sight but not in a pleasant way, this was an angry looking individual who was looking intently at what we were doing. I plucked up all my courage and shouted, "What do you want?" He replied simply, "YOU!" I took in a sharp breath at that as I wasn't expecting it.

Mum tried to push me behind her but there was no way I was going to let her face this thing alone so I did my best to stand firm. His eyes were staring right at mine, it was like looking into the darkness, the sort of thing that every youngster is afraid of in their wardrobe or under the bed – here he was standing at the other end of the attic. He moved forward and his steps were heavy and made a lot of noise. I grabbed a torch, turned it on and shone it at his eyes. He didn't seem to like it and he stopped moving. I walked forward keeping the light in his eyes and retreated a few steps. This gave me confidence I had something to use against him. Mum told me to stop but I was trying to protect her, trying to buy her time to get to the hatch. I told her to quickly go down the hatch if she got the chance as I seemed to be pushing the figure back with the light. Mum moved forward with me as I pushed the man away from the hatch. I told her to go quickly. I knew she didn't want to leave me in the attic but I promised I would follow if she went first. She made a dash and got down the steps and was shouting up for me to come down too.

The figure smiled and stopped retreating. The torch was still shining but it seemed to be losing its power over the presence. He lunged at me and I dropped the torch. He grabbed me by the arms and I heard mum shouting but it was like it was from a distance almost like it was in a long tunnel. I struggled to get free but he had a strong grip. He quickly swapped his grip to my waist and threw me over his shoulder. He had my legs tight in his large hands, I was facing down over his back. He had a firm grip of me and anything I did barely had any effect on him. My heart was pounding, even more so when I realised, we were no longer in the attic. I could hear lots of unfamiliar sounds and some strange smells. The next thing I knew I was onboard a ship. He let me down from his shoulder but kept a firm grip of my arm. He told me there was nothing I could do and no means of escape and that what was to happen to me was up to him now.

I could hear people shouting above and a sense of lots of movement. He let go of me and said his name was Frederick but that I should call him sir and nothing else. With one hand he grabbed me by the throat and squeezed and said he would carry on squeezing if I didn't do what he said. I was only a boy and no match for him so I nodded.

We were in a ships cabin. I could tell by the wood that this was old. He threw some old clothes at me that were just lying around. He told me to take off all of my clothes and put these on. They were dirty and more rags than clothes. I didn't want to think about who had worn them last or what had happened to them. He took my clothes and bundled them into a sack. He shouted for someone who entered quickly and called him sir.

Frederick told him to put me with the others. The man nodded and came over and grabbed me by the arm and dragged me out of the cabin. He pushed me down some stairs which led to some sort of cargo hold. He took some rope and tied my hands behind my back. He put a rope with a slip knot around my neck and tugged hard. I fell over and started coughing. He shouted that if I didn't want a lot worse that I should do what he said and I nodded. He dragged me up with the rope and we climbed some steps.

Finally, I saw daylight as I was reaching the deck of the ship. I was pushed onto a gangway that led to the edge of the dock and walked across. There were some more scruffy looking men and boys already there waiting. I got pushed over to them and tied in by my waist to the one in front. They appeared to be tied together in twos and threes. This was obviously to stop them running away but looking at the state of some of them, they didn't look capable of running anywhere. They were all very thin and looked wretched. Their faces looked as if they had lost all hope, all will to object.

I hadn't had much time to think about what had happened and I didn't have a clue where I was. I didn't know it then but a better question was when was I? Who were these people I was now tied to? What was going to happen? Now my situation began to dawn on me, at least the fact that things weren't looking good. It would have been easy to cry my eyes out but that wasn't going to help me and would probably get me into trouble so I gathered my wits together and decided to try and learn as much as possible about where I was and see if there was any chance of escape. I was in a lot better shape than the rest of the boys I was tied to.

I saw Frederick leave the ship and come towards us. He grabbed one of the boys at random and hit him in the face with his fist. The boy went limp and he dropped him on the hard floor. He shouted if we didn't all want the same treatment that we had to do what he said. He told us to get inside and pointed to some large open doors. A couple of us picked up the unconscious boy and we all headed into the building. There were lots of things being taken in and others coming out of the building on old looking barrows. There were a couple of men standing guard by us on the inside of the building. They had what looked like short whips that had pieces attached to them at the end. Nobody disobeyed as they didn't want to feel what it was like to get a lashing from one of them.

We were herded on further into the building and through some passage way that had no natural light, just candles to barely see where to walk. Everyone just followed the one in front. We were walking for what seemed like forever until we came to a wider part of the tunnel and we were told to stop here. There was some straw spread around on the floor so we all sat down on that. Frederick shouted that there was no point trying to run anywhere as there was nowhere to go and that we should just stay here. There was some bread in large bowls on the floor and some glass bottles filled with water. I got one of the bottles and poured some on my hand and splashed it on the unconscious boy's face. Slowly he came around and I tipped-up the bottle so he could take a drink from it. He drank a little and he was grateful, I got a chunk of bread and gave it to him. He looked at me and nodded a thank you.

We were in a large underground room that had some carvings etched into the stone walls. There was no way I was staying here. It was obvious I was in much better physical condition than any of the other boys or even the men and if I stayed here, presumably I would end up in the same state. I should try and do something before that happened. I decided the first thing to do was to get back inside the first building. There was a lot of boxes and crates of all shapes and sizes in there. I thought if I could get back there, I could hide in one of those crates until I could think of a way to get out completely. It shouldn't be too difficult getting untied as there were lit candles dotted around the room. I guessed Frederick thought nobody would try and escape or have the strength to. He had forgotten about me.

I took a nearby candle and used the flame to burn through the rope around my waist which was attaching me to the next boy. That was the easy part. I did the same with the rope around my hands and got several candle-burns in the process. I took the noose from around my neck with great relief. I told the other boys not to say anything and that I would try and bring help. I hid the rope under the straw as I guessed the men hadn't counted the number of boys they had and hoped if that was the case I wouldn't be missed. I carefully retraced our steps through the tunnel, I had noticed there were a couple of side tunnels and if I heard anyone coming, I would have to make sure I could run into one of those. This was risky as it was a considerable distance, but it was one worth taking.

The candles were still lit so it wasn't hard finding my way, I just had to make sure I followed the same main tunnel and I would be back in that first building. I was as nervous as could be the whole time with my heart thumping in my chest. I could hear the noise of the men bringing in and taking out those crates as I had before. As they were putting the crates into lines, I noticed they were opening them with crowbars and checking the contents, presumably for damage. Once they were satisfied, they put the lids back on the crates loosely. This was making a lot of noise and would give me some cover. I waited for my moment and then ran for all my worth to a spot behind some crates that had been checked. I watched out for the big man who was obviously the boss, the one who had brought me here. There was a large table and chair to one side of the room and I spotted him sat there. Workmen were bringing notes to him and he appeared to be checking things off on a register of some kind.

There were writing implements on the table – several quills, ink and other fancy paraphernalia. There was a lit flame like a candle flame but it wasn't a candle and wasn't for light. I wasn't sure what it was for. I noticed he was wearing this huge ring. It was something you noticed about him immediately and I'm sure that was the idea. I noticed the documents on his table were building up as the men cleared goods from the ships tied up on the dockside. He was working through the pieces of paper carefully and some he appeared to be stamping once he had finished. He was bundling them up and then adding them to a drawer. I had to be careful not to be seen but everyone was busy with their work and not expecting to see me.

I saw him writing and passing notes to one man in particular and on those I found out what the flame was for. He was adding a waxed seal to the bottom of the note, the flame was to melt the wax in a small metal container. He poured a small amount of wax on the note and then took off his ring and pressed it into the wax. That must be adding his authority to whatever was written on the document. I noticed he hadn't put the ring back on so he must have several of these to write and add a seal to. That ring was clearly important and I resolved to taking it if I got the chance. I had noticed when he grabbed me by the waist in the attic he had pressed or handled the ring in some way just as we arrived in the ship. If the ring somehow helped him bring me here maybe, it could be used to get me back. I could see the crates going to the ship were all in one corner of this big space. I picked up a crowbar and as quietly as I could I opened the lid on one of them that was at the back and so be taken on last.

I made a noise but made sure I waited for another, workmen to open one of the new crates – that covered up the noise I made. I needed the ring and I needed to get into this crate. I could see they were no longer taking things out of the ship I arrived on and were taking things in. So, the crate I had opened would be going on the ship I was on, that could be just what I needed. This must have been what the boss was using the seal for, the documents for the outgoing cargo. He called to what looked like his foreman and they went off for a quiet discussion. This was my chance if I could dodge the barrowmen I could get to the table and the ring. I picked up a spare barrow and a small crate, I headed to the table and looked for the ring but it wasn't there. I was desperate and not far off panic. I calmed myself down and looked in the drawers, it was there at the back. Even better, if it was at the back of the drawer, he might not miss it right away. I turned back with the small crate and was going to put it back when one of the others shouted that it had to be on the ship and for me to stop wasting time and get it on board quickly.

This was perfect, my dirty ragged clothes didn't look out of place with the younger men and boys who were loading the ship. I tried to look and act like they did. I kept my head down and barrowed onto the ship. I put the barrow to one side quickly and jumped into the hold as if helping load. One of the men shouted at me and I said the boss had told me to put a note in his cabin. He just looked at me but the mention of the boss was enough and he just shouted for me to get on with it. I went through a door and had to now concentrate and see if I could remember where the cabin was. The ship wasn't huge so it shouldn't be too hard and I remember it was at the end of a corridor. I knew we had gone up some stairs so I had to make sure I was on the right deck.

I went to the right, down the corridor and got to what I thought was the wooden steps I had been forced up. This deck didn't look familiar so I went down the stairs to the deck below. This looked better and I headed to the end of the corridor and sure enough there was the cabin door we had both come out of. I tried the handle and it was unlocked. I quickly entered and breathed a sigh of relief. There was no activity down here as everyone was focussed on loading and that was at the other end of the ship, at least for now. I looked at the back of the cabin and could see a sack on the floor. I looked in it but it wasn't the one with my clothes in. I wondered if it was better to just take these old clothes off, then I remembered, mum had found lots of old clothes in the attic so that should mean they could be okay for me to wear. I didn't have a lot of time it wouldn't be long before they started searching the ship. I had to make some decisions and quickly. There was no point searching for my clothes and I didn't really want to appear back in the attic naked so I decided to try and get back as I was, if it didn't work, I could soon take these rags off.

I was now in the same place as I arrived at, I wasn't wearing the same clothes but I had the ring. What next? I touched the ring but of course nothing happened. I clenched it in my hand and made sure I was pressing on the front of it. Still nothing so I tried to calm down as much as I could and closed my eyes. I focussed my mind's eye on the attic at home. I concentrated on the moment he had grabbed hold of me. I could hear a commotion in the distance. It was too far off to be on the ship and I wondered if Frederick had noticed his ring was missing. This made my heart race but I had to keep focussed, I couldn't think of what else I could do other than hide. I moved to what I thought was the exact same spot I had arrived on and pressed the ring so hard it was hurting my hand. I concentrated so hard that the sounds began to fade away. Then there was no sound at all and my hand stopped feeling the ring.

Whatever had happened I felt a lot warmer, but I daren't open my eyes for fear of still being in that cabin. I stood motionless for what seemed like an eternity but was just a few seconds. Now I could hear a noise and felt arms around me – I had been discovered and God knows what would happen to me. I remembered what had happened to the boy when we first got off the ship. I struggled to get free and opened my eyes only to see my mum and hear her trying to calm me down. Her face was the most beautiful thing I had ever seen and I flung my arms around her. We hugged each other so tightly I could hardly breathe but I wasn't about to let go. We just stayed there for quite a few moments not saying anything. Eventually I looked in my hand and the ring had gone. I looked around to check but I was certain I hadn't dropped it. We slowly loosened our grip and just looked each other in the eyes. Not many words were needed at that point, I think we were both in shock and disbelief so for now, we both went back downstairs. Mum hadn't even bothered to say anything about my clothes, I guess she figured it could wait.

When I told mum what had happened, she confirmed that very little time had passed after I was taken to me returning. To say it was strange didn't do it justice and we both agreed that I should not go in the attic again. She was now determined to find out a lot more about the contents that had been left in the attic and why this man had appeared and why he had taken me back with him. How could he travel through time like this? What did he want with me? Mum wanted answers and she could be a very determined lady when she put her mind to it.

There was little point lingering on what had happened to me with the rest of the family as none of them would believe what we had to say and we knew it so we more or less kept it to ourselves until maybe a more appropriate time.

What I resolved to do was to have another talk with Philip. He could hardly tell me I was making things up after what he had told me about him being sensitive and that he could also travel to different places. Was that different to what Frederick had done. I remember Philip saying he made no noise when he travelled and he was more viewing what was happening rather than interacting as had happened to me. Who knows he might even be able to give me some tips as to what I should do if Fredrick came back. I would certainly be more prepared next time if he did. Not least of all, I thought, I would run in the opposite direction.

I waited for an appropriate day to speak to Philip, when the two of us were alone and he was reading. I told him what had happened, he book marked his page and looked at me intently. He asked me to go through every minor detail, especially about the ring and

Frederick. He said that he believed he had seen Fredrick – the one he had heard making his presence felt in the attic. I now knew he wasn't using the same method as Philip to move around. Philip couldn't make a noise or speak when he travelled or even make people aware he was there. His body was still on his bed throughout his travelling but Frederick was just like an ordinary person moving around but in different times and places. The fact he was able to take me with him showed he was an incredibly powerful entity and that at least some of that power seemed to be focussed around the ring he wore.

Philip seemed very interested in the ring, in the detail, what it looked like. I thought it was because Frederick had clearly used it to aid his travel, but in fact it was because he suspected he recognised the type of ring it was. I would only get to know this later. Philip was at a loss to know why Frederick would want me with him. What possible use could he have for me? The obvious answer was to be sold as a slave and presumably that is what would happen to the others I was tied to. It was certainly the right timeframe for such trade and it was very lucrative for merchants such as him. The thought of being saved from a life of slavery, left an impression on me for a long time. It made me think how lucky I had been and I promised myself never to forget that. Philip said he would pass on my experience to someone he could trust, someone who was very interested in Frederick and his abilities.

I knew if I asked who, Philip would do what he did before and return to his secretive nature, so I didn't bother. Instead, I asked if there was anything I could do to protect myself and Philip said he would ask his friend to see if anything could be done and that in the meantime I should stay out of the attic. I told him I had already decided on that. I left Philip to get back to reading his book and I decided to make myself feel better by playing with Shandy if he was awake. I knew where I would be able to find him, so I went to my bedroom and there he was washing himself on my bed cover. I laid on the bed close to him and stroked him, in response he began to purr. At times like this all was right with the world.

My mum decided it was safer for now to have another look at the old photos and various neighbours and visitors to the house thumbed through them over the next few days and I think they were peaking mum's interest as several people were suggesting the same thing. That the cemetery was one that had been somewhere on the land that the houses now stood on. Nobody was able to pinpoint the spot as there wasn't any visible land marks to follow. Over time it became a bit of a hobby for mum to try and find out more about the content of the photos by visiting several archives, including the city council and the local newspaper.

It turns out that going back to seventeenth century that this estate land was outside the city boundary and had been used as farmland until several human tragedies had come along such as the plague and then later typhoid, to which there was no treatment and a high mortality rate. The people needed a substantial area of land to put aside for the dead. The most recent such event was the so-called Spanish flu just after the first world war. Again, this set-a-side land was called on for mass burials. What must have been happening was that over this extended period graves were being dug one on top of another. The more recent ones had been kept quite shallow for that very reason – they didn't know exactly where the existing graves were so they didn't want to risk digging up the old remains.

Records of where the multiple cemeteries were situated were quite vague, probably because there was an urgent need to bury people and that was the priority at the time. The consideration was that it was outside the city boundary and that there was a large enough space marked out for it. Later nobody had done a survey as the burials were considered so old, there would be no surviving living relatives and it would just be cheaper to leave them. It was decided, according to council records, that if any were disturbed during building developments, they would be reburied in a local cemetery with one joint memorial marker.

I guess in modern growing cities this is the sort of action that would be repeated many times over, when cost and the lack of local knowledge is considered against the benefits of new housing and office complexes. Modern science of course dismisses the paranormal and the possibility of some part of an individual surviving death or indeed the concept of good and evil. Having lived in one such property affected by these decisions it does make me wonder how many people find themselves in a similar situation and having to try and make some sense out of it, let alone get some peace in their house.

Mum did a lot of research about the land our housing estate was on. She went to the local land registry to see if there were any plans that might give a hint to the location of the burials. There were several maps of the city and its boundaries that were dated which helped. This was the east of the city so that was the boundary she was particularly interested in. Water courses were marked and that helped as there was a land drain not too far from the estate. There were lots of old trees dotted around and some in lines which were fairly obviously the remains of old field boundaries. This was good as the maps carefully showed boundaries for farms and old track ways. Not least of all these helped local officials decide on taxes due. Just because they were outside the city boundary didn't mean the city officials didn't claim administrative rights over them. The surrounding farms were meant to provide food for the city and were liable for tax paid in kind for the use of the services of the city. The city also provided plenty of seasonal labour to allow the farms to thrive.

By piecing together lots of these maps over a prolonged piece of local history, mum was able to establish that most of the estate at some point had mass graves on it. The area our house sat on seemed right in the middle of one of the large cemeteries and it was one that had been used several times over for the various waves of human tragedy.

This was not a comforting thought for any of us and she at first wondered whether to inform us of her findings but then on balance she decided to share as we all knew she had been researching this for a long time and expected to learn what had been uncovered. She was at great pains to explain that this was not to be unexpected as the city had a very long history and that this sort of situation was common in a country with limited amount of land to expand.

Looking back, I guess this was meant to make us feel that the house was nothing special and the local history was just something of interest, not concern. I think mum missed her vocation – she should have been a sales person and I'm sure would have been very good at it. She sure sold us all that this was just a normal house. The trouble was, that sales pitch wouldn't stand the test of what was to manifest itself to us.

As part of her research mum decided to contact the previous occupants of our house. She did it officially because she wanted to make sure they didn't want any of the contents of the loft they had left behind. Unofficially she wanted to ask if they had encountered any sounds and if they could shed any light on the photographs and other old objects they had collected at some point. Were these, part of their ancestors' story or just junk from a car boot sale?

She managed to track down the previous owners and decided to meet the mother for a coffee in town. She took some of the old photos and one or two of the smaller engravings with her to discuss. The mother of the previous family in the house was called Eileen and she was a pleasant individual, very warm and kind. She was a little apprehensive when mum said she had brought some items out of the loft with her. Eileen's reaction wasn't what you would expect, after all these were her possessions.

Eileen told mum that she had been a collector of antiques and curiosities and had bought these, what we considered, strange objects in a house clearance sale and an auction. She claimed to know little of the person they had been purchased from other than she had passed away whilst living alone and had no known family and so part of the will had been to sell the possessions and give the money to charity. The plaques had apparently come from an old work-house that was due to be converted and brought back into use as flats. There was no hint at malevolence just of sadness at the situation of no remaining relatives to pass the contents of the house to.

At one point Eileen had owned an antiques and curiosities shop and she said the pieces in the attic were once in the shop but they hadn't sold and Eileen liked them so had taken them home. There had been rumours of an antique shop in the town being haunted, was this the shop Eileen had owned? Mum asked Eileen if she had come across a male apparition. She knew it would sound crazy to anyone who hadn't experienced any paranormal activity but she felt Eileen didn't fall into that category and she felt safe bringing it up. Eileen looked shocked and even worried. She stared at mum as if waiting for her to say more. Mum mentioned the name Frederick and Eileen made a sharp intake of breath. She covered her mouth with her hands as if trying to stop words coming out. She started shaking and mum asked, more sternly this time, what she knew.

Eileen said that she had no idea that he would return and thought that she had got rid of him. She said at one point he had been haunting the shop she had and that any youngsters present seemed to make his presence felt more. Boys in particular had started complaining of feeling threatened and it was putting off their parents from spending any time in the shop. Eileen said she had no idea why teenage boys seemed to cause more activity but she had called in a medium who had come up with the name Frederick as the troublesome presence. They had blessed the shop and Eileen had taken a few objects home and placed them in the loft. That had stopped the activity in the shop at least and she rarely went in the loft and tried to convince herself that the footsteps she would sometimes hear was just her imagination. Eileen said at one point she had been contacted by someone who had worked at an old house, who knew she ran an antiques shop. They said that the owner had passed away and they had been given some old books as a thank you for long service before the person had died.

When she had asked to see the books, she was surprised to see how old they were and in what excellent condition. They were large, heavy with some disturbing illustrations. Eileen said she had no idea of their true worth but the seller was keen to get what they could for them so she had just offered a figure based on them being antiques and possibly desirable for anyone wanting to add to an old book collection. The person had agreed and the next thing she knew a large box of very old books were delivered to the shop. The medium who had come to cleanse the shop had noticed them and said that they were important texts and that I should hold on to them as they could fetch good money in the right auction. Eileen said she had forgotten all about them once the activity in the shop had died down and that they had remained on a shelf for a long time with no interest from anyone.

She said she still had the antiques shop but only opened now by appointment as she was ready to retire but still had plenty of stock to sell. From time-to-time collectors would ask to look at what was left and it was providing some money to help her be more financially secure. Eileen said if spirits were still causing trouble for Marge that she could introduce her medium friend and that maybe she might want the old books to help. Mum thanked her and asked her not to part with the books without talking to her first and Eileen agreed. After all she still had space in the shop and they filled a shelf making it look more presentable to any visitor.

She apologised to mum and said that she hadn't meant to cause any problems by leaving the objects in the attic. She genuinely thought that the spiritual activity had stopped. My mum told Eileen that Frederick had shown interest in me in the attic, (she didn't say he had grabbed me), and wanted to know what he could possibly want with me and the other teenage boys. Eileen claimed she had no idea but my mum insisted that if she knew anything that she should say so now. Eileen was very uncomfortable and clearly upset and said she only had a clue what he was doing by a note he had left behind. She had found it in one of the cabinets she had bought. It had a secret compartment and she had found some old documents with what looked like Frederick's name on them.

They looked like he was researching something, an idea he was formulating to become more, wealthy, and influential. Mum asked if Eileen still had the documents. Eileen said she had kept them just in case they were ever needed and that she would locate them and pass them on to Marge.

My mum asked why she had left so many items behind if she liked them so much. Eileen said she thought the items she left might be of interest to the next family moving in. (If that was true, why was she so apprehensive about those particular objects?)

Eileen told mum about who the house sale had been for and the address and the approximate date it had happened. Mum knew she could use this information to research the history of the family the belongings had come from.

The two of them continued chatting over an extended coffee shop visit with Eileen not offering any more useful information. She claimed she hadn't heard anything untoward in our house other than the normal sounds any house can make, something mum doubted the sincerity of by the way the discussion was brushed away and then the subject changed to something more mundane like the weather. Before they parted, mum asked Eileen to promise to pass on the notes she had mentioned and she said she would. It sounded like she would be glad to see the back of them.

Mum had no idea why Eileen wasn't being more forthcoming with her experience of the house but she did know there was a lot more that hadn't been said. She decided not to mention more of what she had experienced with Frederick as she wasn't sure how much Eileen would believe.

The two women parted company, one feeling she had managed to deflect awkward questions about things she would rather forget, the other that there was another round of researching to be done to get to the bottom of a potentially darkening situation.

My mum had a small circle of friends she could rely on to help out which would be very handy as dad was at work during the week so by teaming up with her friends, they could share the tasks of finding out more about the deceased woman, her estate and ancestors.

It turns out the woman who had passed was called Edith Wilson and had founded a charity to help poor families and orphaned children. On the face of it all very laudable and respectable, but like a lot of things, what you see on the surface isn't always the same when you dig deeper.

The more that was uncovered about Edith, the more mysterious she became. In fact, infamous or even malevolent might be more appropriate descriptions of her character and actions. The family money came from a shipping company that transported a wide range of goods all over the world. Seemingly they would transport anything to anywhere so long as there was a good profit in it. Safety of the ships crews was only considered because the ships couldn't sail without them. Conditions on board could be grim but human life was cheap and profits were good. This was just typical of the time and nothing strange there.

The family had a dozen large sailing ships which made them very rich. As was the custom with successful merchants, they bought a large country estate with a huge house on the land. They put their own stamp on it and to add further respectability, they commissioned landscape gardeners to show off the family's wealth with lavish and ornate gardens complete with orangery and a huge walled garden. The entrance to the estate meandered for miles so as to impress any visitor approaching the house and to provide a statement of power that this family were clearly better than most and had to be taken seriously.

Like a lot of these rich and powerful families, over the years that followed, the wealth was lost by a mix of severe death taxes and unfortunate gambles on stock markets. So much so that by the time it came to Edith's turn to be matriarch, the inherited fortune had dwindled to such an extent that she was living in a large but not palatial house – huge estate sold off to pay debts of ancestors. She had enough money to maintain a well-off lifestyle however and her investments had done extremely well so she was repairing, at least financially, some of the family name.

The house was full of Victorian artifacts and decoration. The house still had all the modern facilities but they were hidden by the heavily ornate and over the top Victorian style. The decoration was very dark and looked like it had come out of a scene from a period drama. The house was meant to make any visitor feel uneasy even inadequate so that when Edith appeared it would be as if a powerful presence had entered the room.

This is of course exactly what Edith wanted – she was in character a throw-back to her powerful and domineering relatives. This was no modern thinking woman fighting for equality. She had a character to match any of her male Dickensian counterparts and struck fear into most people who had the unfortunate circumstance to have dealings with her.

This account of her nature had come from contemporary written accounts in various journals and also from the memory of locals who had completed work for her. Why then had she formed a charitable organisation and left it most of her money? Was she trying to make some amends for the way she had treated people?

Locals were convinced her house was haunted, but that was to be expected when the owner was so unusually dominant and the contents looked like they had come from some gothic film set.

There were some photos of the house both inside and out that had been taken presumably for posterity and they showed each room in detail. If a film company had bought it, they would have a ready-made set for a horror movie. In the end the house had been gifted in trust to be set up as a museum. A perfect example of Victorian architecture and design and only a relatively few of the contents had been sold separately – ones that had been deemed not to be in keeping with the rest of the house or surplus to requirements of the museum.

Some of these items were now in the possession of our family – the ones Eileen had left behind. There was an obvious next step to the research and that was to visit the museum and speak to the curator, maybe even take the items to discuss and find out why they had been sold. They might even be glad to have them back. At that time mum would have been happy to donate the items in return for their story being told so it was decided that is what would happen next – a museum visit.

Chapter 4

One of the items that had been left by Eileen was an old wooden quite gothic, ornate trunk that contained several items of interest along with the old photos. Mum got her research friends together and resolved to go to the museum. They arranged with the curator so they could spend some time discussing the items as well as have a tour around the house.

The grounds surrounding the house were modest indeed compared to the ancestors' parklands but they were still substantial and were laid out in quite a formal style of walkways, borders, hedges and a large water feature. There were several old statues that had lichen growing on them. The museum had tidied up the gardens but were at pains to bring them back to the style they were in when first constructed. Edith had employed just one gardener in the latter days of her life and all he could hope to achieve was to cut the grass and do his best to keep on top of the weeds.

The house dominated the approach to the front door. Its gothic styling, aged stone work and long paths harked back to that time when visitors were supposed to be impressed by the power of the owner and be aware of their superior status. Edith certainly played this card for all its worth. Why anyone would want to do this in modern times was a bit of a mystery, but that was the point, Edith wasn't of modern times she belonged in an era two hundred years passed. She was the only matriarch in the family and clearly did not want to be thought of in any lesser way due to the fact she was a woman.

The house wasn't open to the public yet as the museum was still putting its final touches to the interior, so it was just as well mum and her friends had booked in advance. They were going to be some of the first visitors and the curator was looking forward to hearing their impressions of the house and the way it and its contents were being displayed.

The front door was huge, made from oak with impressively large black hinges – more like something you would see on an old church. There was a large black knocker in the centre but a modern bell had been fitted by the museum presumably to help staff hear visitors. In its heyday the house had quite a few servants including a butler so they would have heard knocking at the door very clearly. Not so much these days with cleaners using loud vacuums and some building repair work happening hence the temporary door chime.

The entrance hall was all about making a statement. Even though it was modest by stately home standards it was still a large building with a long dark wooden staircase off a domineering space that made visitors aware that you were in the house holder's domain and that person was clearly someone of power and prominence. There were various rooms coming off the hall including a hidden one towards the back leading to a hidden staircase for servants to use as access to the kitchen and servant's quarters. The floor was covered in black and white marbled tiles rather than a carpet, which made a lot of noise as people walked on them but would make it much easier for the museum to keep clean when visitors started coming in large numbers.

There was a library where most visitors would be placed to impress before meeting their host. The ceiling was impressively high and the library had lavish plaster reliefs around the door ways, tops of the walls and on the ceiling. They had taken a lot of conservation work to bring back to how they originally looked. Edith had struggled to keep staff, not because she couldn't afford them but because they didn't like working in the house and complained of an oppressive atmosphere. She had no choice but to rely on a core of servants who had been with her for many years and so she had little choice but to let maintenance slide in some rooms.

Equally tradesman, of the quality required, were hard to find and when she did, they complained of tools being taken and one even stated he had been pushed off a set of steps while working off them. That had been the last day he or anyone else had been willing to remain in the house.

Edith seemed to relish in the growing dark reputation of the property and used it to intimidate anyone invited in. This in turn added to her own legend as a woman not to be taken lightly and someone who was cold, harsh, stern and uncompromising. A woman who knew her own mind and that it was her destiny to be where she was and to leave her mark on the family heritage.

She was unable to have children and was unaware of any other living relatives, so she would be the last of the family line. Hence the charity being gifted the house in trust with an endowment to pay for its upkeep – that along with entrance fees to the museum would ensure the future of the house. Instructions had been left that the house should not be changed in any material way, just that it should be maintained to a good standard.

The last servants to the house had been kept on as they were knowledgeable about the house and Edith's family and so could add to the museum visitor experience by showing people around and discussing the history. They had worked and lived in the house for a long time and would now be called visitor hosts. They knew every inch of the overbearing rooms and were well aware of the reputation the house had built up. In some ways they were part of that reputation as they had managed to stay where others had left quickly. They didn't talk much about the darker side of the house, just that it was alive and demanded respect.

Paranormal investigators often say spirits in a house become more active during building or restoration work. This house was constantly active and all the restoration work had done was expose more people to its malevolence. The visitor hosts knew it but played it down by saying old houses with substantial wood panelling always made sounds and that it was people's imagination that did the rest.

My mum and friends had been shown to the library as visitors, just as they might have been years ago. They looked around the library while they waited for the curator. There were large paintings of some fierce looking ancestors, as this was now a museum there were explanations of who each was on notices underneath. There was a huge open fireplace with ornate surround, lots of seating with sofas and chairs. Some occasional tables stood ready to receive alcoholic beverages from the beautiful wooden drink's cabinet.

The carpet was a rich burgundy and heavily designed with numerous birds and flowers. Decoration was everywhere and that was the Victorian style that at least this room had been left in. There were large windows looking out on to the back garden which, like the house, was extensive. Long heavy curtains draped along the edges of the windows, they matched the carpet in colour and design. There was wood panelling along the walls and masses of books, all fitting perfectly on the shelves and probably picked more for that reason than any other.

All of a sudden there was a tremendous bang on the library door – not a knock, but an enormous bang followed after a few seconds by another. The women looked at each other somewhat startled. After the third loud bang one of them went to the door and opened it as quickly as she could to see who would be standing there, nobody was at the door. In fact, there wasn't anybody nearby at all. This put everybody on edge as they assumed it was one of the workmen, now it left them wondering what else it could possibly be. As one of the ladies was closing the door, there was another almost deafening bang on the door and she fell backwards in surprise. They all backed away from the door and left it partly open. The door then swung open and to everyone's relief it was the curator. She introduced herself and asked if everything was alright, the group all said yes and dismissed what had happened.

The curator was eager to know what the women thought of the library. They all said how imposing they thought it was and were of course told that had been the intent of the head of the family who had commissioned it. Very much to display the status and opulence of the owners. My mum, Marge, asked if workman were using any heavy equipment but was told no, all that was being done now was finishings to decoration – painting or cleaning, that was all. Janet, the curator, asked if there was a reason for the question but Marge insisted, she was just being curious.

Now the tour began, Janet leading the way and giving details about the rooms and anything she felt noteworthy of pointing out. The group asked questions along the way and all seemed quite normal, as normal as that house could ever appear at least, until they got to a room on the first floor that was a sort of study that Edith liked to use to relax in. It was this room Janet asked Marge about the photos and the box that had been mentioned over the telephone. Marge had sent over the trunk in advance and it was waiting for them in the study. She opened it and took the box out and unwrapped it. She put it on a table in the middle of the room and opened it.

As soon as she did that there was like a whoosh of air that travelled from one side of the room to the other. All the women looked at each other. It was like a mini tornado that appeared and then disappeared equally quickly.

The temperature in the room had dropped significantly, while the inside door handle started rattling as if someone was trying to enter the room. Everything was quiet until a shrill blood curdling scream rang out loud and long. One of the windows flew open and the curtains moved vigorously. Janet rushed to close the window and secure it with the latch. The curtains stopped moving. She looked at the small group, everyone was open mouthed but not saying a word. Finally, Janet explained that there had been some noises reported by various workmen but they had been discounted until very recently when things seem to have developed and become much more disturbing. Marge asked Janet to check the scream hadn't come from one of the staff in need of help but Janet just looked a little sheepish and said that she had heard it once before and that when she had checked, nobody else had heard it.

They all wondered if bringing objects back into the house that once belonged there, might be triggering a response from something that seemed to be present in certain rooms of the house. They were all shocked about what had just happened and particularly the unearthly scream. Was this Edith trying to make contact or another spirit? Was it just some sort of recording that had somehow been triggered or was it intelligent and intended to scare them. In any event that's the effect it had. That question in itself would seem a ridiculous thing to suggest amongst a grouping like this – until now. The group knew what they heard, the fact that it wasn't being directly discussed, reinforced the after effect on them.

My mum invited Janet to take the photos out of the box and look at them. She did so carefully and placed them one by one on the table. Some had names and dates on the back and it turns out some were of Edith looking very sullen dressed in dark almost Victorian style clothes. Janet was very interested in the photos and asked if they could be donated to the museum as she felt they could be used to add some interest for visitors looking at the more recent family line. Marge agreed as the photos meant nothing to her but she did like the box and wanted to keep that if Janet didn't ask for it. Having said that she was beginning to wonder about the box itself. This was the second time she had witnessed an unnatural reaction to it being opened. Maybe it would be better if the museum had it back after all, at least that way they would be the ones having to cope with any spiritual activity associated with it.

After looking quite intently at the photos, Janet turned her attention to the box. It was of dark wood – mahogany, stained and polished with a key hole in the front of the lid. On opening the lid, the box had a piece that lifted out to reveal another compartment below. Janet removed this but continued to handle the box in quite an intense way as if interrogating it. Marge asked if everything was alright. Janet said that she thought this was a box she had heard about and that if it was that there would be a hidden compartment. Janet was trying to work out from the outside dimensions if the inside matched or if the inside wasn't quite right. She shook the box vigorously to see if there was a rattle from anything. Janet examined the inside and outside of the box very closely.

Janet tried pressing, pushing and pulling every part of the decoration on the box to see if anything moved, it didn't. This was quite frustrating as the inside dimensions clearly were different to those of the outside now it was pointed out. There had to be a mechanism to release something. Janet picked up a magnifying glass and looked at the inside and brought out a small torch from her pocket. She shined it at the inside and the only thing she could find was a very small hole in the corner at the bottom.

She reached into her pocket again and felt for a paperclip. She looked at the clip and started straightening it into a piece of wire. She used it to push in the hole in the box. The wire started to bend under the pressure – clearly a stronger wire or device was needed. Janet hunted in a drawer for something suitable and found a drawing compass. The point was just the right size to fit in the hole. She pushed down and a click was heard but nothing happened.

On closer inspection there was a second small hole in the opposite corner. Janet pressed the compass into it, there was another click and a drawer popped out of the bottom of the box. At the same time there was a tremendous bang on the ceiling, a rush of air swirled around the room as if the outside door had been left open and a portrait fell off one of the walls. It made everyone jump and the air became very cold. Next came a loud thump on a window as a crow had flown into it. The atmosphere in the study changed and felt heavy. The air was electric with anxiety. Everybody was worried that some simple actions were causing such massive reactions by something up to now unseen.

The drawer to the box could be fully removed and was itself a rectangular thin box. After examining it Janet was able to tell there was a sliding side panel which she removed to reveal a hollow compartment and what looked like a folded piece of paper. She shook the box until it fell out. This time there was a loud bang on the table which vibrated, the paper flew off the table as if taken up by a gust of wind. The women all looked at each other disbelieving what they were seeing yet experiencing at the same time. A feeling of dread filled the room. The atmosphere turned damp and a foul smell pervaded the air.

Janet chased after the paper which looked very old, it was parchment or vellum and yellowed with age. It had dark writing on it clearly from a quill – this was no modern printed note.

Everybody was amazed at what had been found from this curious original box that was saved from being smashed up or burnt. Now everyone wanted to know what was written on the document. One of the ladies managed to catch it in the air but dropped it instantly and said it felt hot as if it were on fire. Marge had the peace of mind to throw a small cloth over it that she had pulled off one of the tables, the document stopped moving.

Janet put on a pair of white gloves, the type conservators use, to protect things from human touch. She picked up the artefact and placed it back on the table and very slowly and carefully unfolded it. The item was opened out to form a large hand written document that also contained a large red waxed seal with a family crest embossed in it. Janet recognised the seal immediately. It was from one of the early family ancestors – the one whose portrait had fallen from the wall earlier.

This would take some time to understand as it was written in a mixture of old English and Latin. The first letter was a T and was embellished with colour and was much larger than the rest of the letters on the document. It was similar to an old book written by a monk where they start the page with a letter turned into a drawing with bright colours.

The first two words were, "This Covenant." Janet carefully flattened the piece of vellum and asked Marge if she would photograph it with the camera on the sideboard. It was one of those instant ones that send out a completed photo, no need for developing. This would allow them all to be able to see it and research it whilst the original could be sent for conservation in the downstairs part of the museum. As Marge took the photograph an ornament on a sideboard hurled across the room and smashed against the wall. Clearly something was not happy with them opening the box and then finding the document.

Marge checked the print but there was no image on the photo, so she tried again. This time the photo was badly fogged with white swirling smoke. At the third attempt she looked at the result and let out a cry as she dropped the print. She was shaking so one of her friends picked it up and instead of seeing a written document there was a ghastly face of an old woman complete with rotting teeth and grey wispy hair. The image showed her with mouth wide open and a look of horror on her face. Her eyes were dark and sunk into her skull. A loud unearthly shriek filled the room at huge volume and the hairs on the back of people's necks stood up. The lights flickered and the door slammed shut. Whatever was causing this activity seemed to be very unhappy with what was being done.

The women were getting terrified but were determined to photograph the document, not least of all so they could fold it up and put it back in its box. Marge made another attempt with the camera and this time managed to capture an image of the writing and seal. Janet carefully but quickly re-folded the document and put it back in the smaller thin box compartment so as to protect it from the light. At least that's what she said. On closer inspection of the outside of the small box, there was a seal scorched into the surface of the wood. It was the same as the one in red wax attached to the vellum. This was obviously of some importance else it wouldn't have the seal and be placed in a secret compartment and also wouldn't have created the reaction that it had. Everybody was very tense.

Janet hurried to the door which led to the main stairs and hall way, everyone followed her. The door opened on its own, as they approached. It did so quickly and slammed against the wall. The party virtually ran through to the stair landing as if that was some sort of sanctuary. Janet called down to a colleague, whilst mustering all the decorum she could. She asked the person to take the box downstairs and instructed that the contents be passed for conservation right away.

Janet turned to look at the group who were all watching her intently. They were all breathing quite heavily and all looked shocked. Janet suggested they go to the visitor centre, a converted part of the house meant to be the last part anyone visited so they could buy refreshments and souvenirs. Janet knew it wouldn't be staffed as it wasn't yet open but she also knew they could all have a seat and get a hot drink and calm down from their experiences.

Everyone was more than happy to get to the seating area and have a cup of Yorkshire Gold Tea. The finest local brew that would help them relax and talk about what had happened.

Nobody was expecting any of this morning's events. They thought they would maybe be able to obtain some useful research and background information. They weren't prepared for any of the interactions that had happened. Marge had already decided to donate the box to the museum if they said they would like it. To start with she had just thought it was an ordinary box for placing letters or keepsakes in. Now she would be happy for it not to be in her possession.

When the group had calmed down, Janet explained that she was hoping the box would be the one listed in an inventory of the house. This had been completed by Edith as a sort of catalogue of her possessions in the house but Janet had gone though it carefully and realised some items were missing. She guessed some had either been stolen or given away or wrongly sold without the inventory being adjusted.

In the inventory the box was described as important and personal to Edith and further described by its dimensions, colour and pattern. The one Marge had brought matched perfectly. On hearing this Marge at once offered it to Janet for the museum to keep. After all, to her it was just an old find in the attic that now seemed to have some sort of paranormal activity attached to it. That was the last thing she wanted to take back to her family home.

Marge asked if there were any other items Janet was aware of that were missing. In anticipation Janet had drawn up a small list of items that she thought may have found their way into Marge's attic via the previous owner's collection of antiquities.

There were several items Marge recognised from her rummage in the attic. She was now very pleased not to have thrown any of them away in her haste to tidy up. There was a large black iron key, which seemed a strange thing to put in an inventory but it was clearly important for some reason. Also listed was a small musical box, a child's wooden wheelchair and a Steiff bear.

Marge informed Janet of the items and invited her to visit the attic to check if there was anything else that could be from the house. Janet was very grateful and seemed quite excited about the key. During the restorations of the house and transformation into a museum a hidden door had been found in the basement but they decided not to force it when they checked the inventory and saw a key was listed but no room mentioned where it was for. It was presumed that the key was for this hidden door and that they would try and locate where it had gone. Nothing in the inventory mentioned where the hidden door led to or what was behind it.

Now they had calmed down Marge asked about the image in the photo that shocked everyone. Janet said it was of Edith in a rather ghastly pose and that she couldn't understand how that could have been produced. It was something quite unnerving and for now at least just had to be put to one side. There was lots of thinking going on within the group but nobody wanted to make any suggestions or ask more questions for fear of what the answers might be.

After the women had their tea, they thought they'd had sufficient tour of the house today but that they would go back to Marge's attic to see what could be located that might belong here. They thought it would be a way of leaving what had happened behind, at least for now. Janet had cleared out most of the day to take the women's tour but also to look at anything that they had brought so she was happy to also return with Marge and see if there was anything else from the inventory. They all gathered themselves together and made to leave the museum with haste.

Marge's house was only about thirty minutes car drive from the museum so they set off in two cars and had an uneventful journey. On entering the family home Marge felt a very different atmosphere. This was her family home and yes there had been noises for a long time, there was never a bad atmosphere. As soon as she opened the front door, she noticed an unusual odour and not one that she liked. Everyone noticed it but didn't say anything. The front door opened to a small room with a telephone, and coat storage. The next door opened into the kitchen diner with the open stairs to the left.

Marge hung everyone's outside coats in the hall and led them up the stairs to the bedroom with the access to the attic. She explained to Janet about the room and what had happened there over the years. Marge opened the wardrobe doors to reveal the attic entrance panel. Most of the clothes had been removed while Marge was frequently going into the attic. She pushed the panel up and to one side – as she did a gust of wind emanated from the roof space and the bedroom door slammed shut which made everyone jump. Janet put it down to the wind coming through the loft. Marge said nothing but instead used the metal pole to pull the access ladders out of the attic. They slid all the way to the floor and had a handle along one side. They were quite substantial so nobody felt unsafe using them. Marge turned on the lights to the attic and went up the steps. The others quickly followed.

Marge was very house proud and had cleaned up the attic space and gone through most of the boxes left by the previous owner. There was just four left to go through and she knew she had put the items she recognised from the inventory to one side as curiosities. She showed Janet the four items and she began examining them. An old wooden child's wheelchair. These always looked out of place and so very sad somehow, being so small. A Steiff bear sat on the chair, looking much more cheerful. These could be quite valuable if genuine and he was a good size for the chair. Then there was the large black iron key that had been hung on a hook on the wall. Finally, the musical box made of ebony and inlaid with a floral design.

Janet was very excited and seemed sure these were four items from the inventory. It was the key she particularly wanted in the hopes it would open the hidden door back at the museum. The musical box appeared to be a child's one and maybe belonged to the owner of the chair. Janet explained that Edith had adopted a relative's young girl and that she had become ill and it was her that used the wheelchair and probably owned the bear. It was probably her music box too. The young girl unfortunately had contracted tuberculosis and after a prolonged period of needing the wheelchair, she had passed away.

One of the women pointed to the wheelchair. It was slowly turning; the bear was still sat upright in it and it gave the appearance that the bear was moving the wheelchair slowly around the attic space. As if to make the scene even more tense, there was a squeak made by one of the wheels as it turned. Marge recognised the noise as the family had heard it before but never had a clue what was causing it. Marge had played it down before, as the thought of heavy footsteps from the upstairs was bad enough without considering other unworldly happenings in the house.

The wheelchair was slowly travelling to the other end of the attic. They were all transfixed by the movement of the wheelchair. Janet suggested the boards they were standing on must be sloped in that direction making the wheelchair slowly travel in that way. This sounded reasonable and the wheelchair stopped, everyone looked quite relieved until it abruptly and in one instant, turned and faced them. You could hear a pin drop as the wheelchair began to move again but this time in their direction. It started very slowly but then it picked up speed, they were all rooted to the spot and horrified by what they were seeing. If Janet was right about the floor, the wheelchair was now travelling uphill and quickly. It was as if someone was pushing it until it finally crashed into a cardboard box that Marge wanted to sort through.

Marge looked at Janet and said the floor couldn't be sloping in both directions. None of them wanted to believe it but they all knew this wasn't normal and was certainly nothing to do with a sloping floor. Activity amongst these possessions seemed to be building and they were witnessing it. Marge thought the sooner all of this stuff was sorted through and out of the attic the better. Everything associated with Edith's house seemed to be possessed in some way and she wanted her house to be quiet and no disturbed spirits.

When Marge explained about the last four cardboard boxes Janet became eager to look at their contents and gently placed them on the floor one at a time. The first one was filled with junk items purchased from car boot sales. The second was more of a treasure trove.

There was a pack of Tarot cards, a second Ouija board – made from wood and Victorian in style. There was a broach in the shape of a pentagram, and a large family bible. There was a large hand mirror, a scrying stone on a silver chain and a large copper highly polished deep bowl that was meant to hold water and be used with the scrying stone. Most of these items were on Janet's list from the inventory.

One of my mum's friends picked up the copper bowl not knowing what it was for, she just liked the copper colour. She looked right at it and dropped it making a loud metallic din that scared the others half to death. They paused for a few seconds then asked what had happened. Mum's friend said she saw a face looking back at her. She had been so startled she dropped the bowl and didn't want to touch it again. Janet explained they had been used many years ago to contact someone from the other side. She looked at it directly but didn't see anything, only her own reflection.

They put the items back in the cardboard box for taking downstairs. Janet asked if she could speak to Marge alone so the rest went down the steps to the bedroom and then down the stairs into the kitchen to make a cup of tea. Janet asked Marge if she had noticed anything else about the attic space. Marge said she had noticed some strange markings on the walls. Janet had already spotted some of them but as she carefully looked around, she could see more. She explained they were protection spells.

Janet explained she hadn't wanted to ask with the others around for fear of putting them more on edge but she asked my mum if there had been any happenings around the house. My mum told her about the heavy footsteps coming from the attic and the fact that people in the bedroom below never slept well and had a strange feeling of other people's presence. Janet said that at least one of the spells she recognised as one of a binding spell. It was meant to keep a spirit from roaming. She explained that she had done extensive research as part of her doctorate whilst at university and knew of cleansing ceremonies and said she was willing to help mum with the noises from the attic in return for her being so helpful in returning these items to the museum. Mum was very happy to hear this as it was confirmation of what she heard and felt and that dad had denied ever since they first moved in.

Mum was desperate to tell Janet about what had happened to me and decided, on condition of not telling anyone else, to confide in her about Fredrick. Janet was shocked, she reassured mum that she believed her and understood why she wanted to keep it quiet. Janet hadn't realised that this spirit could be such a danger to certain people. She promised to do everything she could to make sure I stayed safe. That's really what mum wanted to hear. Janet told Marge, that she had experienced Frederick once already at the museum and that it hadn't been a pleasant experience. He was clearly a very dominant and active presence. Was it him these spells were meant to keep in check?

Janet and Marge went downstairs to speak to the others and try and lighten the atmosphere. Everyone was feeling drained from the day's events and badly needed some upbeat conversation. No sooner had the tea been poured than the footsteps upstairs could be heard. Loud slow heavy footsteps walking across the attic floor. Then there was the repeat of what had happened to my mum once before. The footsteps sounded like they were now in the bedroom above the kitchen. They were walking towards the landing and now slowly descending the stairs, one at a time.

Everyone nervously looked at the open stairs. One of them started video recording on a small hand-held device. Nothing could be seen on the stairs but the footsteps continued whilst on the video, a large shadow figure could now be seen. It appeared to be staring right at the group and even leaning over the banister in their direction. It was a terrifying sight. The footsteps had stopped but the shadow figure was still there on the video. Next it appeared to rush at the women, only seen by video but it could be felt as if a gust of wind had suddenly blown through them. Then it was gone again and all was quiet. Mum made everyone promise not to say anything to the family as she didn't want to scare them. She was hoping something could be done to cleanse the house before any of the family knew there was a lot more to the footsteps than anyone had previously experienced.

Janet said the museum wouldn't open for a few months yet and that some days there was little for her to do apart from overseeing the restoration work and so she could spend time researching the newly found artefacts and help with the family home. After all the two now seemed to be linked by the inventory items as well as the paranormal activity. It would be legitimate time spent on behalf of the museum trust. My mum and her friends were very glad to hear the offer of help and were keen to accept but for today they had more than enough activity and wanted to go home and put today behind them. Janet returned to her museum office and the ladies all went home.

Chapter 5

The big house had an extensive cellar next to the downstairs kitchen which had been converted by the museum for conservation work to be undertaken. A conservator was looking at the thin wooden box that had been handed to him by another member of staff with instructions that conservation work should begin right away on its contents. He was intrigued what was inside. After a short time, he realised the box had a section that slid away revealing the cavity and a substantial document. He used some long plastic tweezers to gently pull the document free from its housing. He put it on the table and carefully opened it. This was indeed made of vellum which meant it was very old and should be handled carefully. There was a lot of writing on one side and a large red wax seal.

The conservator, Ian, hadn't noticed at first but the room temperature had dropped considerably in the last few minutes. The lighting in the room was all low intensity which meant it would have little effect on the vellum and the humidity was kept low for the same reason. Ian carefully laid out the document flat so that he could photograph it close up and look at it in detail. This would need to be carefully presented in the museum under low light so visitors could see it but so the light wouldn't damage it. The document was entitled, "This Covenant." A covenant of course can mean several things but in years gone by it was a solemn pact between the parties mentioned within the text. The presence of the seal reinforced that as a binding contract.

Ian looked up as the lights in the room began to flicker. It was as if the power was failing and then coming back on, causing the bulbs to dim and then brighten. It was now Ian noticed the temperature had dropped. He tested to see if he could see his breath in front of him, he could. This was not usual, the room needed to be cool but not cold as this would raise the humidity levels which he specifically didn't want as it could damage artefacts he was working on.

As Ian was used to the style of mixed old English and Latin it wasn't too difficult for him to read the document. What might give him more trouble is the interpretation as Latin in particular, words can change their meaning depending on the context.

On first quick reading Ian thought it referred to some sort of deal, he presumed a business deal between merchants. One agreeing to supply goods of one type in return for payment in different goods and agreeing the exchange rate. Shipping was mentioned but some of the words seemed to be in a form of code making it difficult to understand what was being mentioned. No doubt that was the intent in case the document was to fall into the wrong hands.

The atmosphere in the conservation room was getting oppressive. Ian could feel the hair on the back of his neck standing up and he was getting goose bumps all over his body. He began to feel very uncomfortable. This was something he had never felt working here before.

Ian proceeded with his conservation work, which meant carefully photographing the vellum so it could be studied without the need for the original. It would then be laid out flat and placed between special protective sheets of paper and placed between backing boards. Once there was a proper cabinet constructed to display it, then it could be placed inside for all to see.

The lights continued to flicker as Ian bent over the manuscript, trying to observe more closely. He thought he heard breathing that wasn't his. He could feel someone breathing close to his neck. Next, he heard a slow tapping noise and slow deliberate footsteps behind him. Ian spun round but there was nothing to see. He looked back only to be confronted by the figure of an old man so close he could smell his foul breath. Ian jumped back in shock and horror. He let out a shriek and ran out of the room, slamming the door behind him. He quickly ran up the stairs and came out in the hall way.

This was a scientist who believed in the rational not the fanciful. What had just happened was clashing with his world, his notions of the world. His very fibre was at odds with even the possibility of anything supernatural. To him there was no such thing, only exaggerated stories and legends that could be investigated and debunked as old-world superstitions. He had heard the workmen discussing happenings in the house but he had simply laughed them off as superstitions and coincidences and mere ghost stories to frighten each other with.

Ian went to make himself a strong coffee to try and help him regain his composure. He told nobody what had happened. After all what would he say? That he was scared half to death by the appearance of a ghostly apparition in front of him? Janet, he thought, would think he had lost it and that he wasn't up to his job. He took time to calm down in what would be the visitors centre. He couldn't help but return his thinking to the vellum document. After a while he decided that it was his senses that was playing tricks on him and he began to feel almost silly that he had let that happen. He convinced himself this was an occupational hazard of working alone for long periods and without natural light from a window. A little sheepish he slowly walked back to his work room.

There was no apparition this time, he didn't think there would be. No flashing lights or sudden temperature drops. Nothing to report to anyone. Ian smiled to himself that he was back in his very rational world, one that some might even call dry and dusty, just as he liked it.

When Ian studied the text more closely, it gradually started to show that this document was far darker and more sinister than he had realised. It was a covenant to deliver indeed but the cargo was people and not to be as slaves as might seem the obvious motive bearing in mind the dates involved. This was for the delivery of souls! The shipping company had been paid by the British government to deport convicts to Australia and other colonies. This was a life punishment so it was easy to make unscrupulous deals with corrupt officials to route some of these shipments elsewhere than their official destination.

Early scientists wanted bodies to dissect and perform experiments on. Doctors and those learning the profession, needed accurate books on anatomy to learn from but at this time none existed. There was, only one-way scientific diagrams could be made and that meant the profession needed bodies. They were legally allowed to use those of people who had been hanged but that was a relatively small number compared to the numbers needed for various experimental work. There were also secret societies that worshipped Satan. They wanted souls to make deals to aid their businesses, to become rich and powerful and to gain immortality. There was plenty of opportunity to gain convicts as in these times, the poorest people could be deported for the slightest thing such as stealing a small amount of bread.

It seems the people mentioned in this covenant thought they had created the perfect deal. They would get paid by the authorities to deport the convicts to far away lands for substantial payment. Instead of fulfilling that contract they would route the ships to another English port where they would pay the convicts a small amount of money for them voluntarily giving up their soul and being able to send the money back to their families. Of course, that money was never sent to their relatives. Now all that was needed was to find a way to get rid of these convicts themselves so they wouldn't show up anywhere incriminating. This was the last part of the plan, to sell them to the body snatchers. They would keep the convicts alive until their body was needed and then they would be murdered and sold for experiments and vivisection.

The covenant was very tidy – the shipping company owner would be paid handsomely to ship the convicts, they would also get the souls they wanted freely, and at no cost, and then at one stroke be paid by the body snatchers who supplied the medical profession and that would take care of the evidence of wrong doing. It was a clever plan and one that was so immensely grotesque. Life was very cheap in these times and once a person had been sentenced to deportation, there was no further interest in the individual from the state. Effectively it was a death sentence if they were to be deported by this group.

The shock of deciphering this was bad enough for Ian. However, the fact that hit him even harder was the realisation of the numbers of convicts this happened to. This company was dealing in many shiploads every year. This was thousands of people. Presumably if anyone was to find out about what was going on, all that was needed was either for them to disappear or if part of the establishment, a bribe might be appropriate. This was fool proof and truly evil.

If this were to get into the public domain, the family reputation wouldn't just be considered dark but more like that of mass serial killers who dealt in human misery and the occult. Depending who was named in the document, that might destabilise the local establishment. This was absolute dynamite. No wonder some of the words had been written in code. He would have to find a way of breaking that code if he wanted to fully understand the whole document.

The one thing Ian hadn't been able to decipher was the conspirators' names as they were part of the code. There were names but not of people so any presumption of guilt would be pure speculation and with the explosive nature of this document, speculation wouldn't be a good idea.

Ian knew through his research in previous archives that in the seventeenth century cryptography had got quite sophisticated, partly to avoid revealing such things as shipping details for fear of theft but also in secret societies to prevent non-members understanding what was going on or even who members were. Without some form of key this document would be unbreakable and could even have an element of secrecy within the people noted within the document by use of slightly different versions of the coded names or multiple keys.

Ian told Janet of his findings who was horrified and said they should keep it quiet at least until they were certain nobody would be able to find out who was involved. The obvious place to start would be the wax seal. Unfortunately, all that showed was a symbol of the secret society the parties mentioned, were a part of. The seal was that of the 'All Seeing Eye' but that symbol was used by many societies, meant to remind members to remain vigilant and that their deeds would be seen by others in the society.

Without another document it was likely the name of this group would remain unknown which is just as well. Who knows that society might still be around today and be a charitable one. Revelations of this kind would destroy the reputation of anyone remotely involved. Of course, there was one elephant in the room. This document had come from a secret compartment of a box belonging to Edith's family. Presumably Edith herself knew about it. One can only assume from this that at least some of her ancestors were directly involved and no doubt named in code. Only a few people knew of the existence of the document and only Ian and Janet knew what the contents actually referred to. This was not something to be mentioned even to the trustees of the museum as they would soon likely wish to be ex-trustees and want to distance themselves from such things.

Ian put the piece of vellum away in a special cabinet with large drawers that allowed documents such as this to be kept flat. It would be fine in here until a display case could be made for it to be kept in more permanently, if that indeed is what was to happen to it. For research purposes there was the photographed copies to fall back on. These had been stored on reels and so could be physically passed around to others very easily. Ian had decided to send encrypted copies to his boss Janet and one or two trusted friends and colleague's special mail. He made everyone swear to secrecy as a condition for viewing the images of the photographed covenant. He had used this strategy successfully before and it also meant that the recipients took the contents very seriously. To view the photographs they would have to break a special seal which meant they agreed to the conditions.

One of the colleagues Ian had entrusted said that his package was spoiled as he couldn't read the contents and that the photograph was all fogged and undecipherable. On checking with others, he sent the packages to, they said they same thing had happened to theirs. Ian wondered if the packages had been intercepted and interfered with. He asked the museum's photographic support company to check out the equipment to see if there was a problem. They checked various devices but all was in good order – no damage and no signs of wear.

Satisfied all was well with the equipment Ian sent out new copies again and this time used a special courier. This time when the package was received, the only thing present on the photograph was an image of the 'All Seeing Eye', the same as on the wax seal and a second photograph which, instead of showing the document, showed an old man in a top hat. The photo appeared faded and the image was transparent as though it was a double exposure on a conventional photographic film. This was very unnerving for all concerned as it felt like someone was interfering with them over what should be a secure delivery method.

Ian sent out the packages a third time and used a bonded courier that kept hold of the package from sender to receiver, this time everyone received what he sent. Janet suggested researching the early family history to when they had owned sailing ships. Maybe the ships mentioned in the document were the ships the family owned. After all it seemed, they were prepared to transport anything provided it gave a good profit. The family name was thought to be Wilson – that is what Edith called herself. Of course, that can change through marriage so some detective work would be needed to piece together any gaps in the family tree to make sure they had the right surname.

When tracing a family tree, one of the first things to look at is the local census and that's where one of Ian's colleagues started. Of course, a census is only as good as the information freely given by the individuals. There is a requirement in law to provide the information but no checks are done on the accuracy of that information supplied. Edith was there in the census with the family name Wilson, giving her father's and grandfather's name as Wilson but that's as far as it went. No mention of great grandparents and when they were researched, it was as if they didn't exist. When the name of Markle was researched, that could be traced for several generations before that too came to an abrupt end.

There was no publicly documented link between the family names of Markle and Wilson. This presumably was to clean up the more recent ancestry and put some considerable distance between it and Markle. Either that or there genuinely wasn't a link between the two which was possible but would be very strange considering the inheritance. Of course, what could have happened is that the Markle name died out due to lack of children and the line of inheritance was transferred to another arm of the family. Either way it was going to be near impossible without further evidence to directly link Edith to the original shipping family and maybe that was quite deliberate protection.

The museum of course had family portraits which could also be used to piece together the jigsaw puzzle. The first mention of a shipping company in the family was in the surname of Markle. Frederick was the head of the house hold then and his four grown up sons all joined him in the business. Unusually so did his wife Sophie. Usually, women of this era were not meant to take part in men's affairs of business but it seems she was an integral part of the company, helping keep the finances in order.

From this it was possible to find the name of the company which was changed at some point to 'Free Spirit' which was ironical if this was the shipping company Ian suspected of transporting convicts. He could also now uncover the names of the sailing ships which had been named after Greek mythological characters such as Achilles, Hercules, Medusa and Titan. Ian recognised the names from the document. This was starting to show that the shipping company was the one mentioned in the Covenant and then by default one of the parties involved would be the Markle family. This couldn't have been a lone venture by a rogue member of the family as they all worked so closely with the company, so this would implicate them all in the thriving family business. Was this why the family name had later been changed to Wilson to throw people off the scent?

The first part of the puzzle was coming together and it showed how they were becoming very rich very quickly. Further research, this time of government records, confirmed names of six of the company's ships which were involved in the transportation of convicts. Company records showed the other six were involved in more usual, but high value, trade such as sugar, tea and spices. These ships travelled long distances and it would be very easy for them to have additional cargo from say the orient and brought back to England for sale or keeping by the company owners. Honours were bestowed on the family and as they became richer, they became more powerful. Did they put this success down to the taking of souls or was that to do with something else?

Ian was starting to learn a lot about Edith's early ancestors and the more he learned the darker and more secretive it became. The family name became linked to several secret societies and one had the symbol of the 'All Seeing Eye'. It was the innocuously sounding 'Society of the Eye'. Not a lot could be found in archives about this other than speculation and suspicions of writers of the time. Members were known to be powerful people and there was speculation that anyone who got too close and was about to reveal details about them, suddenly and strangely disappeared. If Ian was right the family had a ready-made production line to deal with any unwanted attention and powerful contacts to shut down any publicity.

It was beginning to sound like the Covenant was the founding document for the society and that it was between the senior members of that society, with any new member presumably having to agree to it.

Ian wrote up his report for Janet. She would not like what had been found and would have to decide what to put in the public domain and what to keep confidential. After all she was not only curator of the museum but in a way, of the family name. Thankfully from Janet's point of view all the staff had signed a non-disclosure agreement when accepting a position with the museum. This had been done initially to help with positive publicity so that instead of any notable findings being leaked, they could be properly announced to gain the maximum benefit for the museum which, of course, would help with visitor numbers. The agreement would suit just as well in this circumstance even though at the time it hadn't been considered.

The lights in the conservation room dimmed. This time Ian wondered if they were having a power problem. He tried to contact someone using his office phone but it was dead. He reached for his radio but the battery was flat. That was strange as he had only charged it a few hours ago. He could here feint voices coming from the room next door the room that had the hidden door running off it. The door that Janet hoped she had found the key for. Why would voices be coming from there? Nobody was in there, they would have needed to go through his room first to gain access, wouldn't they?

Ian grabbed a torch and went to the empty room and up to the hidden door. He could hear voices louder than before. He placed his hand on the door, it was cold, the voices stopped instantly. Ian looked through the keyhole but something was covering it from the other side. He placed his ear to the door and waited. He pushed against it and a loud thump from the other side made him jump. Someone or something had just banged from the other side of the door as if they knew he was listening in!

How could anyone possibly be there? This door was sealed shut and had been for many years. This didn't make any sense to him but he could tell it was colder by the door. The room smelled of damp and fustiness. He felt ill at ease again, as he had done before.

Ian ran back to his room, the lights had totally failed but he still had his torch. He decided it was time to leave for the day and went back upstairs, not telling anyone what had happened. He left the museum and headed home which was a small house in which he lived alone apart from his pet cat called Tiger. Thankfully the only resemblance to its larger cousin was the ginger tabby stripes on his fur. Tiger was free to come and go during the day thanks to a flap in the back door, operated by an electronic trigger on his collar. He was a very affectionate and easy-going cat. The type that was happy to come on your knee to be petted and then fall asleep. He was good company for Ian.

One of the rooms in the house had been turned into a study with books on various subjects along with a microfiche system loaned to him by the museum. Tiger liked to have a nosy and climb on the desk as he didn't get to go in that room as often as the others and cats being eternally curious have to check out to see if anything has changed. Ian decided he would calm his nerves by feeding Tiger and then researching on the microfiche. He wanted to see if he could find any more about that secret society. This would be a slow process.

Once Tiger had decided he had finished his snack he went to assist Ian at his desk. He jumped up and started walking towards the microfiche keyboard. Tiger's tail was standing proud upright as he walked over to where Ian was forwarding through the documents. Ian tried ignoring the cat but of course all that did was make Tiger more curious as to what could be more important than him. Tiger looked at the microfiche screen and let out a loud meow and jumped off the desk. Now he was growling as if there was a threat in the room. This was not like him at all as even in the presence of another cat, Tiger was usually very calm and quiet. Ian wondered what was wrong. He looked at the screen and instead of a photographed document he saw a contorted face of a young man in pain and with his hand outstretched as if pleading for help. It gave Ian a start and he let out a gasp. The cat ran off and when Ian returned his gaze to the screen, it was back to normal. He wondered if he had been working too hard and not been getting enough sleep. These screens could be harsh on the eyes and maybe it was that.

He turned off his microfiche system and poured himself a glass of red wine. He knew that helped him sleep and thought he might have an early night. He ran himself a bath first to make him feel more relaxed. He had candles in the bathroom which he lit and poured some lavender bubble bath into the water. He always left the bathroom door open so Tiger could come and see what was going on, even though the cat was, like most cats, virtually allergic to water and would run at the slightest splash in his direction.

Ian put his clothes in the washing basket and went to the bathroom. He paused and looked at the mirrored cabinet. The mirror doors were steamed up. He wiped them with a towel. He looked in the mirror, thankfully nothing untoward, just Ian looking back at him although a little pale. Hardly surprising as most of his recent time had been spent in the basement of the museum. He needed to get more fresh air and promised himself to get out for a run more often as the weather was improving.

The bath was filling nicely, Ian checked the temperature was to his liking and turned off the tap, which squeaked a little as he did so. The wall alongside the bath was tiled in a mix of navy blue and white. The tiles although not a mirrored effect, still gave a reflection and the candles added an effect of depth to the room. Ian slowly climbed into the bath. He looked at the tiled wall and jumped when he saw another face looking back at him. He spun his head around only to see Tiger looking at him from the corner of the bath. Ian smiled and stroked his cat who obligingly started to purr. Tiger didn't like water but he did like a warm room and the bathroom was suddenly very inviting with the corner of the bath even more so, being warm from the hot water.

Tiger was slow blinking, showing his approval to Ian, as cats do to people they know and trust. Ian had topped up his wine glass and placed it on a recessed shelf next to the bath. The candles glowed, the cat purred and Ian was finally relaxed. He didn't realise it but he had fallen asleep. Tiger decided the lack of attention meant it was time for him to change rooms and to curl up by a radiator. All of a sudden, Ian could feel a cold draft. There shouldn't be any as all of the windows and external doors were closed. He heard the squeak of a tap and felt cold water pouring onto his feet. Then his feet were pulled up sharply and his head went under the bath water. Ian jumped up gasping for air. He scanned the bathroom, the candles were still lit, the tap wasn't running and there was no draft, he had fallen asleep and started dreaming.

The water was still nice and warm so he had some more of the wine and laid back in the lavender scented foam bubbles. He didn't usually have bad dreams and decided this research was getting the better of him. Now he felt something cold around his ankles as if someone had grasped him with icy cold hands. He looked at his feet but there was nothing to see. The next second he was under the bathwater as his feet had been pulled up high to force the rest of him under water. He was splashing with his arms trying to get a breath but his head was fully submerged. He was panicking, thrashing around, then his feet fell back to the bathwater and he was able to pull himself up to get some air. He was struggling to catch his breath and coughing. Again, there was nothing to be seen. No presence of any kind.

Ian decided to have a quick wash, empty the bath and dry himself ready for going to bed. He made sure he had a full glass of wine and that Tiger had food in his plate along with some treats.

He would retreat to bed with a book and his wine. The book was 'Oliver Twist' by Charles Dickens. Ian had read it many times before but liked the characters and he needed something familiar to drift off to sleep to.

His wine helped him relax and the book helped him feel sleepy. Ian drifted off into a deep sleep, he started dreaming about a large sailing ship being loaded with supplies at the dock. Then he saw men and some older children being brought on board, they were in chains and had two large and angry looking men herding them like animals. They each had a cat o' nine tails that they could use to keep order. Looking at the state of the convicts, it was highly unlikely any of them had the strength to put up much of a fight. They were thin, dishevelled with rags as clothes, beards and they looked like they hadn't been washed in a long time.

Ian's dream was very vivid and it was as if he was watching through some sort of portal, where he wasn't taking part but he could hear and see everything going on.

He saw the men in the hold of the ship, chained to each other and to hoops in the ship. He saw several of them brought to the captain, one by one. He heard the captain shout at them and that their lives were already over so they might as well do something good for their families. Each was told a sum of money would be paid to their relatives if they signed the document in front of them. Most couldn't read or write so the captain read out a summary saying that they consented to their souls being given up in exchange for the money and better food on the voyage. Each man looked scared at this point but agreed as what use was their soul to them and again most didn't really understand what a soul was and they were virtually starving from their incarceration so the thought of some real food meant they readily signed – what more could they possibly lose, and if it helped back home?

Once they had signed the document, (or made a mark with their cross), they were returned to the hold and given some hot food. The ones still waiting saw this and were eager to be taken to the captain as they were so hungry. They didn't care what they had to sign to get it. The next part of Ian's dream saw the ship coming into a dock, one that he recognised. It was an old but very busy version of the one with train tracks. He saw the men being taken off and being led off to a warehouse. He couldn't see any name just a very large number 12.

Ian's dream seemed to move on and he saw some of them, men, moving crates around the basement of the warehouse. They were checking crates of goods that presumably had come off the ships at the dockside. He saw others being led down a tunnel to a large chamber with inscriptions on the wall. There were lots of symbols but he couldn't make them out. They were being plied with gin from a large barrel for some reason. Then a figure appeared making incantations and the men were each forced to give up some of their blood by a dagger being drawn across the palm of their hand. Their hand was held over a gold bowl until some of their blood was added. More incantations were said and the blood was poured into a large vessel. The men were given a final small drink and after a short while they began to fall to the floor.

The bodies of the men were placed in white sheets and placed side by side on hand carts. Ian saw these being wheeled through the tunnels. Before anything else happened, Ian was woken up by a furry tail swishing against his face. Tiger was purring and happy to be on the warm bed laid leaning against Ian. It was a nice wakeup call and was just before the alarm clock went off so was good timing. Ian was quite relieved to have been woken up from this nightmare and it took him a little while to shake off the foreboding. After cuddling tiger for a few minutes, Ian got ready for work at the museum.

Ian felt very troubled by what had happened at the office and even more so at his house. He decided the latter must just all have been part of a dream, that was the only rational explanation. A dream brought on by intensive research mixed in with his personal knowledge of old sailing ships and conditions convicts were kept in.

Chapter 6

Janet was desperate to try out that huge black key that Marge had given her when they were in the attic sorting through items. Janet thought it only right to invite Marge and her group of friends back to the museum to see if the key could open the hidden door. The ladies had all eagerly accepted the invitation as they were just as keen to see what was behind the door. Janet had arranged for Ian to be with them as she thought he would be interested and might be able to comment about anything they found. She also thought it a good idea to have a couple of workmen, from the restoration team, with them in case there was any poor support work that might need their attention.

It was early morning and everybody was gathered together in the hall way and Janet had suggested that Marge have the honour of trying the key in the lock and hopefully then opening the much talked about door. This was going to be very embarrassing if after all this anticipation, the key didn't fit the lock. Everyone quietly considered the possibility but nobody dare speak it. After all what else would a key that size fit? It was an unusually large sized key for an internal door which only led to more intrigue and speculation.

When everyone was ready, Janet led the party down the stairs, through the conservation lab and into the next room where there was the door that had been hidden seemingly for many years. It was at the far end of the room and so people had assumed this was the end of the basement but apparently not.

The workman only found the door by accident when they were emptying this room, it was obvious some of the brickwork would need some repairs and while checking the walls they noticed something not quite right. There were clearly some differences in the age of the brickwork in this particular corner and when they had tapped it with a hammer, it had sounded hollow. A decision was made to check it out and remove some of the bricks in case there was damage behind them which may lead to a structural issue. When the team had carefully removed part of the brickwork, it was then they discovered the door and they had looked for the key ever since.

The workmen had rigged up some temporary lights ready for the occasion so at least that wouldn't be an issue. Marge went over to the door with Janet and placed the large black key in the lock, it fitted perfectly. Now to see if it would turn the mechanism. Marge turned the key to the left, it was very stiff, so she brought both hands to bear and it turned with a sudden clunk. Immediately the temporary lights began to flicker. The two workmen went to check the connections, everything seemed in order but the lights continued to flicker for a while.

Voices could be heard and they appeared to be coming from the other side of the door. This was somewhat alarming as they had no idea what to expect on the other side. Janet shouted, "Hello?" but no response. The voices on the other side stopped and everybody in the room went quiet. Now it sounded like there were whispers in the room they were in, but it wasn't coming from anyone in the group. It wasn't audible what was being said, just a low-level whisper that couldn't be made sense of. Janet asked, "Whose there?" Again, no response and now the whispers had stopped.

Marge got the nod from Janet and turned the large handle and pushed on the door. The door opened with surprising ease but as it did so, there was a rush of cold air that passed over the group. It surprised them all, why would air need to leave the room? They were unnerved and the hairs stood up on the back of their necks. There was a feeling of foreboding but surely that was just everybody feeling nervous about what might be beyond the door.

Janet had a torch and she used it to see what was on the other side of the door. It was very dark but it looked like it was a tunnel lined with brickwork. The floor appeared to be made from terracotta tiles. If this was in keeping with the rest of the house, these tiles would be very thick and stable. More torches were used to light up the passage, which seemed to be in very good condition. This was raising more questions than it was answering. What was the tunnel for? Where did it lead? Why had it been sealed off? Who had built it and for what purpose?

It was thought safer to let the two workmen lead from this point as they could check on the stability of the tunnel and warn of any likely dangers. They had been prepared and had some very large torches. They also had a mallet they could use to strike the brickwork to test the sound and movement, if there was any. It all seemed very secure. The tunnel had a high ceiling and was surprisingly wide. This had been a major undertaking when constructed. If this was just for people traffic then a lot of people could move around the tunnel at the same time. The group slowly continued moving forward until they came to a crossroads with tunnels of the same quality to the right, left and straight on. The obvious thing for now was to carry straight on and that's what they did. The last thing they needed was to take a turn and then get lost underground.

They continued on for quite a long way until they entered a large chamber. There were symbols all over the walls and dead ahead above another open tunnel, carved in stonework was the symbol of the 'All Seeing Eye'. This had been seen before in the research in to the 'Society of the Eye'. Was this to do with that secret society?

Ian was getting deja-vu, this looked just like the tunnel opening and chamber he had seen in his nightmare. He couldn't see the symbols properly then, but he could now. He felt a cold shiver run down his back and he felt very uncomfortable. Janet noticed his reaction and asked if he was alright. He reluctantly explained that he had seen this chamber in a dream that he had and that he had suspicions of what went on in this room. It was some sort of anti-chamber where people might gather before presumably going on into the next tunnel that had been lined with stone.

The far tunnel entrance was clear and just as large as the previous tunnel but now lined with a light-coloured stone, probably sandstone. Everything was in remarkably good condition and was obviously built to stand the test of time. The direction of travel appeared to be towards the dock area of the city. This was going to be a longer exploration than anyone could have anticipated.

Janet discussed with the group the possibility of turning back and leaving further exploration for a later date with a properly prepared set of workmen. Nobody liked the idea of just heading back after they had come this far, they all wanted to know what this was about and what they might find. The workmen however suggested returning to the museum to lay out a string of lights in the tunnel. It had been noticed that there were fixings built into the walls, presumably for candles and these could be used to support strings of lights they had on long coils in preparation for just such an underground discovery. While they were busy on that task the rest of the group could examine the anti-chamber and discuss its possible function. They would need many reels of lights but they had plenty in store and being made for this purpose there was a lot of cable on each reel.

It didn't take long for the workmen to set up a continuous lighting rig. They joined lots of coils together and powered them using an electric generator they had placed just outside in the museum gardens. They brought extra coils, loaded on sack barrows, to rig up in the tunnel that was at the far side of the anti-chamber. It was now a lot easier to see the detail in the walls, the decoration and symbolism.

The group pressed on out of the anti-chamber and into the next tunnel. It was not clear if the quality of the tunnel surround was meant to inspire or intimidate the people travelling through. Before long they arrived at a huge space faced in large stone blocks with many symbols and images carved into the walls and ceiling. This would need a lot of light to fully illuminate but to everyone's surprise there were doors leading in different directions. Each had three heavy metal bolts keeping them shut. They were certainly meant to stop people entering this space. The doors looked like they were made from iron, in which case they would be very heavy and also very strong. Nobody would be able to easily get past these.

It was decided they would try one door that was in the opposite side of the room to where they entered. The workmen carefully examined the doors for damage and slowly slid the bolts to the open position. They pulled on the door and it opened remarkably easily considering the obvious weight and age of the door. The hinges had clearly been well made and the door well balanced. The people who built and fitted this door knew what they were doing and spared no time or expense on it. One of the workmen shone a torch which revealed a stone stairway leading upwards.

The group slowly ascended the staircase, there were more symbols on the stone clad walls. As with the previous tunnels there was plenty of space both in height and width for a considerable number of people to move along at once. After navigating the stairs for some time, they came across a landing and then a door equally as impressive as the earlier ones they had encountered. Again, the bolts were on their side and they slid them open and swung the door towards them. There was a large thick curtain covering the doorway, they pushed it to one side. It suddenly dawned on Janet where they might be. The room they just entered was cavernous and seemed to be a storage area for a wide range of items. It was a basement room to some old building. As the group looked around Marge found a light switch and turned it on.

The storage area was huge and right away similar symbols could be seen on the walls. There was a stairway on the far left. Janet asked the workmen to check it out, on ascending the stone stairs the two workmen came up against yet another iron door, this time a double one, bolted from the inside. They pushed the bolts over and pushed up at the doors. There must be some sort of counterweight helping as the doors pushed up easily, despite their obvious weight. The men found themselves outside at the back of a large house, more like a small mansion house. There was a road leading towards an impressively tall iron fence and a large set of gates.

When the men returned and told Janet what they had found, she instantly knew her hunch was right. They were in, what was locally known as, the Chapel. Janet had researched the history of the place as part of her doctorate. It was a mysterious building in its own grounds surrounded by a high, decorative iron fence which in turn sat on a thick brick and stone wall. At one point in time, the building had stood alone but gradually land had been sold off to the growing town, not for housing but commercial and civic buildings.

The most curious thing Janet had found about the 'Chapel' was that its ownership had been placed in trust to some anonymous organisation and a large sum of money had been left for its maintenance. The only thing local people saw was teams of gardeners and the like who would perform routine maintenance and then leave. If anyone asked who had engaged their company and paid their bills, they would be told it was a confidential matter and they couldn't discuss it.

Janet realised they were in a strange situation, technically they were trespassing in the basement of a local enigma. When they examined the basement, they realised it was very orderly and used as some sort of storage facility. There were lots wooden storage boxes. It looked like an Aladdin's cave, a treasure trove, but they had no legal way of finding out what was actually there. Janet thought it was high time she gathered the group together and that they retreated back towards the museum. She made sure the curtain was once again covering the doorway as it was closed and she also made sure it was bolted from their side so nobody from the 'Chapel' could enter.

It took a good hour to walk back to the museum. They closed each of the heavy doors behind them and the workmen reeled in the lighting rigs but left the spools in position so they could be used again soon. The tunnels were dry so there was no fear of damage to the lights. The brick and stonework were in perfect condition which, was in itself, intriguing. Someone had been maintaining these passage ways up until quite recently.

The group of explorers entered the room adjacent to the conservation lab back at the museum. As they did so they got the fright of their lives. There was a boy in the middle of the room looking away from them. Janet asked if she could help and who he was. She knew of course there should be nobody down here, it was a restricted area but something wasn't right. The boy was dressed in shabby, dirty Victorian style clothes. When Janet beckoned to him again, he spun around on the spot. He looked ghastly, almost like a skeleton and he shouted at them in a terrifying demonic voice, "Why didn't anybody help me?" several of the group let out a shriek and then covered their mouths as if to stop them accidentally making a noise.

The apparition's eyes glowed white and he ran at the group. Instinctively they moved out of the way and they saw the boy run through the solid iron door, they had closed moments earlier. Everyone was shocked and looked at each other speechless. The workmen insisted they wanted to leave and that the women should as well. They all quickly went into the lab next door and up the stairs to the main hall. They slammed the door behind them and Janet locked it. She told the workmen to take the rest of the day off and suggested the rest should go into the, soon to be, visitor café area.

Everyone looked very thoughtful and concerned about what they had just encountered. Marge asked Janet what was going on. Reluctantly Janet explained about her thesis she had written whilst at university. She had extensively researched the local area regarding commerce that had helped pay for the town's and now, city's development. Inevitably there would be some myths and legends about local business men, especially as this was a port, and so she had researched them as well.

She had spent years looking in local archives and interviewing anyone she thought might be able to shed some light on local history. Time and again fingers were pointed at this 'Chapel' as being at the centre of some unsavoury happenings. Her research showed up some key figures almost founding fathers and she had formed suspicions around some of them. At least some of it was connected to the shipping family – the one Edith and the museum itself were descendants of. It was this work that had allowed her to gain the position of curator and had impressed the trustees of the estate.

During her research Janet had come across mention of a tunnel under Edith's house. It was gossip as much as anything and hearsay but when the hidden door had been discovered during renovations, Janet had suspected that it led to the tunnel. She also heard mention of this large iron key that Edith was supposed to keep in a small chest in her room. When Edith became ill, one of her servants came across it when looking for something. How it ended up in the house clearance sale was a mystery. It seemed the key had been treated more as a curiosity than anything else and that the lock it opened had been assumed to be lost over time.

Marge promised to have another search through her loft to see if there was anything else that might be of interest and maybe belong to this house. She knew there was still two substantial boxes to go through. Janet offered to help as it was helping unravel the ancient history to the museum and possibly to the town.

Ian desperately wanted to tell Janet about the rest of his dream, although it had felt more like a nightmare at the time, now it was looking more like a planted memory or even a vision. This sort of language isn't the sort that would be expected from someone in charge of conservation and someone with a reputation to protect, so for now he kept quiet.

Once the women had composed themselves sufficiently, they agreed to call it a day. Marge and Janet set off in search of more artefacts.

Chapter 7

The two women got to Marge's house and entered the kitchen. Immediately there was a loud bang from upstairs. The two looked at each other. Marge called out to see if any of the family had returned home early but no one answered. She shouted again but no response other than a thump from the bedroom above the kitchen. The two of them fortified themselves and then went up the stairs very slowly. As they approached the bedroom, Marge noticed the door was shut. That was strange because she knew she had left it open earlier to allow air circulation. Maybe that was the bang they heard when they came in, that a draft had slammed the door shut.

This was a comforting thought as she reached for the bedroom door handle. The comfort however was soon shattered as there was a tremendous thump on the door from inside the bedroom. They decided to leave the house and Marge called her brother Roy on the way out. She told him they would be waiting for him in the back garden. If they needed to leave quickly, they could as there was a gate in the fence that led straight onto an open green area.

Roy was employed as a security guard so wasn't phased by doors banging. It was his two days off so he agreed to come over right away. He was only about a twenty-minute drive away. He told them to stay where they were and that he would meet them by the back gate. While they were waiting, they looked up at the bedroom window – the one above the kitchen. They could clearly see the shape and face of a young boy. It looked menacing and the eyes were looking right at them. It made them both jump – was this an intruder or something else?

They waited for Roy to arrive. When he did, they told him about the boy but when they looked back at the bedroom, there was nobody there. Roy reassured them and told them to stay where they were as he went to check out the bedroom. Roy got to the bedroom door and there was a repeat of what had happened to Marge, a loud thump on the inside of the door as if someone was inside the bedroom and was telling him to keep out. Roy thought this must be the boy and quickly and forcibly entered the room. He was keyed up and ready to shout at the intruder. Roy was trained in martial arts and was a physically dominant presence which he used to his advantage in his job.

To Roy's surprise there was nothing untoward in the room. He quickly looked out of the window and waved to Marge and Janet. The closet door was shut and there was a bed – both points were possibilities where someone could hide. Roy used his most authoritative voice and instructed any intruder to come out and leave peacefully while they had the chance. There was no noise, no response. Roy bounced on the bed hoping to surprise anyone who might be hiding underneath. When there was no response, he went towards the closet door and pulled the doors open. They did so with a click and a whoosh of air. Roy could see at a glance that the loft access panel was open and pushed to one side. He moved the clothes to see if anyone was hiding, again nothing.

He decided there was only two possibilities after what the two women had told him. Either there was indeed someone under the bed or they had gone into the loft space. The latter seemed the obvious spot with the access panel being open. Roy resolved to quickly look under the bed and did so with speed so as to startle anyone there, nothing. Now there was only one place left.

Roy had been in the loft on a previous occasion when Marge and her family first moved in. He had helped carry boxes and put some of them up in the loft for later sorting. He knew there was a set of ladders that pulled down. He used the hooked pole and pulled the ladders down. Any minute he expected someone to show themselves and to try and fight passed him. He would be ready if they did. Roy tuned on the lights in the loft and climbed the ladder. His aim was to enter the loft as quickly as possible as he would be at a disadvantage just slowly showing his head above the access panel. He quickly put the top half of his body into the loft space and looked around. There was nothing obvious to start with, no person, although there were a few large boxes someone small could hide behind.

Then it happened – a large cardboard box was sent flying through the air towards Roy, this was his intruder. The trouble was Roy was expecting a teenage boy. What he actually saw was two red eyes, looking like fire staring right at him. Roy was so startled he slipped and feel back down the ladders. He was only bruised but was also petrified. He wasn't used to this feeling and quickly composed himself and got back on the foot of the ladders. He climbed into the loft as quickly as he could. He was short of breath but ready for anything. This time there were no eyes, red or, otherwise looking back to him.

He quickly and loudly searched the attic space hoping to scare anyone to rush down the ladders and out of the door. He moved boxes and deliberately banged around but there was no one to be seen and nothing unpleasant to be found. He searched twice just to make sure – looking at every inch of that space, there was nothing. Roy decided there was nothing left to do but to go back downstairs. He also now remembered that his sister and her friend were still waiting in the back garden. He went out to talk to them and reassured them that he had searched the bedroom and the loft and found nothing. He somehow managed to forget the loud noises and red eyes he had encountered. He didn't want to scare anyone and he certainly didn't want them wondering about his mental health.

They all decided they deserved a hot drink and something sweet. Marge was an excellent cook and made a large pot of tea and brought out some home-made chocolate cake which fitted the bill perfectly as it was delicious.

As it was a day off for Roy and he was partly concerned and partly genuinely interested he said he would help them with their investigations for the rest of the day and between the three of them, they could go through whatever was left to sort in the attic. There was a table in the loft which was handy as it could be used to stand boxes on one at a time and then empty the contents onto before deciding what would happen – charity shop, sell, donate to the museum or keep for the family if it might come in handy. These were the final boxes the previous owner had left behind so Marge had no idea what was to be found in them.

Roy gathered up some empty boxes so items could be sorted as they went. He kept one of the boxes empty and that would be used for the charity shop. Another box was items for sale. Not surprisingly it looked like the charity shop was to benefit the most. Marge was happy with that as charities need all the help they can get. They setup a mini production line with Janet going first to see if there was anything she could recognise. Anything she did, she put to one side. Next was Marge deciding if it would go to charity etc. Roy was then placing the items in the different boxes. He could take the charitable items into the shop on his way home.

They finally came to the end with Janet having a group of items put to one side for further scrutiny. One was a wooden box with inlaid decoration. It was in excellent condition and Janet recognised it from the inventory Edith had produced. This hadn't been mistakenly put in the house sale. It was listed as missing in the inventory and Edith presumed it had been stolen by one of the servants or workmen that had been in her house carrying out maintenance. Edith made a note that she was more bothered about the contents than the box itself. At the time it had a ring that belonged to one of her male ancestors. It had circular gold bands with two rows of small diamonds flanking the central motif of the 'All Seeing Eye'.

Janet was keen to open the box and see if there was anything inside. There was the original key still in the lock at the front and it opened with ease. There were some seals of the type you would use with red wax to conclude a contract, there was no ring. Janet had got used to the way this family worked. She began looking for a hidden compartment. She shook the box but nothing rattled. She felt the inside of the box and tried sliding the what was supposed to be the bottom. Slowly she managed to slide the piece of wood to one side and it revealed a secret layer about an inch deep. It was divided into several small compartments, in one of them was the ring. It had been wrapped in a piece of felt to stop it making any sound if someone had shaken the box. She guessed that's why it hadn't been noticed by the person who had taken the box then sold it presumably disappointed there was nothing more valuable inside.

The ring was beautiful and was obviously meant for a male finger. Janet was very excited and told Marge that, if she was willing, the museum would offer a good market value for the piece and that it should be worth in the region of twenty thousand pounds, possibly more. Marge thought that was more than fair as she wasn't even aware she possessed it. Roy asked about its provenance and Janet told them that it belonged to the Grand Master of the Society of the Eye. It was used as a symbol of office and as a seal of authority that many would recognise including those outside. If this seal was used on a document, the instructions within would be followed to the letter and with great haste. All the tradesmen of the time knew this was the family seal of the Markle's. The powerful shipping family.

The ring had passed to Edith through the generations and she was most upset to have been parted from it. There was also a medallion with ribbon attached. On checking the front, the engraving proudly stated, "Grand Master."

The ring had a glow and a sparkle to it, the artefact was truly beautiful and was an emblem of power and wealth. It felt strange seeing it out of context like this but it was a good feeling knowing it would be reunited with the estate to which it belonged and for it to be part of a museum collection.

The remaining items, Janet had placed to one side included a planchette from a Ouija board. It had the eye insignia etched into the wood and a clear glass centrepiece so, when used with the board, the letter underneath could be seen. Janet picked up the planchette and looked through the glass insert. She was shocked to see a tall man looking straight at her and then walk quickly towards her, his face very close to hers. She reeled back and dropped the implement. She looked as white as a sheet and was breathing heavily.

Janet had recognised the man she had seen and knew there was something seriously wrong. It was the head of the Markle family at the pinnacle of their power. She presumed he was the one who was the Grand Master. How could this have happened? How could that image be there, even if it was just a recording? How could he have reacted to Janet's presence – her head was spinning.

The last significant item was, what looked like, a mini strong box that was highly decorated but with no apparent way of opening. This was another one of these hidden compartment boxes, only this time you had to find a way to open it in the first place. Janet had composed herself by now and was closely examining the ornate work on the box. There had to be some hidden point to press or slide. This wasn't listed on Edith's inventory so she either wasn't aware of it or didn't want to draw people's attention to it.

The box was quite heavy and would take a lot of effort to break into. Its contents then would be valuable in one way or another, else why go to all this effort and expense. Janet used her pocket magnifying glass to search the surface of the metal box. There were lots of what looked like holes built into the design of the decorative work. She felt this was part of the disguise of where the opening mechanism might be found. She asked Marge if she could use force to open it. Marge had no attachment to the box and was just as intrigued to see what might be inside and so agreed.

Janet took a nearby hammer and struck the box with it. They all soon regretted those actions. There was an almighty crash in the house, as if a huge thunder clap had struck close by. The entire house vibrated and the sound was deafening. The box was intact, the hammer had rebounded in Janet's hand and was lying on the floor several feet away. Janet had an idea and slowly and hesitantly held the planchette up to the box. She prepared herself to look through the glass. As she did, she saw the same face close up and very angry, seemingly shouting, at least she was prepared for it this time. She focussed and could see a twin of the box on a desk in the room with the angry man. It was open and there was a device inserted in the left side towards the back. This had to be the opening point.

Janet slammed down the planchette, only to receive another loud bang in response. She opened a little box of tools she had in her pocket. There was a pointed item similar to one a watch repairer would use. It was pointed at one end. Janet used it to probe the various holes on the left side of the box and to the back. Non seemed to do anything until she tried one that the implement slid further inside. She pressed it harder, as hard as she could and the lid to the box opened ever so slightly. She lifted the lid to find a red velvet inlay to the inside of the box. There were rings and broaches and a necklace, all heavily jewelled inset into gold all fitted on mouldings within the box to stop any movement and to display them properly.

If these jewels were real, and there was no reason to think otherwise, considering the container they were found in, they would be worth a fortune. Janet reached for one of the large pieces containing a huge gemstone. It was some sort of pendant, meant to be worn like a medal on the coat chest. As she picked it up an apparition appeared. It was that same man she had seen through the planchette. This time he was a full body towards the end of the loft space. He looked fierce. He was in some sort of uniform, some regalia. He was wearing the pendant on his left-hand breast pocket. He had a ribbon and medallion around his neck and the ring on his finger. This must be the 'Grand Master'.

The temperature had dropped suddenly and the air was filled with what felt like static electricity. The three of them couldn't believe what they were seeing. Nobody said a word but they all had their mouths open in disbelief and horror. This thing was looking right at them and was clearly not pleased. As the spirit slowly moved forward, each step sounded like it was made by a huge weight being dropped on the floor. As the spirit drew closer it let out an ear-splitting cry. Marge grabbed the pendant from Janet, threw it into the box and closed the lid. Instantly the apparition disappeared. She turned to Roy and Janet and nearly passed out with relief.

They took the items down the steps and firmly closed the entrance to the loft. They all needed some reflection time and to talk about what had just happened. They decided to do that at the museum rather than stay in this house.

Marge wondered if it was this box that was causing the disturbances in her home and she would be pleased to see all of these items be taken away. She didn't want any of this to affect the family. She wanted everyone of the items associated with Edith out of her loft and out of the house. If apparitions were somehow connected to these items, she wanted them a long way away. It was high time the house went back to being a family home, warm and welcoming and hopefully, quiet.

Chapter 8

Marge, Roy and Janet had reconvened at the museum the following day. Marge's family only knew that the loft had finally been sorted through and some items were going to the museum and that there would be an improvement in family finances as a result. Everybody liked the sound of that and so no more questions were forthcoming.

Janet had asked Ian to get involved with the find and so they all went down to the conservation lab. Janet insisted everyone should wear gloves and that they should not touch any of the gems directly. She didn't want a repeat of what had happened in the loft and thought it might be triggered by human touch.

The beautiful strongbox was opened and the contents spilled out on to a piece of black felt laid on a special sorting table. The edges were raised so that small items couldn't fall off. Janet took charge of arranging the items and told Ian just to pass any comments and observations if he recognised anything. She used a large pair of tweezers to move the items around and display them properly. Thankfully this time no apparition appeared – maybe her theory was right. There were some impressive jewels set in some complicated gold settings. There was some amazing craftsmanship on show. These were one off bespoke pieces, that would fetch a great deal of value on the open market.

Janet asked Marge if she was ok to sell to the museum if they were given an official impartial valuation. The museum trust had plenty of funds that could be called on for the purchase and Marge was happy for them to be part of the Markle / Wilson family story, especially after what had happened yesterday. She also knew the funds would be very useful for her family and so agreed. The items included the large pendant, a heavy gold chain necklace supporting a large gold disc that looked a little like an Olympic medal. There were three gold rings inset with various stones. Also present were some lapel badges with different symbols on the front. Ian speculated these could signify some rank within the top echelon of the society.

Neither the strong box or the contents were listed in Edith's inventory. This meant she either didn't know of them, which seemed strange or more likely, that she wanted no mention of them in any records. In that way if they got lost, they couldn't be traced back to the family. You would only want that to be the case if these were in some way dangerous to their owner's reputation. There were several links to the Society of the Eye including an inlay on the inside of the strongbox but no direct links to any of the Wilson family.

Ian photographed the pieces in close up, while Janet gave Marge a receipt for them. The strongbox itself looked like it was worth a lot of money. It was a bespoke piece and of the highest quality. When Ian looked at the photographs he got a shock, at first, he thought there was a mark on the camera lens or it was light flare but when he enlarged the photos, he could see a face snarling back at him. He showed Janet who then told him what had happened in the loft with the apparition. Ian looked apprehensive he was still reeling from his last encounter.

Janet arranged for an independent valuation but insisted they come to the museum and not physically touch anything unless they were wearing gloves. After consideration of the weight in gold and the value of the gems plus additional for the amazing craftsmanship, the valuation estimate came back at just under a million pounds. When Marge heard the good news, she was delighted and Janet arranged for the money to be paid. All had been quiet in the loft and bedroom lately and Marge was hoping, whatever it was had left with the museum items.

Mum and dad discussed what to do with the money and they decided to put some in trust for each of us and then buy a bigger house with a nice sized garden that would be more private. We all hoped the new place would be quieter but time would show that not to be the case.

Janet didn't dare put the strongbox and contents on public display, instead they were kept in the museum safe when not being researched. Now Janet wanted to find out more about the tunnels and the other building one of them led to.

There was a physical connection between the museum and the 'Chapel'. Janet figured this must have belonged to the Markle or Wilson family at some point so she researched the trust that the 'Chapel' now belonged to. After a lot of painstaking checking with archives and the land registry, Janet was able to finally prove that the trust beneficiary was none other than Edith's estate. That transformed everything as Edith's estate had been put in trust to the museum and its trustees, subject to any remaining relatives being found. That meant that through a very complicated route of trusts and wills, the Chapel house actually belonged to the museum. Janet was put in overall charge of both buildings as it was her hard work that had uncovered the findings.

Edith had effectively set up both buildings with their own trusts and finances so they could stand alone as if owned by separate entities. That felt like a very strange setup but there must have been a good reason. Edith obviously didn't want the two buildings associated with each other. Was it another way to keep the family names distanced from each other? Did it have anything to do with the contents of the crates in the chapel basement? Now at least these could be opened and catalogued and maybe then some of the answers might be forthcoming.

Janet was tasked with learning everything she could about the 'Chapel' and employed additional staff to help. The museum opening was put on hold until the nature of the connection to the two properties could be ascertained. Janet tasked some staff to empty and catalogue the contents of the many crates and boxes in the basement of the 'Chapel'. The official name was Maple Hall. The boxes contained many rare antiques that had been carefully placed in the storage crates that had been in position for many decades. There was another fortune in these crates and it was decided a second museum should be created so as to be able to put the contents on display. A new building was to be constructed within the grounds of Maple Hall for that purpose. It would have to be built in a style in keeping with the main Hall but finance wasn't an issue and a design was commissioned and the necessary permissions given.

Janet continued looking into the archives and trying to find out more about the illusive and powerful Markle family and the Society of the Eye. If they had felt they needed to be so secretive and had at least two properties linked underground but did their best to keep the collective ownership hidden, maybe there were more buildings and or connections, possibly even more tunnels still to be found.

There was an obvious candidate in a building close to the river. It didn't appear to be used by anybody yet it was well maintained. This was getting to be a familiar story. Sure enough, the archives uncovered the building was in trust and had been so since it was built by none other than the Markle family. The trust was still in force and could be traced back to Edith as the beneficiary in an ancestral will. This building made perfect sense for the family shipping business, being so close to the river, it could be used to store goods for transport on their ships. This was a third building that was now under the over-arching trust that benefitted the museum.

The riverside building was a large warehouse facility with several floors and a basement. It had no official name just a number, 12. When Janet told Ian of the latest acquisition, his face drained of all colour and she could tell he looked worried. She asked him what was wrong and he told her of the rest of the dream he had about people coming off a ship and being led to a warehouse with the number 12 on the side. He said he expected that there would be a hidden door found that would lead to a tunnel and that would take them back to the anti-chamber they had been in before.

Janet was fascinated with Ian's revelation and she herself had already made the leap into assuming there would be underground links connecting the now, three buildings. She set men about searching for a hidden door. They eventually found one. They had to break into a wall to gain access as this one had been bricked up and only revealed itself when careful room measurements were taken and it became obvious there was something that didn't match up. They carefully removed the brickwork and revealed a door. It was a heavy metal one as before and was counterweighted to make it swing relatively easily.

When they opened it, they realised this would take longer than expected. The tunnel behind the door had been filled with rubble. Someone had decided to block off the connection between Warehouse 12 and presumably Maple Hall. They had found the same thing when they had looked at side tunnels under Edith's house. Due to cost and lack of evidence they hadn't been excavated further but now there was a case to clear the debris and uncover more of the story.

Construction work can apparently be key to awakening supernatural activity and cause it to increase substantially. There are plenty of contract staff involved with clearing those tunnels that would testify of that being the case. This is one reason why it took so long, several people refusing to carry on working on them because of how oppressive the atmosphere was and others claiming they had either seen or heard things which they didn't want to talk about. There was also the fact that there were a lot of symbols etched into the tunnel walls which generated lots of rumours of satanic rituals.

One worker claimed he had been chased out of the tunnel he was working in by an evil presence and swore never to return. Another said he was excavating the infill when a face appeared in front of him and told him to, "Get out!" Several of the construction staff complained of sudden drops in temperature and the feeling of being watched. Others said they heard voices and presumed it was their colleagues until they checked and nobody else was nearby. For safety reasons, lots of lights had been strung in the tunnels but these would often dim and flicker for seemingly no reason. At the same time there would be a rush of air making the hairs on people's necks stand up.

One tunnel in particular caused a lot of the excavation staff to feel uneasy and some even refused to enter it. This was the last one to be cleared of debris and it didn't head in the direction of any expected buildings or the river. This was very long and in a lot of ways quite disturbing. How could a tunnel make grown men feel uneasy and a lot worse? It was the nature of this tunnel. Unlike the others, it wasn't lined with stone. It was hone out of the bedrock and you could still see the marks made by the pickaxes of the men who built it.

It was thought in this tunnel a lot of the debris on the floor was natural and had occurred over time from the sides or roof collapsing. It was quite damp in parts and plenty of props had to be put in place to shore up the tunnel roof to make it safe for people to use. This potentially would take considerable time to make safe. A specialist team were brought in to spray concrete on the cleared part of the tunnel walls to stabilise them. As the clearance team moved forward in sections, then they were followed by the concreting team. Both groups of workers complained of feeling uneasy and of being watched. Between them they were making a lot of noise and vibrations in the tunnels. According to experts in the field, this sort of activity is the perfect mix to experience previously dormant paranormal activity.

On one particular day the team clearing the rubble thought they could hear water rushing almost like a waterfall in the distance. This wasn't the sort of sound anyone in a tunnel wanted to hear. Did this mean there was a cave-in that was letting water into the tunnel from somewhere? There were no maps to work from underground and no records of anything, at least none they had been able to find. The men became more and more nervous and decided to call a halt until someone could investigate what was going on and make sure there wasn't going to be a sudden wall of water heading for them. This was a common hazard in the old days during digging of new mines. It was an ever-present fear of miners as they could easily be cut off underground by a sudden breach in a wall allowing water to rush in and drown the men. They reported back to Janet who sent in some mining experts to check what the excavators had found.

The miners were experienced and used to underground water and had knowledge of the areas underground workings dating back to the industrial revolution. They used some specialist mining equipment to carefully clear away fallen debris and the excavation team took the material away. The miners were able to push on at quite a pace and the noise of the running water got louder as they moved forward. They felt confident in what they were hearing wasn't heading straight for them but they had lots of monitoring equipment just in case.

As the team got closer to the sound of the water, the atmosphere seemed to get far more unpleasant and the feeling of despair was becoming overwhelming for some of the men. They couldn't explain it other than it felt very unpleasant and filled them with dread. The miners were used to digging underground around here and they had experienced this sort of thing, on occasion, before and so were ready for it but the clearance team weren't and they got more vocal about possibly leaving and saying the job wasn't worth feeling like this. Two walked out and Janet had to find replacements at short notice. The mining team were determined to press on and wanted to find out where the sound of water was coming from.

Then one day they all got a shock. They heard what they thought was a large underground explosion and they all stopped what they were doing instantly. They listened intently, at first all was quiet but then they heard men's screams in the distance. They could hear tapping coming from the rock. There was the smell of gunpowder, the sort of smell you get these days from used fireworks. All of the men hurriedly left the tunnel after the chargehand miner shouted for them to do so. He had come across this situation before and in his mind there had been an underground explosion set by someone that had gone wrong. He wasn't about to take any risks with anybody and so had ordered an evacuation.

Everyone got out of the tunnel safe but shook up. Ralph, the chargehand, insisted the emergency services be called and that an underground explosion needed to be investigated and possible trapped men rescued. He figured there must be a mine of some sort still operational somewhere close by. Mining and cave rescue teams were called in as was the police and the first task was to try and find out where the mine workings were. The local authority insisted they had given no licences out for underground mine workings and that the only mines they were aware of were around two hundred years old. Maybe this wasn't a legitimate operation, that they were mining for some valuable deposits they had found only to cause some sort of explosion, presumably from a build-up of gasses such as methane or other combustible material. If this was the case it could have destabilised the area, especially if they had been excavating without a license – nobody would know how extensive their workings were. Mining was one of the most dangerous occupations and many thousands of men had died over the years in collapses, explosions and crushing accidents.

The rescue teams decided to enter the tunnel the miners had been clearing. They had sensors for gas build up and wore special equipment that would help prevent causing any sparks. The local authority urgently searched its old maps of the underground mines and found one close by with a record of an explosion which had killed many men after a fuse and dynamite had set off prematurely. The rescue team carefully entered the tunnel and made their way to the end where the miners had heard the explosion. There was no fresh debris, no collapse, it was just as the earlier team had left it. They had special sonic devices to listen for distant noises in collapsed rock. They had used them before in caving accidents to locate injured people tapping on rocks with tools or shouting out. The team listened in silence and placed a listening device on the rock. They could hear the sounds of men moaning, injured, that was the confirmation they needed and quickly headed back to the surface.

The head of the rescue group insisted there must be some mining going on even if it was unlicensed. He asked two of the mining team if they were prepared to help break through the remaining rock that was in the way of this mine working. They agreed, and in the end, the whole team bravely agreed to help to clear the tunnel. They knew they would have to be careful but also knew there was a need to act quickly. Everyone formed a chain to clear as much rock by hand as possible, so as not to cause any more vibration. Ralph was put in charge of watching for any possible weak spots in the tunnel as early warning signs and they all worked feverishly. When they needed a break the rescue team would listen for the hurt men and they could still be heard which gave them the urgency to push on.

Fresh workmen were brought in to help with the debris clearance and to give the others a rest. This went on for hours and the rescuers were getting exhausted. They had a lot of temporary lights strung up, on a continuous cable, so they could see what they were doing but just as they were having a few minutes rest and started listening for noises, the lights began to flicker. Ralph shouted for the light connection to be checked and the instruction was passed back and a conformation from the surface returned saying all was plugged in and should be working properly. The lights continued to flicker so Ralph called for more torches to be sent down which was duly done at double quick time. As the torches were passed down, some of those began to fail. All had fully charged batteries but by the time they got to where they were needed, they were getting fully discharged. Nobody had any idea why and the only suggestion was some sort of anomaly in the rock causing the discharge.

With all of the work going on in the tunnel it had got to quite a warm temperature, everyone was sweating. Then suddenly one after the other they noticed a huge change and the air had got a lot cooler. That shiver that goes through your whole body affected most of the men and they couldn't understand why. They looked at each other to get conformation others were feeling the same thing. The lights continued to flicker in fact it was more like they were slow flashing on and off. Almost as if there was a dimmer switch being used to raise and lower the lighting level.

Ralph called out loudly and excitedly to the rescue team at the front of the clearance face. He had spotted something, some movement. It wasn't clear at first what he had seen with the lights acting as they were. When they focussed on the fallen debris, they could see a hand reaching out, at first Ralph was startled but then he ran forward and reached for the moving hand and called out to the fallen man under the rubble. His entire body went cold when his hand made no contact with anything living. He thought the light had made him misjudge his movement so he shuffled his position and reached again for the slowly waving hand and again missed human contact. Ralph was puzzled and asked for the lighting to be pulled closer to where he was. Everyone nearby could now see the hand coming out of the rubble and they tried clearing some more of the loose rubble. As they did, they could see more of an arm and ralph called out to try and reassure the buried individual and again tried to make contact with his hand. This time several of the group could see what happened, Ralph's hand went clean through the rubble covered arm.

The people that saw what had happened all looked at each other shocked and said nothing. They frantically cleared more of the rubble in silence and more of the man became visible.

He was clearly injured and was covered in rock dust and blood. No matter how much of him they uncovered they couldn't feel him. They didn't want to distress the rest of the team so they called a break and said they should go back and have some hot food and drink before continuing. Nobody argued as they were all exhausted and could do with some natural light. Due to the problem lighting, and the number of rescuers at the rubble face, only a few people had seen what had happened. The ones who had, were saying nothing but were pausing from leaving the tunnel. Once they were the only ones remaining, they returned to the rubble face and the buried individual had gone. They looked around to see if somehow, he had freed himself but there was no one new. No injured miner, nothing.

The men looked at each other, at first saying nothing. Then Ralph spoke to break the silence and said he knew what he had seen and that he had seen an injured man partially buried. There was no response from the others stood there until finally one of them said that they had seen him too. One of the others suggested the light had confused things but Ralph quite angrily said the light couldn't make him see things like that. They decided to start excavating again, they had all heard voices, they could all agree on that, so they began removing the loose rubble as before and once the others had taken a break, they were called back to re-form the clearance chain. They had no idea how much was still left to be done but the sound of running water was definitely getting louder.

The team kept checking with listening probes to make sure the running water wasn't coming towards them, and they were placing expanding props to support the roof to try and prevent any repeat of a roof fall. They still weren't sure what had caused all the rubble, but they assumed some sort of underground explosion probably from a build-up of gases. The sounds of the men had fallen silent, which was a worrying sign. The rescuers kept battling through until they could feel a draft of air. Ralph called out to see if anyone would respond but there was silence. They cleared more debris until there was enough space for Ralph to crawl through safely and see what had happened on the other side of the rock face.

Ralph shone his torch around the area he was stood. To his amazement it was a large chamber that had been hollowed out of the rock by a mix of miners and natural means. There were no bodies of miners, no injured calls but there was a loud noise coming from running water, even though he couldn't see it. He went back to the rescuers and told them to complete the rubble clearance but then to send the majority away for a break while the senior ones figured out what to do next. He knew the situation would need to be managed as this was a rescue of trapped and injured men by people who had risked their own safety and yet there was nothing for them to see to get closure with. They would have to come up with some sort of cover story that sounded more plausible than paranormal activity.

Once the senior rescue organisers had cleared their way through and reached Ralph, they quickly realised there was an issue even though they didn't understand why. They had broken through into a worked out underground cavern that had a wide walkway and a manmade canal. There is nothing particularly unusual about this sort of setup and there are several examples around the country such as in the Black Country near Birmingham, but none have reported a disaster or collapse with injured men screaming and needing to be rescued only to find they are ghosts. Once the team began to discuss what had happened and what they now saw, they where at a loss as to what to say.

The sound of running water was very loud and, to people not used to it, was very disconcerting. It was happening at a different level to that canal close to where they stood but it was echoing through the hollow rock as if it were in the same chamber. Ralph suggested a plan and they all agreed it was a good one. They would tell the rest of the rescuers this had been an elaborate training exercise, meant to be as realistic as possible including having voices of injured men calling out. They would be told the rescue had been successful and the training had been a very positive exercise in liaising with multiple organisations and that they could now stand down and debrief in their teams to reflect on the positive work.

The organisers knew this would not be questioned and that everybody would be relieved that there had been no loss of life. They also agreed once the bulk of the team had left the site, that they would speak to Janet and research what had happened underground. They wanted some answers, not least of all because they had been scared half to death several times on this so-called rescue.

The wider rescue teams were disbanded, and all went home with a sigh of relief that in reality no one was hurt and that everybody had successfully worked as one co-ordinated team to get through an extensive and well put together training exercise. It would give them valuable experience in a real-world situation and something to discuss with their families when they got home. That part of the plan had gone well and was true at least in part.

Now came the discussion with Janet and the awkward conversations about what had happened. Ralph and the others had arranged to meet Janet and inform her about what had happened. They were a little sheepish as they didn't expect Janet to believe them. Of course, they were wrong as by now, Janet had experienced enough strange goings on not to dismiss any reports of paranormal activity connected to the tunnel network. The men were relieved in the fact they had been believed but they were then at a loss to reconcile what had happened with what they had expected and what they were used to. Janet thanked them for the efforts and promised a generous donation to the rescue organisation which, after all, was a charity and the men were trained volunteers. That went down well with the men and they agreed not to say anything else about what they had seen and heard. Apart from anything else, who would believe them?

It only took a little more time to clear the tunnel network. The debris had mostly gone but each tunnel had to be checked for safety. They were found to be in good condition and now linked the Warehouse to Edith's tunnel and so the one to Maple Hall. It was now clear the family had an underground network of tunnels for some sort of commerce but also for possible escape from whichever building they were in at the time. All three were connected and each had secret entrances with heavy tunnel doors that could be locked, preventing anyone catching the fleeing occupants. This was very elaborate but the family clearly felt it was a necessary precaution. Plus, there was the one with the underground canal which warranted a lot more investigation.

Mines were supposed to be listed in detail on various documents so their presence can be used to see if there would be a problem for the construction of houses for example. These are what solicitors look for when you pay for "searches" they are looking through archives to see if there are any underground voids that may affect the value of the property. The trouble is not all of the records are as accurate as they might be. This one was documented in quite a lot of detail. It had originally been a coal mine started from the surface about a mile from the cavern area. A lot of money had been made by the owners extracting the coal that was needed in the industrial revolution.

Eventually the coal had begun to run out but then various other minerals had been found in sufficient quantity to keep the mine valuable. There were deposits of iron ore and lead, both of which had a good market value at the time. The mine continued until it ran into this naturally created open space. It was full of valuable ore and so was mined extensively until it had become this enormous cavern. They had built a canal simultaneously with the mining to provide an easy way of getting the material from underground. There was also plenty of water so it gave somewhere for that to go rather than causing a flood or it needing to be pumped out.

There had indeed been a record of a mining disaster that had killed many men but the owners simply paid some compensation to the families and work carried on. The owner even went to the extreme of hosting social events in the cavern. A piano and various other musical instruments were transported via the canal on several weekends throughout the year along with musicians and various servants to entertain important guests at this novel atrium that had amazing acoustics. Of course, the guests were transported in the most luxurious of canal boats in convoy.

Lots of lighting was provided and even magic lantern shows were held making the cavernous open space very atmospheric for the partygoers and a great talking point. There was nothing else like this around so it gave a special feel to any event held down there, which of course was the very idea.

Champagne and caviar were lavished in great quantities on local dignitaries to show off the wealth of the owner and garner influence for the granting of future licences. It all added to the influence of the mine owner who eventually sold the cavern and mine to the Markle family. It wasn't clear why they wanted it but the valuable minerals had all been mined out so the transfer wasn't of much financial value. It seems Frederick, who was the likely new owner, wanted the working for other means. Presumably to link it up to his already spreading tunnel network and this would also add a canal to allow easy movement of goods and maybe people with nobody able to see what was moving around. This fitted his need for secrecy perfectly.

When looking on a map of the area and the three buildings positioned on it, if lines were drawn between each one, a perfect equilateral triangle was made – like the one often seen in the image of the 'All Seeing Eye.'

There would be plenty of research opportunities for Janet now the tunnels were cleared and she could investigate the symbols. There was also the question of the triangle – what was the significance of that? What did it mean for the land within the triangle? She also needed to consider whether or not to engage a paranormal investigation team and maybe even a psychic medium. Janet was a woman of science but she also had an open mind and paranormal activity intrigued her. During her years of research, she had encountered lots of references to activity from beyond the grave and when she considered the darkening history that was unfolding about the Markle / Wilson family, all of a sudden, a paranormal investigation almost became a required tool to try and complete the family story especially after the things that have happened that she herself had witnessed recently.

Janet contacted a paranormal team and asked if they would investigate the tunnels for possible spiritual activity. They were only too pleased to accept the invitation especially as Janet had insisted on everything being recorded and documented in a very scientific approach which would give any findings more credibility.

At the same time as Janet was getting a team of investigators together, she was also researching the many symbols that were etched into the walls of the tunnels as well as that anti-room she had been in. There was also writing in places that, just like she had seen before, was a mixture of old English and Latin with some code words which made understanding all the more difficult. The Society of the Eye was mentioned several times and the anti-room looked like it was used to hold secret meetings underground away from unwanted attention. There were lots of crosses in the symbols presumably indicating this was some sort of pseudo religious group.

Janet discovered a motto associated with the symbol for the society. It read "Your future depends on your deeds." She took this to mean, the more committed you were to the society, the better your future would be. This is a common theme in such societies as they want devoted members and ones who will do major favours for one another. The more you do for others, the more you can expect them to do for you. Of course, this means the likes of the Grand Master can expect near God-like devotion from followers. It was becoming clear, the Markle family were powerful in open society due to their wealth and the influence that gave them but also on a hidden level they were untouchable through their control of this society that enabled their secret network of soul taking, murder, the selling of bodies and who knows maybe satanic worship. These were dark discoveries but after recent events, nothing was surprising Janet about the rich and powerful family.

Chapter 9

The paranormal investigating team arrived at the museum. Janet had briefed them on the fact that there was lots of spiritual activity and unexplained happenings within the museum itself and told them there were tunnels to investigate but they had no idea what was to come, what they would find and the profound effect it would have on them all.

The team were given free access but had to sign a non-disclosure agreement so that any publicity or making of a programme, had to be done with the permission of the museum estate. They were a very experienced group regularly coming together to undertake paranormal investigations. This would be by far the biggest they had ever encountered. They decided they would make some preliminary investigations before calling on the services of their regular medium.

Janet told them about Ian's dream and they were keen to talk to him before setting out. At first Ian was quite reluctant as he wanted to be taken seriously and not thought of as some crazy scientist. He was reassured with the non-disclosure and he made sure they would not make reference to him by name or position. Once he realised, they were genuine and wanted to undertake a serious investigation, he began to open up about what had happened at his house and in his dream, which these days was feeling more like a premonition.

As there was lots of activity around the various properties, the team decided to spend some time in the tunnels and focus on the anti-room chamber. This had been uncovered and then due to lots of other things happening, had more or less been left. It was a large space with a high ceiling and was finished in light grey polished stone. There were lots of symbols and inscriptions in the stone. Some of these symbols were clearly of the occult, such as the horned ram's skull, inverted crosses and inverted pentagrams.

The team wanted to document any activity in this area and so brought masses of equipment with them. They had cameras on tripods for recording, infra-red cameras for detecting changes in temperature, movement detection devices, EMF meters for detecting changes in magnetic fields. They were setting up cross over grids to help detect movement. This was a once in a lifetime opportunity to investigate something so historic and so active, they wanted to make the most of it. They could make an entire television series out of this network if they were given permission. For now, they would just have to gather as much evidence as they could.

They decided to bring in their medium once they had set up all of their devices. Her name was Dena, she wasn't a household name because she investigated quietly with no fuss or fanfare, she lived by independent means so didn't ask for any money for helping out genuine cases of demonic possession. She had an impressive portfolio of investigations, all of this led to her having a lot of credibility.

Dena didn't want to hear too much of the background as she felt it could cloud her judgement. This wasn't about her demonstrating her abilities it was about her conducting a thorough untarnished investigation, one that wouldn't be tainted by hearsay or embellishments. A lot of what she had dealt with in the past was either fake or unproven and she could deal with these very quickly and move on. There was a significant core of cases, however, that were troubling at best and downright terrifying at worst. Dena always kept an open mind but assumed there must be something paranormal going on here with the team who contacted her being so enthusiastic for her to be part of this, "serious and genuine," investigation.

On arrival at the museum Dena met with the head of the team, Eric who introduced her to Janet. They shook hands and instantly Dena felt something unusual, there was some tension yes which wasn't uncommon under the circumstances but this was deeper, darker and unsettling. Not what she expected from someone who invited an investigation.

Dena could feel a lot of energy in the museum building. The hall felt oppressive and she could readily feel the presence of an old woman, not a pleasant character. She could spend more time up here later but right now she knew the team wanted to focus on an underground feature so the paranormal team walked down the stairs to the conservation lab. Dena could feel a strong malevolence as they got nearer the lab. On entering she could feel a heavy presence. She told Eric who quickly turned on a hand-held EMF meter. The needle went high up the scale as did the coloured lights and it sounded a high-pitched electronic warning.

Then suddenly they were confronted by a large angry looking male spirit. He looked Dena right in the eyes and snarled that they should leave, that they had no business here. Dena asked who he was and he replied angrily that he was the Grand Master and that they should all leave while they could. Eric managed to get some of it on a voice recorder. Everybody was on edge and they hadn't even got to the place they wanted to focus on. Dena told everyone to keep calm and that they all knew nervous energy would feed any spirits present. She looked at the Grand Master and shouted that he didn't scare them and that it was him who didn't belong. She threw some holy water in his direction and for the time being at least, he was gone.

The team looked at each other with a mix of apprehension and excitement. This was just the beginning and they had already seen a full-bodied apparition and documented some of its responses.

They walked to the next room with Eric leading the way as Dena had no idea where they were heading.

She spotted a young boy dressed in rags and looking dirty and half starved. She was the only one who could see him. His hand was outstretched and appealing for help. She went over to him and promised that she would help. She told him not to be afraid but he shouted back terrified telling her not to go through the door. He said there was a nasty man in there who was very mean and strong. Dena told the boy that everything would work out and that he mustn't be afraid any more. She asked the boy's name and he said he was called Luke. He said he had been killed by an evil man and that he had tried to warn people about him ever since but that most people couldn't see him. She thanked him and asked him to help her if he could.

The team could hear Dena but only her side of the conversation. She explained who she was talking to and when they checked with their EMF meter again it went high on the scale. They were getting excited but she was getting more concerned. This clearly wasn't a fake and it wasn't a few unexplained noises. This was full on paranormal activity and she knew that could get dangerous, she just didn't know to what extent yet. When Dena looked back the boy had gone.

The group went through the heavy door and into the tunnel which had by now been fitted with electric baulk lights so they could clearly see where they were going. Dena could feel a heaviness, not just from one spirit entity but from a large number. They kept on walking until they arrived at the anti-room. Dena was virtually overwhelmed with a sense of sadness and foreboding. The negative feelings were overpowering. She told the team this was a key area to setup their equipment and that it was very active with spirit entities.

The investigation team set about covering the whole area with various monitoring equipment. They included panels placed on the floor that would detect if someone or something, walked over them. These were placed in all of the tunnels so if something approached the anti-room from any direction, they would hopefully be caught by the panels and seen on camera. They were far more enthusiastic than Dena – they wanted their proof for their investigation but she had to deal with the pain and misery she could feel coming from the very walls of this place.

There were inscriptions and symbols everywhere. Now there was some substantial light they could be more clearly seen. Dena recognised some but there seemed to be layers of them for different reasons. Some were clearly for satanic worship, while she thought others were binding spells aimed at keeping malevolence anchored to the space and to stop them entering our world. Why would there be seemingly contradictory inscriptions – unless they had been written at different times and with very different reasons in mind.

Dena looked at the inscriptions carefully, there were lots of references to Satan and the Grand Master and something about a bargain, no a sacred covenant, payment in souls in return for success in commerce and long life, no extended life. At that point she felt a malevolence, an intense heavy atmosphere. She called out for the team to be on their guard. The touch panels in one of the tunnels began to react, the cameras began recording, they picked up a dark entity coming towards them. Dena could see it, she threw holy water at it and made an incantation to expel it from this earth. In a fury of sound, it turned transparent and disappeared. Eric looked back at the recordings and they showed a white streak of light coming from one of the tunnels and approach Dena. It seemed to evaporate when Dena cast her spell.

The team took instant photos of the inscriptions so they could look at them when they got back above ground. They left the equipment in place and Dena insisted they take a quick look at the other two buildings. They used the tunnel to get to the Chapel so Dena could experience more of the underground network. When they were approaching the Chapel Dena could feel oppression, a feeling of people being forced to do things against their will. Also, a feeling a helplessness and of being trapped. This was not a pleasant place for her to be. She told the team what she was feeling and they documented it. Dena looked around the basement and saw lots of wooden crates. As she touched them, she got a short vision from each one coming off a sailing ship and placed elsewhere. She guessed that would be a warehouse.

She went up the stairs and to the outside of the Chapel. She looked around the building and could see lots of activity, both inside and outside the fenced off area. She was seeing life from two hundred and fifty years ago. The Chapel was surrounded by open fields, very few buildings around. She could see a cemetery in the distance with lots of grave markers – most weren't headstones but wooden crosses. There were lots of trees, this must have been the very early days of the Chapel's existence. Above the front door she could see the symbol of the eye inside the triangle, this must have been an early meeting place for groups of merchants and maybe masonic. She knew it didn't have to be anything to do with the Masons as at this time there were lots of secret groups who were formed to basically be a mutually beneficial societies in pursuit of wealth, power and influence.

Dena was getting a fascinating insight to the Chapel and as she went back inside and wandered around the main hall, she was getting a sense of the meetings they held with senior members almost holding court. She saw a glimpse of a new member being initiated, of a meeting of a substantial number of men discussing issues of the day. This was all very normal for the time and even carries on today in certain circles. Then she saw a much smaller group gathering and she heard them mention tunnels. She could only make out a few words of what they were saying. She heard ships and imported goods and then a discussion about contracts and souls. It was difficult for Dena to make full sense of what they were saying. She did see some of them wearing large rings and medallions.

Dena told the group what she had been seeing and they recorded what she said for future use. They were getting ready to leave when the atmosphere changed dramatically. Eric and the others had brought a few hand-held recording devices and meters with them and one of the EMF meters went crazy.

Everybody was on their guard but there was nothing to see. They were in one of the main rooms of the chapel. The meters were saying something was there but still nothing to see. The temperature dropped in the room and Dena could sense a presence but nothing was manifesting. Dena called out to the spirit, to show itself, nothing. Then out of the blue a ghastly figure suddenly appeared in front of them. It let out a terrible wail that echoed around the room. The face was distorted and snarling with rotten teeth and black tongue. The group recognised the clothes in an instant but they didn't match the entities actions. It wore the habit of a nun but there was nothing good about this apparition it brought a sense of evil and its sudden terrible appearance reinforced that.

Dena tried the holy water and incantation but that had no affect other than to annoy the spirit. It lunged at one of them so Dena held out a crucifix and started reciting the Lord's Prayer. The nun, if that's what she was, looked at her, she had the most grotesque features. The nun's eyes were black and stared intently. It had such a malevolence and evil intent. Dena's intervention caused it to move away. It raised its hands in a threatening way as its spidery fingers became distorted. The team could hear the sound of bones breaking – it was a sickening sound. The nun started to move forward again in an awkward jerky way. Her hands and arms sounded like they were breaking and twisting. Dena changed the prayer to the Hail Mary and pushed out the crucifix towards the nun's head. This caused the entity to reel away as if in agony. It let out a blood curdling scream and disappeared.

The team looked at each other and checked that they were all ok. They were very nervous and scared half to death but physically they were fine. One of the team had managed to capture a still photo of the nun and it looked absolutely terrifying. They all needed to take a few minutes to calm down. Eric asked Dena what she thought about the nun. She said there were a lot more religious orders hundreds of years ago and that sometimes nuns would be sent out as missionaries but also that they often performed as nurses as they were seen as helpful and caring. It was also a good disguise for someone who had more malevolent intent and one that could be easily used to trick people into a sense of safety and reassurance. This is what Dena suspected of this nun and that she was now paying for her deeds.

Dena wanted to make a full day of useful investigation but gave the team time to recover from what had happened. The time also gave her the chance to clear her thoughts ready for the next on the list which was Warehouse 12. When everyone was ready, they headed off in that direction.

From the outside it looked like any other old dock-side warehouse. It had dark red brick but was clearly in a well-maintained state. This was no dilapidated old building ready to be knocked down or turned into luxury flats. On the inside it had a lot of space, a large amount of which, was filled with crates of different sizes. There was no activity here which surprised Dena as she felt this place was key to what was going on.

The team went to the edge of the dock which was still pretty much in the state it would have been when vessels were loading and unloading their cargos. There was no lifting equipment, all that had long since been scrapped. There were train tracks still, presumably from a time when steam trains would move freight around. There was a turntable at the head of the dock so train engines could be turned around. The dock itself had been cleaned up by the local council and had been made into an overspill marina. It was linked via a set of lock gates to another dock that was the main marina and this in turn had lock gates leading to the river and open water.

There were information boards dotted around with diagrams and even some old black and white photos of what the dock was like when sailing ships had filled it. It was an impressive sight and many people must have been employed servicing the ships. They also showed more dockside buildings – other warehouses, ships chandlers, dock offices. Some had been preserved and were impressive stone buildings but some had fallen into disrepair and had been demolished. One of the signs said that this was Railway Dock, hence the train tracks. This was once a bustling, noisy, dirty and smelly place to be and potentially dangerous with locos moving large heavy wagons around. There were no barriers to protect or warn people, only their wits.

Everyone was fascinated with the local history as it would still be in living memory for a lot of people. It was relatively recently that the docks had become disused but then thankfully had been recognised as a potential asset and turned into local facilities and attractions. They decided they had seen enough for now and called it a day. Dena knew she would need to return here but for now there wasn't much more she could do today.

Suddenly there was the scream of a railway engine whistle. It startled Dena who stumbled back in response to the high-pitched sound. She looked around and the dock side was filled with men with wooden barrows containing multiple boxes and crates. They were working to unload a ship of its considerable cargo. There was a steam loco being turned around on the turntable. When Dena looked at the water, she could see the dock was full of masted sailing ships. Cranes were unloading ships using rope nets, they would descend into the ship's cargo hold and come back up full of crates or sometimes loose items, depending on the cargo. In the distance it looked like an army of young boys were moving things around on smaller barrows into dockside sheds for short term storage before being sent on to their final destination.

She could see Warehouse 12 had its main doors open and barrow after barrow was being taken inside and unloaded. Dena was puzzled as to what had happened. She didn't know if she was seeing a recording of what had gone on or if somehow, she had been transported back in time to see events unfolding. She tried to take in as much as possible and she noticed a well-dressed gentleman overseeing the work at W12. She couldn't tell if anyone could see her but as she walked slowly towards the warehouse and tried to make out what the gentleman was looking at, all of a sudden, he looked her right in the eye and stared. Nobody else seemed to see her but he clearly did. She recognised him and was filled with dread. This was the spirit that had made itself known to her as the Grand Master. Only now he looked very much alive and in his rightful time. She managed to get a glance of what he was reading, it was the ships manifest and he was checking crates off as they entered the warehouse.

He stopped what he was doing and started to walk towards her. Dena quickly backed away and headed towards the edge of the dock. There was a loud shriek of the train whistle warning her to get out of the way. She ran forward and the slow moving loco and wagons passed between her and the man. She looked around and realised she was back with the investigation team who were all fussing around her. She asked what had happened and they said she had gone into some sort of trance and that they were worried. She asked how long she had been in that state and they said just a few moments. It had been long enough for her to get a good glimpse of the goings on at the dock and see the grand master when he was alive. She told the team what had happened and they all had a mixture of excitement and concern. Dena made various observations to the team. She had interacted with the past not just seen a recording of past events. How could the grand master see her but nobody else could?

The team wondered what had triggered Dena's experience, she didn't even know herself but she knew if it happened once then it could happen again and if she thought about it maybe she could be the one to initiate it and hopefully find out more of what was going on and leading to the hauntings. The day had been very eventful and demonstrated to her that this was the most interactive paranormal activity she had been involved with. It also showed the connections between the three buildings and the tunnels. Obviously, the Grand Master was key to all this as he was the only one who kept showing up in all locations. He seemed to be much more mobile than any of the other apparitions. He also seemed to be in charge of everything. Everybody needed a rest and went back to their hotel and agreed to carry on the investigation the next day.

Chapter 10

Dena wanted to follow up what had happened in the underground mine. Nobody had been in there since the rescue team left and the rubble had been cleared. She arranged with the investigation team to meet up and walk through the tunnel until they came to the cavern. They took plenty of meters, gauges and recording equipment with them. They wondered how the mining disaster manifestation had been triggered. Dena thought it would be due to the clearance of the rubble by men and machine and all the vibrations that had been caused for a prolonged time. The team had taken a special piece of equipment this time to generate a form of static electricity to the surroundings to help spirits use the energy to manifest themselves. It was similar to ones seen in school science labs.

They got to the end of the tunnel near the cavern. It had been raining hard for days and the noise of the hidden running water echoing around the cavern was extremely loud and quite unsettling unless you were used to it. Eric setup the ion generator inside the end of the tunnel and another just outside so they would overlap their emissions and they dotted around several more on the floor of the cavern. They set them going and then started to explore a little. The team had plenty of torches between them and they could see the canal which stopped at the cavern but carried on out of sight in the other direction. Nobody had yet traced where the canal came out and they could only guess it was originally constructed to remove quarried material out of the cavern. It seemed a lot of work just to remove material but that mine had worked for years providing a lot of valuable ore and other deposits used around the industrial revolution. Presumably this canal would be a side branch off the wider main canal that would take goods to the foundries around the area.

As this had been linked with the tunnel network, it must have changed use at some point, no doubt when the cavern had been emptied of its workable seams and would provide a continuous route from the river, through the tunnels and then the canal network and back again. This could be a very valuable transport link for the family and one that would not draw any attention to, perfect for their ungodly trade.

For anyone who doesn't like water underground this was a nightmare place. There was the still canal, quite wide so at least two boats could be side by side. Then there was the noise of gushing underground but invisible waterfalls and the lack of light. This was indeed not for the faint hearted and all of the team were on edge. It felt and sounded that any minute you would be washed away in a torrent of water above your head. Suddenly they heard a tremendous noise that shook the ground. It made everyone jump and wonder what had happened. The tremendous crack echoed around the cavern, filling the space and making the group cover their ears. Eric checked his air pressure meter and it was showing heavy rain conditions likely for the area. What they were experiencing was a thunderstorm even though one hadn't been forecast and when they entered the tunnel the sun was shining.

None of them had experienced underground sounds like this and it was nerve racking. The cavernous space was acting like a sound chamber, amplifying any loud noise. Another massive crash filled the air and everybody could feel the vibrations in the rock and cavern floor. The team's meters started to fluctuate wildly, indicating various energy fields. Dena called to the team to be on their guard as she could sense activity building. The lightening was filling the air with charged particles and the hairs on people's arms were standing up due to the static electricity. The gauges were sending out loud bleeps and flashing brightly. Dena called out for any spirits to show themselves. Eric started sound recording to capture any EVP response to Dena. When he played it back, he got the unmistakable call for help.

Dena called out again but this time asked who needed help and what could they do to help? Eric played back the recording and this time there were several voices all calling for help and it sounded like there was the noise of a rock fall. With that the cavern echoed with another ear-splitting crash and then there was the sound of falling rocks as if the walls were caving in on them. They all looked terrified, they were recording and all of their equipment was screaming different tones causing further echoes. They desperately looked for where the rocks were falling but there was no sign of any debris. Immediately following the sound of the rock fall came the shouting from men they couldn't at first see. It was as if they were off in the distance. Then there was the sound of a second, closer explosion. The team huddled close together and Dena said they should go back to the tunnel entrance. As they did, they could see movement on the floor and around the tunnel. They shone lights so that just a reflection would hit the area and there they could see and hear several men calling apparently injured in a rock fall. This is what Ralph had witnessed previously and had told the team about. It was a terrifying sight, seeing men struggle, reaching out their arms and calling for help. There was a heavy dusty dry smell in the air from the rock dust. Then another enormous crash of lightening rang out.

The cavern was filled with cries for help, the lightening combined with the team's gadgets was filling the air with electricity and it was causing the massive manifestation of a previous mining disaster that had clearly killed a lot of men and boys. The scene was one of utter carnage with fallen rocks everywhere and arms reaching out for help. It was a form of paranormal recording due to the type of rocks present in the cavern. Given the right conditions, like right now, the recording plays again just like on the day the disaster happened. It was a terrifying scene and all of the team looked shocked they weren't prepared for this on such a huge scale.

Dena was getting a horrible and sickening feeling that somehow this was less of an accident and more of a deliberate act. She had no idea why she was feeling this, surely no person would want to cause such injuries and death on others. They looked around the cavern and everywhere they could see was strewn debris and bodies mixed with smoke and dust. There were also the flashing lights from the team's various meters. They had several cameras recording but how could this scene be shown to others? The sight would leave a lasting effect on anyone who saw it. They looked towards the canal and they could see men on boats clambering to get to the landing platform to rescue the fallen men. They had ropes and pick axes and candles and stretchers. These must have been from the original response team to try and get everyone out.

None of them were aware of the investigators, they were apparitions of what had gone on and to add to the terror for Dena and the team, these ghostly figures were transparent and couldn't be interacted with. Another loud crack of thunder filled the cavern with noise like a massive explosion. This caused the scene to be reset. The canal rescuers had disappeared and the apparitions were back to the first moments after the disaster. This was confusing but absolutely terrifying for the investigators. Dena just explained to them that the power of the lightening was starting the manifestation of the men each time it hit like a jolt on a record player making it play part of a record over again. She suggested they turn off their energy creating gadgets so there was less electricity in the air.

The lightening had stopped, much to everyone's relief and with the energy inducing machines turned off, the mining manifestation was starting to fade and the sounds coming from it was reducing quickly. It was just like an old movie that was starting to fade until it disappeared completely. None of the team were in a rush for this to return.

Now they were left with the other nerve-jangling noise of waterfalls close by that was getting louder, presumably due to the heavy rain and it was adding to the team's distress as it was causing a feeling of claustrophobia and adding to the fight or flight response that they were all feeling. Usually, you're expected to run away from explosions and nearby overhead gushing water. In all likelihood the water was coming from a hollowed-out level below them, maybe from previous mine workings or from the water's actions on the rock. It was the structure of the surround to the cavern that was making it sound like it was coming from above. Without lights this would be a scene that nightmares are made of.

The team were mentally exhausted from their ordeal and they were all ready to leave. Dena and Eric agreed to call an end to the investigation but then Dena told them to wait. They all looked at her, she looked worried. She said she could sense something else another presence was moving closer. She told the team to stay close to each other and to be careful of this presence. They were all looking but couldn't see anything yet. From nowhere came a tremendous shout, "GET OUT!" The words echoed around the cavern and the team's meters began to light up again. Unlike before, there was nothing to see until a sizeable piece of rock appeared to be thrown in their direction from the back of the cavern. This wasn't a recording this was an active response to their presence and a malevolent one. Dena told them she sensed this was an angry and domineering spectre and one who was clearly powerful enough to do them harm.

Dena called out, "Who are you and why do you want us gone from here?" The only response was, "GET OUT!" and several large stones thrown into the canal generating splashes. Once again Dena called to the entity, "You don't scare us, we mean you no harm we haven't done anything to hurt you. Tell us your name." This time silence but now they could see a barge on the canal. They were all sure it hadn't been there before. It wasn't moving, just moored alongside the landing platform. Eric pointed an EMF meter at it and the needle went off the scale. Suddenly a dark entity, a shadow figure appeared on the boat. It wasn't possible to see any features just a thick black mass in the shape of a large human figure. Dena called out to it, "What do you want?" There was no response but it appeared to be watching them. She raised a crucifix and threw some holy water from a small bottle she was carrying. There was a loud roar from the shadow figure as if it were some sort of wild animal being taunted.

Dena moved closer to the dark figure and kept the crucifix firmly in her hand with her arm outstretched. She threw more holy water at the figure which again roared in response. She commanded the figure to be gone and began repeatedly reciting the Lord's Prayer. The figure violently lunged at Dena screeching a terrible blood curdling scream as it did so. At the last second, she could see it was the figure of an old hag with rotten teeth and pock marked complexion. The figure evaporated as it touched the crucifix and at the same time the boat vanished. Now Dena looked at the rest of the team and much to everyone's relief she said, "Let's go." The team gathered up their equipment in double fast time and they all headed back down the tunnel, back to the surface.

Chapter 11

Dena was very keen to get a full meaning of the symbols and writings in the tunnels and she wanted to see how much Janet could decipher through her past research. The two of them working on it together along with the investigation team should be able to shine a light on what had occurred in the past so they could do something to stop the hauntings and put the spirits to rest.

Now Dena had experienced a taste of what was going on with the museum and was convinced this was a serious case and one she felt she should help with, she talked more with staff members about their experiences. Ian told her about what happened to him at home and in his lab. She could tell he was being sincere by the way he explained and by the look on his face. He was at pains to point out that he was afraid for his scientific reputation, so Dena reassured him that everything was confidential and that he could help decipher some of the writings so they could all get to the bottom of the mysterious happenings that way much quicker and that a cleansing could take place and he could get back to the work he was used to. That all sounded music to Ian's ears so he readily set to work.

Dena already had some serious suspicions about the apparitions everyone had reported and the writings. She wanted to try something and gathered the investigation team in the underground anti-room to document any happenings. They took a table and some chairs underground and set up for a séance. They took lots of large candles so they could detect any drafts.

The candles were positioned around the large room and the electric lights were turned off. This created a more natural atmosphere and one that would recreate the light levels experienced by the creators of these underground structures. When all of the tunnel doors were closed the ventilation came from two side tunnels which terminated in what looked like iron portcullises. They were fixed in place, anchored to the base rock, so as not to be a weak spot. They were disguised from prying eyes by surfacing within the estate land and made to look like disused mine shaft ventilation, secured for safety. This sort of ventilation was highly unlikely to create too many air currents.

Dena had the team sit around the table and hold hands. She insisted no matter what happened that everyone had to keep a grip on each other and not to break the circle or to speak. Before they started, they made sure they had various devices recording including several video cameras fixed at certain points. Dena began asking if there were any friendly spirits that wanted to make their presence known. She encouraged them by saying they would be safe and that the group meant no harm. Once again, she asked for friendly spirits to show themselves. Everybody was expectant but stayed quiet as they had been instructed. The circle of holding hands meant that energy could pass around the circle from one member to another and be used by the spirits as a sort of living battery so they can manifest themselves.

The temperature around the table began to drop, they could feel it but they could also see it on a gauge placed close by. There were several candles on the centre of the table and these began to flicker, even though others around the room didn't. Dena gently asked if there was anyone present and the middle candle began to burn brighter and very straight. Dena smiled and thanked the spirit.

Dena assured the spirits they meant no harm and asked if there were any children present. Suddenly they could hear children running around the room as if they were playing with each other. Dena asked if they would share their name and one shouted, "Peter." Dena thanked them and asked Peter to come closer and to talk to them. She told Peter he could use her body to communicate if he wanted to. Dena closed her eyes and a childlike voice came from her mouth, "I'm Peter." Was what they heard. One of the investigators asked how old Peter was. "13" came the reply. Another investigator asked Peter why he was there. He replied, "I'm stuck here." Peter also said, "I have to go the nasty man is coming." Dena's face went back to normal and she opened her eyes. She tried to get Peter to come back but had no luck. They looked at each other and everybody wondered who the nasty man was. Dena already had a good idea who it was.

The movement detecting pads on the floor lit up, the candles in the middle of the table flickered and blew out. There was a gust of wind that came from one of the tunnels. This was a heavy presence, very different from Peter. There was a loud bang on the table as if someone had slammed down their fist. The sudden noise made several of the team jump but Dena managed to keep them holding hands. Dena asked who was present and what did they want. They all heard a very deep and guttural voice say, "Master." Dena asked if the spirit present was the master and it replied, "Yes."

Dena realised this was probably the Grand Master she had heard about and even seen earlier. She asked why he was still here and not at rest. His reply was, "I need souls." That sent a shiver down people's backs and made everyone feel very uncomfortable. Dena said she was going to close down the séance with a blessing on everyone including the spirits. She had found out at least some of what she wanted to know. She felt if they carried on, some of the team could be in danger. She was the one who always tried to keep everyone safe. She told the team to gather their recording devices and to go back to the museum so they could have a debrief.

The team were more than happy to comply. They returned with some of the equipment and turned the rest off ready for another day. Once they were back in the museum, they used the visitor centre as their base of operations. They played back sound recordings and looked at the video footage to see if anything had been captured. Several orbs were captured on camera at the time they first sensed children playing. An orb could be seen approaching Dena just before Peter began to speak. Finally, there was like a white streak of light that came from one of the tunnels when the movement lights turned on. It swirled around the table before disappearing. They listened to the EVP, (electronic voice phenomenon), recorder and what they heard was chilling – the message was a very slow, deliberate and deep, "GET OUT!"

The team were all grateful to Dena for closing down the séance when she did. They were also pleased they had some useful evidence of spirit activity. Dena asked the lead investigator, Eric, if he would stay back for a chat when the rest had gone. He said he would be happy to. The team finished by having a celebratory beer and drifted off, ready for more research the following day.

Once they were alone, Dena told Eric of her suspicions. That the "nasty man," was the Grand Master and that his presence wasn't just a recording triggered by events but was an intelligent spirit. She held back one thing for now as she had no way of knowing for sure she was right.

The next day Dena asked Janet if she could see the basement of the warehouse where some of the crates of artefacts were stored. Rather than using the tunnels they used a more conventional route by car. It gave a very different perspective approaching by road rather than underground. Plus, this way they hoped not to invoke any paranormal activity. Janet was intrigued what Dena was looking for but was happy to be part of the investigation. After all she hadn't seen that much of the contents of the crates yet herself.

Janet had warned the porters in the warehouse they were coming and for them to be on standby to help open the crates if needed. The short journey was uneventful and they parked alongside the dock. They walked up to warehouse 12 and had a good look around. The warehouse was separated from the dock by a road and some old railway tracks. It wasn't much of a distance from the warehouse to where the old ships would be unloaded. The warehouse would be able to hold a large volume of cargo of different types and the multiple floors could be used to segregate goods depending on their end destination and use. Most of the other buildings had now been demolished as unsafe but W12, as it was known, had been well maintained and was as strong as when it was first built. It was a bit of a mystery locally why it was in such good condition but locals figured it must be just some businessman with too much money who eventually would sell it for turning into expensive apartments.

These days, from the outside at least, there was no discernible activity in or out of W12 other than periodic maintenance visits. Dena asked several dock workers if they had ever seen anything being taken into or being brought out of W12. They all replied that they hadn't as long back as they could remember. Janet had no real idea what Dena was getting at and for the time being, Dena was keeping her cards close to her chest but she reassured Janet that all would be revealed when she had more evidence.

They entered the warehouse and two porters greeted them. W12 had a large footprint and each floor was a large open space with high ceilings that gave a lot of flexibility for what could be stored there. There were eight floors and a basement. Janet asked where the majority of crates still left, were stored. She knew a lot had been transported underground to the Chapel. This was done to stop any media interest as there was still a huge story to be uncovered about the buildings, their contents, uses and the tunnels. The chief porter said the majority were in the basement and he was a little hesitant to say much more. Both women noticed his body language and it was clear there was a lot more he wasn't saying.

Janet asked if there was an inventory of the basement and the chief porter became very defensive, saying there hadn't been time and that he hadn't been told there was a need for one. He was about to carry on when Janet assured him there wasn't a problem and that she had thought it might have been done as a routine matter and not to worry. The chief porter, Carl, seemed to relax quite a bit after Janet had said that. He now knew he wasn't in any trouble and so showed the two of them down to the basement. There were plenty of electric lights fitted on each of the floors and it was clear part of the warehouse maintenance was to keep the building up to date with technology. That included the addition of a freight lift. They used it to get to the basement, even though it was only one floor down, as Carl wanted to demonstrate how it worked so they women could use it if he wasn't around.

The freight lift was large and had big hit and miss wooden doors that met in the middle. The frame of the lift was in criss-crossed steel. This was meant to be capable of handling large and heavy goods and its design meant you could see through the lift as it moved. This was clearly retro fitted a long time after the warehouse was first built and meant movement of goods around the warehouse had been speeded up tremendously from the old days of ropes and pully.

They entered the lift and descended to the basement. The lift had a very smooth movement and it took only a few seconds to get to the basement. Carl showed them that the crates had been arranged in batches. Some contained pottery while others had glass or ivory, others had items of jewellery but the largest crates held furniture and paintings.

Janet asked for two from each section to be opened so they could examine the contents. While Carl got another porter to help, Janet and Dena had a good look around at the rest of the crates. There was a lot to look at. They examined the stamped writing on the outside of the crates. Most of them just said, "Markle W12." Some had additional stamps stating, "Fragile." Others appeared to show the country of origin. A lot stated Australia and some said China. There were crates from all over the globe including, Europe.

The porters started opening some of the crates. When they were examined for contents, it became fairly obvious that the items had been kept in their original shipping crates, moved to W12 and left there until now. The crates, the contents and the packing were in pristine condition. This is what Dena had suspected all along. Dena approached Carl and said she had a delicate question to ask. He paid attention and waited. She asked him if he was aware of additional crates arriving in recent times. Carl went a bit quiet but said yes there had been but that he had no idea who was bringing them in. He said it varied but that there appeared to be several new crates every few months. He said the newer items always appeared on the upper floors but he had no idea why. Janet played a long and told Carl not to worry and did he know of anything special in any of the crates. He said there were some particularly heavy small ones that were marked up with red stamps. He took them both over and opened one and left them to examine the contents.

Janet pushed back the packing material and could see several metal boxes. She pulled one out, it was very heavy. There was a large seal on the front. When she examined it, there was the tell-tale sign of the eye inside a triangle. Janet broke the seal and opened the box There was a foil covering over the contents. She peeled it back to reveal beautiful shiny gold coins. The box was full of them and this crate was full of identical boxes, presumably each with similar contents. There must be many thousands of gold coins in this one crate. Janet placed one in her pocket to examine later and put the closed box back in the crate and put the lid back in place. She asked Carl to fix it down and he nailed it shut.

Janet and Dena looked at some of the pottery. It was flawless and looked like valuable antique. They checked some of the paintings. They were like new and from accomplished artists. Some had been thought to be lost to history as they hadn't been seen for such a long time. A theme was developing, how could items be so old and yet in such perfect condition and how had they shown up in the warehouse? Bills of sale and ownership were present showing they had been transferred to the Markle family legally and all paid for. This was no tax or import scam everything appeared to be above board. There was a vast amount of wealth in these crates. It was beginning to look like the family's lost wealth hadn't been lost at all only transferred into the contents of these crates or used as funds to purchase them at least.

Janet had a huge mystery to unravel but at least she didn't have any urgency or worry to inform the authorities. When news of the contents got into the public knowledge this would be sensational and she wanted to be well prepared for when that happened.

The two of them had seen enough for today, Janet decided to take back a large vase and a piece of jewellery to the museum so that research could be done on them to trace their origin and estimate the value.

On returning to the museum, she handed the three items, including the gold coin, to Ian to try and trace. When he saw the coin, he could tell this was something special. There wasn't any wear on it and this had clearly been bought as an investment. It was a George III gold sovereign, marked with the date 1817. Ian's quick research showed these are very rare and worth a lot of money. They were only minted for three years. What he didn't know was that there was at least one substantial box full of them. He told Janet of his preliminary findings for the coin and she couldn't help but let out a chuckle. She was desperate to tell Dena. When she did Dena just raised an eyebrow and nodded. Janet exclaimed that this would put the finances of the museum into a whole different league. Again, Dena nodded.

Chapter 12

Dena wanted to know more about a workhouse that had been mentioned to her, she wanted to know what the connection was between it and the estate. They were very common at one time but not many had survived. That was hardly surprising as they weren't looked on in a favourable way and were usually demolished to make way for developing towns and cities to grow. These buildings can be recognised very easily from the outside and this one was no different. It was huge in dark brick, almost black with age. There was nothing fancy about it but there was the usual motto etched in stonework at the front entrance. "Hard Work is Honest Work." They all had something equally as condescending and misleading. Workhouses were not good places to be and a lot were far from honest in their operation. If for some reason you couldn't earn a living, the workhouse was supposed to be the social safety net. Once in, it was difficult to get out as you built up a debt for each day you stayed. You were paid for work done internally but that wasn't enough to cover your bed and food payments. This of course provided a workforce for the owners or trustees and so a good profit.

The work was deliberately very hard and menial so as to put off people wanting to enter. Profits were supposed to go back into the provision for the poor but in reality, a lot of it went to the trustees either directly or on their pet projects regardless of the needs for the poor they were supposed to be supporting. Food for the inmates, as they were known was basic and just enough to keep them alive. The mortality rates inside these institutions were extremely high but the local parish didn't mind that as it reduced the number of people needing, "poor support." Or as Scrooge, (one of Charles Dicken's characters put it), "decrease the surplus population." These places were often run on a similar basis to a prison, whole families could be taken in but then split up along gender lines and age. The children would be separated and given different work that their small fingers could deal with. They were horrific institutions that were full of misery and despair that would generate a lot of potential for paranormal activity.

Due to the high mortality rate from such an institution nobody would miss or even care about additional deaths or disappearances. Nobody would question what happened to the inmates and that's what made Dena wonder. The workhouse was well within the triangle formed by the other buildings and she set about researching its operation and management. She found out that several of the Markle family were on the board of trustees or Guardians as they were called. There was a note in the accounts that good work was being provided for a good number of the inmates, by the Markle family and it was praising them for doing so. The fact the family were clearly benefitting from very cheap labour wasn't mentioned of course, just that it was an act of kindness from a business family not forgetting their societal responsibilities. Such was the thinking of the time.

Of course, what actions like the Markle's did was free up the responsibility and cost to the parish which is why it was seen as such a positive. What happened to the inmates themselves wasn't considered beyond the fact that they should be grateful to have been given the chance and privilege to work. The workhouse the family controlled was a very large one with over a thousand inmates. There was no shortage of people needing to enter so there was a steady stream of unfortunate poor families that could be taken advantage of.

The official records weren't going to show Dena what she needed to know, beyond the fact that the Markle's had easy access to a large amount of the poorest of people that wouldn't be noticed if they were no longer around. Maybe Dena had it all wrong and the family truly were being philanthropic to their fellow man, that thought didn't linger long in her mind due to the little she already understood about the patriarch.

One thing Dena did notice in the archival records for the workhouse was that there was a lot of children entering the institution. That was nothing too unusual as there were a lot of orphans due to parental mortality or just that the parents couldn't support their children. If the names of the children were followed through the records, very few of them ever left the institution into adulthood. That was a lot of children dying each year. The causes listed were the usual reasons such as tuberculosis, influenza and various childhood diseases we think nothing of today. These were all certified by a doctor but one of that time could soon be persuaded to complete a death certificate on the flimsiest of evidence as to the cause.

Dena wondered if she could somehow communicate with the young boy apparition she had seen at the museum. She returned to the museum and tasked the investigation team with setting up a vigil in the room next to the conservation lab. This wouldn't interfere with any of the museum work and she hoped they could entice the young boy to talk to them.

They decided the best thing to do was to set up a Ouija session as Dena wanted to ask some questions and they couldn't think of a better way to communicate with the boy's spirit. Dena had heard the boy speak but it wasn't clear if that was more like a recording or was just the limit of his verbal communication. It takes a lot of effort for a spirit to manifest like that and a young boy would struggle to maintain it for very long. By holding a session with a Ouija board, the effort from the spirit is a lot less as they are just affecting the planchette and not trying to appear as an apparition.

The team lit some candles around the room and had arranged some cameras to record any happenings and also set out some voice recording equipment. There were no windows and both the doors to the lab and the tunnel were closed so there could be no drafts or air movements. The flames on the candles were still and upright and they created a peaceful atmosphere. Everything was very quiet as they took their positions around a large wooden table. Dena had everyone place a finger on the planchette and then she closed her eyes and called out to the boy spirit to make his presence known. It didn't take very long for the candles start to flicker. At first it was just one and only slightly but then more were affected as if a blast of air had somehow entered the room. Dena asked if it was the young boy and the planchette slowly started to move to, "YES." The group were excited they had got such a positive response and they knew it was being recorded.

Dena asked what was the boy's name. The planchette slowly moved to the letter, "L" and then slowly and carefully spelled out the name Luke. Dena made sure by asking if they were talking to Luke. The planchette moved to, "YES." She thanked him for the effort he was making and for telling them his name. She asked if he had any parents and the pointer moved slowly to, "NO." Dena asked if Luke was alone and he responded with the pointer moving to, "YES." She felt very sad for the boy and she guessed the answer of the next question but wanted it confirmed. She asked if he once lived in the workhouse. The planchette moved to circle the, "YES." Dena asked what had happened to Luke. There was a pause and then the pointer spelled out, "KILLED." Dena asked if he was saying that someone had purposely killed him. The pointer moved to, "YES." Dena said that she was so sorry to him. She asked Luke who had killed him. The pointer moved to just two letters, "GM." She figured who this meant and was actually quite loathed to speak it in full but then she decided she had to confirm what Luke was saying. She asked if GM meant the Grand Master and the pointer circled, "YES." Dena warned the group to keep calm and in contact with the planchette. She again thanked Luke for being so helpful but at that point there was a loud metallic bang on the tunnel door.

This is why Dena hadn't wanted to verbalise what GM referred to. She knew it might cause a reaction they didn't want. The candles suddenly started flickering vigorously, some were blown out but the team had individual small torches in their pockets in case something like this happened. They all used their free hand to reach in their pocket and turn on their torches and laid them on the table. This at least would provide light for them but also for the cameras recording the session.

A dark entity suddenly manifested in the room, most of the investigation team looked shocked and let out various gasps. Dena told them to hold it together. She spoke in a loud voice, "Is that you Grand Master?" The dark entity bellowed, "YES." She didn't want to provoke what had manifested as she knew it had the potential to harm them. She needed to undertake a lot more research before she would be ready to take on the GM. Dena stated that they meant no harm or disrespect and that they would leave the room if that's what he wanted. Again, came a very abrupt and harsh, "YES." Dena thanked him and said they would shut down the session with a blessing, which she did. At that point she told everyone to slowly leave and to gather in the meeting room. This was code for meeting up in the team's camper van. This was stationed in the museum car park and was big enough for the team to use as a base of operations and also for sleeping in.

When they were able to sit together in the van, Dena explained she didn't want to tell the grand master where they intended to move to. She didn't want him following them. One of the team asked if she felt he could do that and she thought he was very capable of a lot of things and that he wasn't an ordinary spirit entity. She said she would let them no more as she could back up what she was saying with hard evidence. She summarised that they now knew the little boy was an orphan who lived in the workhouse at some stage and that he believed he had been murdered by the grand master. This started a discussion among the group as to why that would be. Dena said that she felt there may be a lot more like Luke and that the reason why would become clearer after they had done more research.

They had managed to bring back the cameras and sound recording equipment and they now set about playing them back on monitors. All the time they were talking to Luke, there was nothing to be seen other than a little flicker of a candle. Everything seemed quite peaceful and they had captured the movement of the planchette in response to the questions Dena had asked. When they grand master showed up, at first there was lots of orb activity. Orbs are often associated with paranormal activity and are thought to be proof of the presence of at least one apparition. Then a large dark mass appeared at one end of the room. It was in the shape of a tall human body. The two yeses were captured on the sound recording equipment and sounded very guttural and intimidating. The group were ecstatic they had captured such good evidence but at the same time were concerned at the apparent level of malevolence demonstrated by the second spirit. They asked Dena what had happened to Luke and she guessed that he had disappeared quickly on the arrival of the grand master and was probably scared of him.

Dena knew at some point she would have to face the dark entity but she only wanted to do that when she was ready and, on her terms, not his. She asked Eric, the lead investigator, to show what they had captured to Janet to keep her up to speed. He agreed to do so while she went back to her camper van to get some rest. Leading these sessions was always draining as the spirits often used her energy when responding to her questions. She hoped she would have a peaceful night and just to make sure she lit some sage in the van and recited a blessing, before having a glass of red wine and retiring for the night.

The next morning Dena met the investigation team for breakfast and said she wanted to undertake an investigation in the workhouse. They knew she would want to do this at some point and so had already sought permission to do so from the authorities. The building was now disused but was still structurally sound and safe to walk around. They had been given the keys on the understanding that anything they did was at their own risk and that they took full responsibility for their actions. This was standard stuff and more to do with insurances and removal of liability than anything else. The team had agreed all this in advance and so could go with Dena that day as she had requested.

They finished their breakfast and loaded up one of the vans with all of the gear they would need. Their tech guy always made sure there was lots of charged batteries so they could go investigate at a moment's notice. They were very organised and well equipped so off they went to the workhouse. It took them about twenty minutes to arrive as they had made sure to avoid rush hour.

First, they had to get through the substantial metal gates that were made of wrought iron that had an impressively large lock built into them. The metal railings surrounded the whole building plot and were painted black. There was nothing cheerful about them. They were as much about keeping people in as they were about keeping people out. Once you went through those gates and heard them clang shut behind you, it would leave you in no doubt that your freedom was now going to be severely curtailed. The grounds surrounding the building were covered in granite sets that were dark grey, almost black in colour which reinforced the dark and harsh surroundings.

They parked up and looked around the building to check what state of repair it was in. The windows and doors had been covered with metal shutters to stop vandalism and anyone gaining entrance who wasn't supposed to. It made you feel like anyone bothering to get passed the iron fence deserved to get inside but the owners clearly didn't share that view. The building had a substantial footprint and had large wooden arched entrance doors painted in dark red. The building had been fitted with electric lighting but they had no idea if the power would be on and if the light fittings were still in working order. With that in mind they took plenty of torches with them just in case.

As they went through the entrance they were immediately greeted with a high ceiling and huge open space. There was drab coloured paint on the walls that was faded and some sort of reception office on the right. There was a huge winding staircase with a massive thick wooden banister. The treads were also made of wood and were bare of any decoration. They were wide for lots of people to pass both ways presumably but also very functional, nothing remotely fancy. The whole reason for that entrance area was to dominate and intimidate the newcomer, for them to feel small in this huge institution. Straight on was a massive room that must have been used for meals and also workspace. There were lots of writings on the wall about being silent and working hard. One said, "The harder you work the closer you are to God." That was probably true in the fact that the inmates would eventually work themselves to death. This was not a happy space. It was cold with windows starting above head height so inmates couldn't see what was going on outside – they mustn't be allowed any distractions. The ceiling to the room was way up high making anyone present feel very small and insignificant.

Dena thought what a miserable existence the people living here must have had. High up on the far end wall there was a familiar symbol painted in gold It was a very large eye inside a triangle. This might refer to the society the team were investigating but it could also be a warning to the inmates that they were being watched. They all wondered why such a horrible building with wretched history had survived in such good order. The local council had in fact listed the building to give it protection from demolition or major structural change as it was such a fine example of its type. They all agreed the best thing that could happen was for it to be turned into a museum for visitors to see how barbaric living could be without proper social care.

This building had been used as a dumping ground for orphans and unfortunates who for whatever reason couldn't work. That included anyone with a disability or severe illness. There was nowhere else for them to go. This was the welfare state of the time and right now it didn't feel like there was anything to be proud of. What it did do was take away the sight and thought of these people away from the better off in society so they didn't have to encounter them and that was the idea. They could feel smug that their taxes were taking care of the less fortunate in a way that they deserved. True they would have to work hard but that was the same for most people and they had food and shelter, what more should they want in their station? Such was the thinking of the time. Any right-minded individual today would be appalled at the human misery that would play out in these places. There could be no hope for any of the inmates as there was no way of them working their way to freedom. The only respite would be death and some of the people here must have longed for that release. All the team felt this was a lesson from history that had to be kept alive for everyone to see today so that no such institutions were ever allowed to thrive again.

The staff in these institutions had quite a hard time too, they were paid little but had better food than the inmates they supposedly looked after. They worked long hours and kept order, where necessary, with sticks or canes they would use to beat particularly the children with. Anyone causing too much trouble would be thrown out onto the street. That threat, the lack of good food and the hard monotonous work to break their spirit was enough to make sure the inmates did what they were told.

The team went towards the stairs and looked for the light switch but there was nothing nearby. They looked for cables and noticed several went to the reception room to the right of the front door. Dena went inside and saw there were lots of switches that were labelled for lots of rooms. This must have been where staff controlled the daily lives of the inmates, at least from a lighting point of view. Early in the morning the lights would be switched on to help get people up for a meagre breakfast before starting work and at the end of the day the lights would be turned off to stop them roaming around. Every minute of the day was controlled by the staff and was very regimented.

It was still early in the day but the huge stairs were still quite dark so Dena flicked the switch that said, "stairs." And most of the large central stair lights turned on. Some must have faulty bulbs. The building was only being maintained to a minimal standard to stop it decaying and becoming dangerous.

They decided bringing the torches was a good idea after all as no doubt the lighting in the other rooms would be equally as bleak. Electricity was an added cost and one thing that was focussed on above all else was the reduction of costs wherever possible. The team got their bulky shoulder mounted cameras ready along with the EMF meters and slowly started walking up the stairs. They creaked loudly, they were sound but old made of heavy oak timbers, nobody would be able to use these stairs without making a considerable noise. There were no doors on the landings, which were intentionally very open plan making it easy for staff to see what was happening on each floor. There were various dormitory style large bedrooms with different floors for different sexes and ages. Inmates were not allowed to mix once lights were out. The lowest floors were for the oldest women, ones further up were for the younger females then males and children, often orphans, were at the top of the stairs.

There was a rudimentary hospital room on each of the floors where anyone too sick to work would be housed. This was often just a place for them to wait to die as any treatments would be very basic and cleanliness left a lot to be desired. The team wandered around the first floor, calling out to any spirits present and looking carefully at their EMF meters. So far all had been quiet although the atmosphere didn't feel good. They moved from room to room slowly and carefully, well aware that a lot of people had passed through these spaces and having an awful time of it. Each floor had a staff station where they could sit and watch the corridors making sure no inmates left their room. The team approached the first one. Staff at these stations wore like a nurse's uniform. They weren't medically trained but it gave them an air of authority. Some, were nuns, as the institution was also meant to protect the inmate's spiritual well-being as well as the physical.

The stations were basic and most were just a substantial desk come work area where staff could complete administrative tasks that helped them pass the tedious nights. This first one was thick with dust and had a basic wooden chair by the desk. There were few staff comforts too, after all they shouldn't be allowed to be too cosy else, they might fall asleep on the job. A solid un-cushioned chair would encourage them to do their rounds as they were supposed to.

They entered one of the dormitory rooms and much to their surprise it still had several bed frames lined up against the walls. They were metal and looked basic. They had rusted metal springs and had peeling white paint around the frames. These had been built with a lasting quality not one of comfort for the user. Each room had sixteen beds, eight down either side, all very regimented and orderly. There was no privacy in these rooms, not even just visual screens. Everybody could hear and see everyone else in the room which added to the misery of being here as an inmate.

The rooms were painted in a dull grey colour with windows high up to again discourage looking at the outside world. The floors were bare tiles and so easily swept clean. This was all about minimum maintenance and cost and the inmates had to be thankful for what they had. You couldn't help feeling depressed as you walked around this place which was the very reason the local authority had wanted to preserve it and turn it into a visitor attraction. Not for enjoyment but for education of the current population so as to make sure society as a whole never forgot the treatment of the poor up until relatively recently. It was partly a political statement but also one to refer to when arranging annual budgets so that social care didn't get forgotten. It's all too easy, unless you're on the receiving end, to forget the social safety net and think of it as an easy area to reduce as there are few votes in it. Inmates using these facilities aren't likely to protest loudly on the streets or make a stand at the ballot box.

The team inevitably had got quite down and gone quiet whilst walking around the dormitory and thinking about the lives that had occupied the space. It was difficult to do any other and it was a hard person indeed that could visit a place like this and not be affected by it. They figured each of the floors would be similarly laid out with multiple dormitories on each floor. They wandered around the other rooms and found a washroom which was in keeping with the rest of the place, and was very basic. Each floor had a communal washing area where cold water would come out of rudimentary group showers. No money was wasted on hot running water for cleaning. The toilets were grouped in one room on each floor containing ten stalls with side dividers but no doors. These had been updated over the years and conventional flushing toilets with hard wooden seats were still in place. They looked rather disgusting. The walls were covered in off white tiles for ease of cleaning. The facilities seemed more reminiscent of a Victorian prison than anything else.

All that can be said as a positive about the institution was that people could survive here but anyone having any knowledge about the conditions would certainly fight tooth and nail not to be admitted here. It was well known that some people committed suicide rather than take up a place here. That didn't bother the authorities of the time as it was one less of the poorest in society that they had to provide for.

The team decided they had looked enough at this first floor and wanted to check out the top one where children would be housed. It was quite a trek and of course no lift, walking up and down the stairs was good exercise and good for the soul.

The major difference with the children's floor was that the dormitories had bunk beds and so each room had double the number of the adult ones. There was also more of an infirmary on the top floor as the children were expected to be ill more often. Mortality was high as infections spread quickly amongst the cramped conditions and a lot was due to poor nutrition. There was more staff based on this floor to deal with the various issues to do with the children and the dormitories could be used to double up as workrooms so the children could stay away from the main institution's population.

As the team walked around, they noticed their EMF meters were getting more of a response on the top floor as they had expected. Children often create more paranormal activity. Then suddenly one of the EMF meters screamed its alarm and the needle went right over to the highest reading. Eric looked at it and slowly waved it in different directions. The tone it was giving off went deeper when there was less activity and high pitched when there was a surge. It was reducing when he pointed it around the dormitory but going to near maximum when he aimed it towards the entrance to the room, (there was no door so you couldn't really call it a doorway).

Three of the team had EMF meters and they all got similar readings when they copied Eric's actions. They all pointed to the entrance and the meters went off the scale. Everyone moved closer to the dormitory entrance at least until they saw the most hideous and grotesque figure of a nun stood there. It was staring right at them with black rings around the eyes. Its skin was decaying and the contents of its mouth was black. It was wearing a black and white nun's outfit and moved silently. It was tall and virtually filled the entrance way. The group were terrified and Dena instinctively held up a crucifix she was wearing around her neck. "You have no right to be here." She proclaimed.

The spirit didn't seem to agree as it howled like a banshee the most skin tingling noise any of them had ever experienced. They were trapped in the dormitory but the tech guy Aaron was recording. On his screen there were several orbs and a dark figure, you couldn't make out it was a nun just a tall dark entity and it was picking up the sounds. This would be amazing proof for their investigation. The nun seemed to sense what was going on and turned to look at Aaron, he was shaking with fear. She lunged at him with great speed and went right through his body. At that point Aaron passed out, both he and the camera fell to the floor. The nun had disappeared and the team tried to revive Aaron. He quickly became conscious but didn't want to stand until he felt more confident about doing so. Instead, he propped himself up against the wall. The rest stood by protecting him in case something else manifested itself. Dena looked around as she could sense something else, another entity. She told the team to be ready, they all looked around the room and Dena moved more to the middle. She could feel a cold spot and had a sense of being frightened. This wasn't her feelings about the nun, this was something else. She closed her eyes and in her mind's eye she could see a young boy. He was calling her name and telling her to be careful and that she was in danger.

She spoke out loud and asked what the boy's name was. He said it was Peter. Dena asked how old he was and he replied that he was ten years old. In her mind he was very small and thin wearing not much more than rags for clothes. She asked if he lived in this room and he said yes. He told her not to upset that nun as she would get very angry and hit the children with a stick. Dena told him not to worry and thanked him. She promised that they would help him be at rest so the nun couldn't hurt him anymore. Dena told the team that before they left the building, she wanted to cleanse at least this room to help Peter be at peace.

They all agreed and Eric said the whole building would need to be cleansed, room by room to stop any evil entities from returning and potentially taking control of unsuspecting visitors.

Aaron had managed to stand up by this time and had been recording what Dena was saying. They all knew if they got the cleansing wrong, it could actually make things worse as it could just antagonise any malevolent spirits. They would have to be very careful. They left the room and could see a painted arrow on the wall with writing underneath, it said infirmary. Most of the children wouldn't be able to read and so it was obvious the sign wasn't for them but to make any visitors feel better that there was some sort of facility to support the children. The group decided it would probably be a good place to get more activity as potentially, youngsters will have died in there.

The nearer they got to the infirmary the less light there seemed to be so they all turned on their torches. Aaron looked back towards the dormitory and instantly wished he hadn't. The ghastly nun's head and shoulders was leaning out of the dormitory entrance and snarling at him. He couldn't help but let out a shriek and everybody turned to see what was there but the nun had gone. They were all getting very hyped up and this is just what apparitions want so that they can use the energy to manifest themselves. Scaring people provided electrical energy they could use.

They approached the infirmary, which seemed to be one of the few places that had an actual door and right now it was closed. There was no glass in the door so it wasn't possible to see what was on the other side. Eric tried his EMF meter and it flickered to about half way then reduced back to zero. It did that several times. They all looked at each other and Dena said that she wanted to go in first while the rest took readings and made recordings.

Dena placed her hand around the circular door handle and just left it there for a few seconds to see if she could feel anything. She took some good deep breaths and prepared herself for what might be on the other side. She turned the handle slowly and the mechanism clicked. She slowly pushed the door and it gradually started to open. The room was very dark and the door creaked loudly as it was opened. She swallowed hard and pushed the door fully open as she let go of the handle. It looked like there was a table towards the right-hand wall but there were various things, shapes and the poor light masking what was there. She took a torch and shone it at the table. There were various books stacked up on top with a chair behind and what looked like a human shape motionless. Dena slowly entered the room backed up by Eric. Now her eyes were getting used to the low light she could see that the figure was actually an old nurse's uniform on a stand. She felt relieved as did the others.

They all slowly entered the Infirmary, the only windows were high up and were covered over by roller blinds. The low light was presumably to help the patients sleep themselves better – that was probably the best treatment they could get at the time this would be in use. Medicines were too expensive to be wasted on these poor wretches. There were several beds still in place with a few pieces of equipment and a side office with windows to the infirmary and a door. This was presumably so a medical person could see someone individually without bothering the rest of the patients. It would also allow them to see what was going on in case they were needed quickly.

Eric and the rest of the team spread out and were holding their EMF meters at arms-length as they went. Dena asked if there were any friendly spirits that wanted to make their presence known. She asked if there were any children and then they heard what sounded like a child crying. They all stopped and listened and they could definitely hear crying, it was so sad, the atmosphere had started to feel oppressive and the disembodied child's crying made it feel all the worse. A common cause of death at the time would be tuberculosis and pneumonia, both caused through poor health and lack of good nutrition and also highly contagious.

They were picking up the sounds on their recording equipment but there was nothing to see, no dark figure or even an orb. Then from nowhere there was the sound of scraping of a chair on the floor. They all turned around to look at the table and there was the full-bodied apparition of a female nurse in full uniform she was sat there motionless but looking right at them. Eric turned his video recorder towards her, all it was picking up was a dark shape but there were two red eyes reflecting back into the camera.

The nurse was dragging her nails across the table, this made one of those awful sounds that puts people's teeth on edge. She slowly began to stand but as she did, all you could hear was the sound of bones cracking. She moved stiffly, awkwardly, inhuman. Dena waved her hands at the team for them to move towards the corridor. The sound of the child crying had stopped, now the focus was on the nurse. Dena pointed her torch at the nurse's face, they were all shocked as the only features they could see were two red reflecting eyes, no nose and no mouth. She began to noisily move side-ways behind the desk as if she was getting ready to come towards the patient area. Dena urged the team to leave the room and she quickly followed. As the team looked back, they could see the nurse suddenly pick up speed and rush towards the door with the unearthly sound of bones cracking filling the air, it was sickening. They slammed the door behind them just as the nurse had reached the door way. Everyone expected her to walk through the door but she didn't and all went quiet. They decided not to hang about and to head to the main stairs.

Dena wanted to check something before they left the workhouse. She wanted to see if there was a tunnel from the basement linking it with the three other buildings that the Markle family owned or controlled. The basement of the building was used for utility purposes such as washing of clothes, preparing food and a morgue. Not the most pleasant of uses to have on one floor but this building was all about necessity not nicety. Each of the three functions had to be carried out and by having them in the basement they wouldn't take any space away from the other floors. This would maximise the number of inmates that could be housed there. The planners of the time were quite proud of that fact. They had installed a version of the dumb waiter system in the walls to help the staff transfer bedding sheets from the top floors to the basement and to get fresh bedding and food upstairs from the basement. Again, this was more about efficiency than being helpful or thoughtful. Less staff were needed by using a system like this so it would pay for itself by reduced staff wages.

The group followed Dena into the basement, they would need all of their torches as most of the lights weren't working. At least the rooms down here had doors, it was a staff only area and the first rooms they came across looked very grey, much like the rest of the building and was a big open space. There were several sinks and the floor area was tiled. This presumably was the laundry. Not that the inmates had many clothes or that they got washed regularly – this was more about washing uniforms for the staff. In turn that was more about looking presentable to visitors and also added an air of superiority between the staff and the inmates, seen as essential for keeping good order and discipline. Being underground there were no windows and so no natural light in the basement rooms. The group couldn't help but imagine the hard work that went on down here, no doubt exclusively women for the laundry area. The people who worked here would be menial staff on less wages than the rest, which is ironic as they worked physically a lot harder than the rest. That set a divide though between basic working staff and those who took care of the inmates. The two groups had minimal interaction and working conditions in the laundry were fierce. There was the sheer hard work but also the heat from the washing and the damp atmosphere combined with long hours. This was barely one up from being an inmate.

They moved to the next room which also had some sinks and lots of raised benches. There were some gas pipes with fittings in the wall so presumably this was the food preparation area. To call it a kitchen seemed too strong a description as proper hot cooked food was rarely given to the inmates and was almost exclusive for staff once per day and more so the trustees during the meetings which they made sure lasted all day and so caused for them to indulge themselves with hearty hot meals and plenty of them. No expense would be spared for them and they saw it as an expectation for them carrying out their civic duty by overseeing the good deeds of the workhouse. The cost of this would be shown in the accounts but these were never questioned as the only people who could do so was themselves. There was no oversight beyond the trustees and its very existence was enough to reassure the local authorities that all was well.

The next room they entered was a large open space with drains in the floor. Again, the floor was tiled so as to make it easy to wash down. The same was to be said for the walls in this room. The staff weren't obsessed with cleanliness just the ease of keeping the rooms reasonably clean to look at. There was only one use this room was meant for and it would be the last room that any of the inmates would occupy. This was the morgue, there was no need for signs on the doors, the staff would know which was which just from memory and most would probably only use one of the rooms anyway. If there was to be a linking door in the basement, Dena expected it to be in here as it would make perfect sense.

They searched along the walls for any obvious signs of a door. All of the others had been hidden so it was a fair guess that this one would be too. However, this building hadn't been so well maintained so it should be easier to find it. Having had no luck from the initial search, Dena remembered a little trick which sometimes works with hidden rooms. It would depend how well this door was covered up as to whether this would work. She suggested creating some smoke and gently passing it over the walls. Fingers crossed, when they came to the door the smoke would disappear into the wall. One of the team had a lighter and some sage and volunteered to blow smoke over the walls. This might take a while if the door was well covered up but they thought it was worth a try. One wall adjoined another room so it couldn't be there, another led out to the stairway, that only left two possible walls. No luck, none of the smoke disappeared, no giveaway sucking in of smoke. They all looked very disappointed. Maybe there was no door after all.

Dena pondered the problem for a while as the rest carried on looking around the morgue. Finally, she asked the team if they all had water and they all said yes for drinking. She asked them to form a line down the narrow side of the room. They spaced out as she asked. Now she asked them to walk forward but look at the floor at the same time and check for any damaged floor tiles or cracks in the grouting. She told them if they found a crack to splash a bit of water at it and watch what happened. They all did it but only a couple of them figured out what she was doing.

They had only got about a quarter into the room when one of them said they could see the water draining away but it wasn't going through one of the floor grates. Dena went over to look and poured more water around. It was disappearing under the floor tiles not through a floor drain. She stamped on the floor and listened to the sound. If she stamped heavily enough, she could hear it was slightly hollow and even had a bit of an echo. Eric took out his strong utility knife and scraped away at the grout around the tile. He managed to lift it out of the way and there was some dry plaster underneath. He scraped it away and tapped the butt of his knife on the surface he had uncovered. They could all hear it had a hollow sound, they felt they had found their hidden door, not in the wall after all but in the floor. If this linked to the other tunnels, it would allow inmates to be taken out of the workhouse without anyone else ever knowing. This would need more exploratory work and they would have to be careful as it wasn't owned by the museum.

The team couldn't come this far and not go down the tunnel, they would need all of their torches as there would be no light down there. As this wasn't owned by the museum, presumably the tunnel hadn't been maintained like the others had so they would need to be careful of that too. This was just about in the middle of the other buildings on the map so they shouldn't have too far to go before they came across the other tunnels. Eric continued working on the tiles and the plaster underneath. He found a recessed metal handle and cleared the plaster from around the edge of the hatch. Now it could be made out there was some rather large recessed hinges for the, what appeared to be, a heavy hinged sub-basement entrance. Someone had decided to cover it up at some point presumably to keep its existence a secret. Eric pulled on the metal handle and he needed considerable force to free it from all of the surrounding plaster, the hatch was thick and heavy made of metal. He could see there were some steps leading down from the workhouse hatch. Dena went first closely followed by Eric and the others. The tunnel was substantial, just like the others. It would be easy to lock the morgue door from the inside, open the hatch and then pass bodies down the hatch into the tunnel without arousing any suspicion. If anyone made any enquiries, all that had to be said was that the body had already been buried and site health reasons. If anyone found the hatch, they could just be told it was used for cleaning the morgue.

There was no debris to be removed from this tunnel and they carefully navigated along it, watching out for anything unusual. So far all was quiet and the tunnel was in good repair. They did come across a characteristic heavy metal door, which they opened and low and behold this led to the anti-room. Like the others it could be locked from the other side which would block anyone gaining access from the workhouse tunnel. They could now draw a line on the map between the workhouse and the anti-room. All of the buildings the family used were interconnected. They could operate with impunity all underground and away from anyone's gaze. They had a continuous network from ship to the tunnels, even to the canal network. They could smuggle anything they wanted yet the contents of the crates had all been paid for. This was to make sure they didn't attract any unwanted attention. The real smuggling was in people – men and boys for their souls and it was despicable. They must have been responsible for the deaths of hundreds if not thousands of men and boys, was this so that Frederick could move through time? This is what Dena suspected but hadn't confided in anyone as it sounded far-fetched not to mention gruesome. Presumably he felt he had gained immortality by doing this. There had been lots of other people in history who had chased that dream and none had been successful, so far as anyone knows at least. There was also of course the insidious trade in corpses that, in these numbers, brought in a considerable sum. Presumably that was the reason for the hatch from the morgue. None of the low-level staff would have any idea what was going on with the deceased and wouldn't care. Only one or two senior staff might be involved and their silence could easily be bought with a little extra money.

The team had achieved what they set out to do so they decided they would return to the workhouse and cover their tracks. As they got close to the entrance, they could hear a strange noise echoing in the tunnel. They couldn't make out what it was but it didn't sound good. They kept on going but now slowly and the teams EMF meters started to flash and make the high-pitched sounds meaning there was an entity present. Dena could feel a presence too and it wasn't a positive one. She didn't feel this was one of the workhouse children. They carried on going slowly and then they recognised what the sound was, they had heard it before. It was the sickening sound of bones breaking. They thought the nun must have followed them down but when they got closer and their torches reached the spot, they could see it was a nurse. She was posed awkwardly, not looking at them at all, she was looking at the floor, arms out with fingers all spread out in a misshapen way.

The entity was between them and the hatch and it seemed to respond to their sounds. Eric threw a stone so it would pass the nurse and she twisted backwards to follow the sound, then she stopped. Maybe it was the dark tunnel or some other reason she couldn't see them in the same way other spirits had. The group tried to move forward as quietly as they could. Any sounds made the nurse move almost in a twitching and then cracking movement. When they got close enough, they could see she had no eyes, just black holes where they used to be. Dena waved a torch around but the nurse had no reaction. Eric threw a larger stone that landed well behind the nurse and she spun around quickly and headed in the direction of the sound. She was now beyond the hatch. They now had to keep their nerve, get to the steps upwards and out of the hatch, all while not alerting the nurse to their movements. This would have to be done one at a time. Eric signalled for Dena to go first and that he would go last. If necessary, he would throw things to keep the nurse occupied.

Dena was light on her feet but it took a lot of nerve to do this in the presence of something that looked like it should be in Hell. Who knows what it would do if it actually caught one of them. She held her breath and slowly headed towards the steps. She took her time and gradually got out of the hatch into the morgue. She beckoned for the next member of the team to try. There was a lot of hesitancy but they all managed so now it was Eric's turn. He had seen the nurse quiver and turn in reaction to the others and he had kept distracting her with objects thrown behind her. Now he was getting close to her, he could smell the stench of death coming from her. She was a truly gruesome sight, partly decomposed. Eric paused and Dena beckoned him to come up. He gently started to climb the steps but then one of the team in the morgue sneezed. Eric looked shocked and Dena called to him instinctively. The nurse instantly spun around and grabbed hold of Eric's leg as he was trying to rush up the steps. She had managed to get his lower leg with both of her hands and she wasn't letting go. He was kicking back, trying to push her off but she had a firm grip of him. Dena reached for some holy water and threw it at the nurse who snarled in response.

Everyone was cheering Eric on trying to encourage him. He was trying to pull himself up but was being pulled back down by this entity. At the same time, he was calling out, it was clearly hurting. Not to mention scaring everyone. Dena passed Eric a crucifix and he pressed it on the nurse's head. He could see it burn and she made a blood curdling scream as she let go and Eric was able to pull himself up the steps at double-quick time. One of the others slammed down the hatch and stood on top of it. Nobody knew if that was enough to stop her entering the morgue but it was an instinctive thing to do.

Eric pulled up his trouser leg and everyone could see the heavy red marks left by her grip, they looked very saw but Eric was pleased to get away with just this. They all took a few minutes to collect themselves. This had been another shocking experience, one that was making them all question if they wanted to carry on. As Dena pointed out, it was no good being a paranormal investigator if you didn't want to come across what you were supposedly investigating. Everyone knew what she said was true and so they took a breath and replaced the tile and the plaster dust and tried to disguise the hatch as best they could. Surprisingly they hadn't been bothered by any apparitions in the basement itself. Dena thought that wouldn't be the case once they started digging up the floor.

There had been some disturbing activity that the group had managed to document and record in the most part. They were all feeling expectant about the door and relieved that they had been left alone in the basement. The institution might be able to be purchased cheaply from the local council if they were convinced it would be preserved and opened to the public. Once the floor had been taken up for investigation, it could always be replaced before any of the public were admitted. Dena thought that the museum may well be keen to buy it if it helped protect the Wilson family name and that of the secret society. After all, the museum had lots of funds available to it now and it would complete the story at least for them, even if they didn't make everything public. The key to the purchase would be to convince the local authority it would save them a lot of money making the building safe for the public. Dena knew that would be an easy task for someone like Janet.

In the meantime, Dena wanted to cleanse the room she earlier promised she would. She burnt sage and recited blessings. She called on Peter and told him he would be safe if he moved towards the bright white light. He took some convincing as he had been afraid and trapped for a long time but eventually, he followed Dena's words and passed over and was at last at peace. The rest of the building would need a whole team and ideally a priest to bless the rooms one by one. The stronger entities may need an exorcism to remove them and that would be critical before any of the public were allowed in. As they left the building, they could hear sobbing coming from one of the upper floors, it was the sad disembodied sound they had heard before. They locked the door and the iron gates behind them. They took one final look at the front door only to be scared half out of their wits by the sight of that ghastly nun stood by an open door. They all ran to the van and drove off as quickly as they could.

Chapter 13

Dena reported back to Janet about what they had discovered at the Workhouse and she set about writing a bid to purchase the building and preserve it and then opening it to the public. Janet knew it wouldn't cost much to purchase if it was to be opened as a museum. The local authority would probably let it go for a peppercorn payment in return for it to be made safe and kept for posterity. This, Janet hoped, could be completed very quickly as it was the parish council who could make the decision and they had very little funds, so they would be glad to see something positive being done with the workhouse as at present it was somewhat of a local eyesore and they were under pressure from locals to either demolish it or sell it for flats.

The transaction in principle was completed at lightening speed, certainly by council standards. The signing of the contract meant that Janet could instruct workman to take up the floor of the building and find out about the door and tunnel.

Dena had checked on a map and realised the Workhouse was more or less centre of the triangle formed by the museum's other three buildings. This can't be a coincidence and must have had some significance to the Markle family at one time. It certainly helped them keep what was going on away from prying eyes. Janet had checked with the land registry and all of the land within the triangle and some beyond, was owned ultimately by Edith's estate. Over the years parts of it had been rented or leased out providing a substantial annual income for Edith. This wasn't London but it was still prime site land that could command high rents.

The investigation team said they would return once the door at the morgue had been cleared and checked out. Dena wanted to do some investigating of her own and asked Eric to help. They went to inspect the local archives to see if they could find anything more about the 'Society of the Eye.' Dena knew it could be still around today but probably in some different form, especially as Edith didn't seem to have any modern-day link to it.

They spoke to a local historian who knew about buildings in the area and that's where they got a good lead. Dena had told him they were looking for buildings associated with secret societies that had historic links to the local area. The obvious place to look was Masonic lodges and there had been plenty spread around. For some reason quite a few of them had now been sold and had been put to alternate use. They were still quite easy to recognise as they often had the name of the lodge and Masonic symbols on the buildings.

After spending a couple of days looking through dusty records and then another physically checking out actual properties, they narrowed the search down to one prime candidate. It was within the museum triangle and it was still in use as a Masonic lodge. It had the symbol of the All-Seeing Eye surrounded by a triangle etched into its front stonework. Dena and Eric would need to tread carefully. This was a group that even in modern times liked to stay away from the public eye and what they were trying to link to the society could well be devastating news. They needed someone to act as an introducer, but who? There was no immediate urgency but Dena wanted to follow this up as and when she could.

Dena and Eric also took some time to research some of the symbols they had come across in the tunnels and the various buildings they had looked at. There was a repeated theme with some of them. They were the ones that were aimed at limiting the movement of spirits. They weren't supposed to stop a spirit from appearing but they were meant to stop it from having free movement in the immediate area. This would only be done when you have strong and powerful entities that can manifest themselves and where you want to limit their ability to roam. This was in contrast to others that called on evil spirits to take the souls of the living and others that were forms of satanic worship and ritual. The limiting spells seemed to be the most recent as some of them had been carved into earlier more satanic verses, presumably to try to block those out.

There were lots of pentagrams and protection spells in the tunnel leading to the museum. Someone was clearly trying to restrict what the evil entities were doing and give themselves some protection at the same time. As this was associated with the museum, a fair guess would be that it was Edith who was doing this. Dena was keen to go back to the museum and look in more detail at the rooms Edith used most. Janet had told her what had happened in Edith's study, that it was very active with spiritual energy and so she asked Eric to gather the team and to meet up the next day at the museum.

The next morning, they all met in their camper van in the grounds of the museum. Dena explained she wanted them to set up their recording and sensing equipment in Edith's study but then to search the study for any spells or symbols. Look for any documents hidden in books, hidden pentagrams and to document what they found. Once they had chance to get breakfast from a local café, the team started rigging up their equipment and then started looking for symbols.

Dena wanted to leave no stone unturned so it came as no surprise, when they pulled back the carpet, that a huge pentagram could be seen that had been painted on to the floor in the centre of the room. Contrary to popular belief, a pentagram is a form of protection from evil spirits. When they looked around the walls, there were lots of symbols both carved and painted, used for protection. There were also binding spells written on parchment and secreted in various books on the shelves. As this was one of the main rooms Edith liked to spend time in, presumably it was because she felt safe in here and maybe more in control. The question was, who was it that she was trying so hard to limit?

Dena thought back to one of the items Janet had shown her, the planchette from the Ouija board that Janet had looked closely through and seen a fierce looking man seemingly in a room similar to Edith's study. What if it was actually the study? He might be marching angrily up and down because he had been trapped by one of Edith's spells. Janet had assumed the man was the Grand Master the original head of the Markle family. It would be ironic if he was been restricted by one of his own descendants.

Dena went to find Janet and asked for the planchette. They both went back to the study, held up the glass part and looked through. Nothing to start with apart from it looked like the study but it was empty. Then moving it around the room revealed the Grand Master himself looking particularly gruesome and appeared to be shouting at the viewer. Dena asked Eric to turn on the recording equipment. When he played back the sound recording, there was a terrible angry voice which repeated, "GET OUT!" Dena told everybody she thought now that this was the voice of the Grand Master and that they could see him through the planchette.

It would seem that Edith's binding and protection spells were working and it would also explain why her study was one of the hot spots in the house. Dena wondered if they would be able to contact Edith if they held a séance in the study. They all seemed to think that was a good idea and Janet was quite excited at the thought of hearing from Edith. After what they had discovered under the carpet they knew where to later position the table they would sit around. They would put it over the centre of the pentagram.

They continued documenting all of the symbols and spells they could find in Edith's study. Then they allowed themselves a break in the staff area, which was to be the visitor centre if the museum ever opened to the public, until then it had been designated for staff use as there was now a considerable number of people using the museum as their base. Once done they would set the room up for the séance.

Lots of candles were lit and the electric lights turned off. Dena would lead with Eric looking after the equipment while Janet and the rest of the investigation team would form the circle to try and provide energy for any spirits to use so they could communicate. Dena had everyone hold hands, she took some slow deep breaths and closed her eyes. She gently asked if Edith could come and talk to them. The room was calm and nothing on any monitors. Next came a high-pitched electronic noise, it was one of the EMF meters detecting magnetic activity. This happens as a spirit entity appears, other things can cause it but the team had already done background noise checks in the room as part of their preparation.

Dena welcomed the spirit to the gathering and asked if it was Edith. There was no reply but Eric whispered he could see an orb on camera moving around the room. Dena asked the spirit if it was at peace. There was no response but at least there was no negative activity which they had experienced so many times during this investigation. Dena told the spirit that if they were respectful and did no harm, they could use her body to communicate to the people in the room. Then Dena's face changed and seemed to age significantly. She called Janet's name who was now transfixed by what was happening. Dena called, "Janet?" again, who responded with, "Yes!" "Janet I'm Elsie your great grandmother you know who you really are, don't you?" The spirits voice said. Janet replied, "I'm not sure I understand what you mean." Elsie said, "You will." Dena's face slowly returned to normal and all went quiet. Dena steadied herself and again called for Edith to come forward and speak to the room.

This time a bell on the sideboard rang and Eric confirmed he could see another orb. Dena asked if it was Edith to confirm by ringing the bell again. The bell rang and Dena thanked Edith for responding. Dena asked Eric to take over the questioning and asked Edith if she wanted to use her body to communicate. The bell rang again. Dena sat back and asked Edith to be gentle. Dena's face changed for a second time, aging but in a very different way. This was quite a stern face and said she was only here because Janet was here. Janet looked surprised but pleased with the rest not knowing what to make of that.

Eric asked if Edith was the one who had placed the binding and protection spells in the room. She replied, "Yes." Eric asked why she had felt the need to do it. Edith responded, "To limit his power." Eric asked who she was referring to and Edith replied with, "The one who calls himself the Grand Master, my ancestor, Frederick. Janet, I know this is what you wanted to hear." Eric looked at Janet who shrugged her shoulders. Eric thanked Edith for responding and asked if she was afraid of Frederick. She quickly smiled and said, "No!" At that moment a book flew off one of the shelves and struck the wall at the other end of the room. Eric asked, "Edith is that you?" She replied, "No, it's him." Lots of the candles were flickering and the temperature in the room was dropping like a stone. Something was sucking up the energy in the room.

The sideboard bell began ringing loudly and repeatedly. It seemed to jump off the sideboard and hit the floor. A window flew open and the curtains began jumping about. Eric rushed to close the window and fastened the latch securely. The curtains stopped moving. Then the doors on a covered in bookcase flew open. Edith shouted, "Stop!" That just seemed to make things worse. Everyone in the room was getting very apprehensive and Eric was getting worried for Dena. One of the wooden sideboard drawers flew open and the papers inside began circling in the air above the table. The drawer slammed shut with a bang making everyone jump. Dena stood up but still was being controlled by Edith who shouted, "Frederick STOP! I command you!" With that another book flew off a shelf and struck Dena in the face. It caught her on her eyebrow and it was a strong enough blow to make it bleed. Edith didn't move and quietly said, "Janet is here." Eric was looking on the camera and he could see there was a dark entity that was moving towards Janet. He told her not to move and not to break the circle.

Edith spoke one last time with a very stern voice, "Frederick, leave this place!" There was a terrific bang on the table and a side table was thrown over but then there was quiet. Edith sat back down and slowly Dena's face returned to normal. She opened her eyes. Eric smiled at her as she asked if everyone was okay. He told her they had got some great responses and that she would love what they had captured on the monitors. She closed the séance using a blessing and told everyone they could relax and break the circle. Dena hadn't been able to ask many questions through Eric before Edith had disappeared but she had got a vital confirmation of something she had suspected for some time. That Edith was the one who had placed the limiting spells around and that it was the Grand Master she was seeking to limit. Edith also seemed to be able to stand up to him and win which was very interesting. This also confirmed Edith had full knowledge of the Grand Master and that she knew he was the original head of the family. She was confused about the references to Janet but that could wait for now. Frederick clearly had a lot of freedom of movement as he had shown up in various places. However, Edith seemed to have managed to limit those places. Dena wanted to get to the bottom of all this history and intrigue. It was obvious Frederick was a bad character and one to be very careful of but why was he still haunting the buildings and seemed to be protecting some of the possessions?

Dena wanted to know about the contents of the crates from W12. There were a lot of objects, worth a huge amount of money, that hadn't been touched for a very long time. Who had bought them and why? What was their purpose? The obvious place to start would be the warehouse itself but not just looking at the crates, Dena had already done that. She wanted to know if she could somehow trigger what happened before, where she managed to witness a recording of real events that had happened two hundred and fifty years ago. On one or two previous occasions, Dena had managed to visit a sort of spirit realm where she could witness events and interact almost like she was a ghost herself. She had only done it when she knew for certain she had a serious haunting and needed some answers to try and make it go away. She knew it was dangerous as spirit entities could affect her much easier on that plane – it was like they were more equal and it would be all too easy to be so badly affected that she would be unable to return to her normal state.

She arranged with Janet to have full access and permission on all sites and co-operation of any staff as needed. Dena discussed her plan with Eric as she would need someone to be with her, not least of all to keep watch over her body while she was on the spiritual plane. The rest of the team could carry on research and investigating as they saw fit.

It was now that Janet thought it appropriate to tell Dena what had happened to me. She knew that Dena had experienced lots of paranormal activity and had learned for herself a lot about the history so she figured Dena would believe what Frederick had done and could maybe prevent it from happening again. Dena was very concerned for my safety and the fact that Fredrick somehow had the ability to snatch me and take me back like that. She wanted to know what was enabling him to do such a thing. She said she wanted to hear the details first hand and so me with mum told her every detail and mum told her all that she had witnessed and about the timescales. Dena knew the next thing she wanted to do was investigate more of the warehouse. She considered asking me to go with her but decided it was too dangerous. She gave me a protective amulet to wear around my neck and a crucifix and said if he showed up again to let her know. In the meantime, she would go to the warehouse to see if she could see what I had experienced.

Dena and Eric went to W12 and took some comfortable chairs with them along with a table and candles. They setup on the top floor of the warehouse which would be out of the way of any estate workmen. They lit the candles and Dena asked Eric to watch over her and make sure nobody interfered with her body while she appeared to be asleep. Eric set up a camera just in case and promised to stay by her side. This would take a lot of concentration from Dena to begin with but after that the main fear was other spirits. Dena closed her eyes and cleared her mind and began to focus on what she had witnessed at the docks previously.

Everything went dark and silent, Dena felt very alone. It began to feel like that strange out of body experience we can all get occasionally, where you are looking at yourself from a distance. That feeling demonstrates we could all do what Dena was doing if we trained ourselves to do it. Dena was very attuned to this because of her family line and she realised that feeling meant that she had travelled to their realm where she was now in real danger and would have to be on her guard.

She could hear lots of noise gradually coming into focus. She could hear lots of voices mostly from outside but also some inside – she was still in the warehouse and on the top floor. There were plenty of windows, so she went to see what was happening outside. The scene was like one out an old book or film. The dock was full of sailing ships and the ones closest to the quayside were having their cargoes unloaded. The air was filled with smoke as this was the centre of the industrial area with lots of factories close by and there were several steam engines making awful clanking noises. This was early for railway engines, they were the beam engines, Dena recognised the sounds. They were partly covered by sheds but it was fairly obvious what they were doing, they were powering the cranes that were lifting the cargoes out of the ships.

There were men and boys everywhere transporting barrows full of goods to the dockside warehouses. The smell was disgusting, a mix of the various cargoes such as fish and guano but also the factories and tanneries, then oil and coal to keep the engines going. The scene looked chaotic but the work was getting done. She needed to explore closer if she was to find anything meaningful out so she slowly descended the stairs but checking each floor as she did. This top one was virtually empty apart from a few large white bales. She went over to have a look at what they were. They were bales of cotton, which was a major trading product of the time and entire shipping routes were based around its production and processing.

The two floors beneath were full of the same type of bales, presumably waiting to be moved on to one of the mills for processing. The next three floors were full of wooden barrels. When Dena checked what was marked on them, some said rum, some gin and some said molasses. All common traded and shipped items of the time. The first floor was different, it had lots of large wooden shipping crates with various stamped writing on. Some said fragile, while others said a country like India or Egypt and were marked up antiquities. This is what she was looking for, they were the same sorts of crates as were in the Chapel basement and the ones I had mentioned to her. She looked around for something sharp and found several nails on the floor. She took one and scratched a letter D into the top edge of the crate on all four sides. The one she had chosen was stamped with "Fragile" and "China." Both in large red letters.

The question now was, where was Frederick? She was presuming most of the people around wouldn't be able to see her, just like when she had the vision before, after the loco whistle sounded. She also remembered that the Grand Master could see her presumably due to some extra power he was wielding, so she would have to be careful and avoid him.

She went down the stairs to the ground floor where there were lots of people coming and going. Just as I had described to her, items were being unloaded into one part of the warehouse while others were being taken out from another section ready to be loaded on to a ship. Nobody was taking any notice of her so it looked like she was right – she didn't exist in their time so they couldn't see her. She figured the reason they could interact with me was because I had been brought back by Frederick using some powerful magicks. Dena wanted to try and get the name of at least one of the ships that goods were coming in from. The doors to the warehouse were wide open so there was plenty of space for her to slip out and take a look.

She looked at the dock and it was full of sailing ships and frantic activity as lines of men and boys were taking goods on carts and barrows in one direction or another. She made sure she watched out for obstacles and went close to the edge of the dock. She could see the name of one of the ships as, 'Medusa.' The next in line, tied up alongside said, 'Titan.' These were definitely two of the Markle family ships she had read about. She wondered, as there was lots of activity going on, if Frederick would be around. She remembered what I had said about a table, so she went carefully back inside. She could see a table at the other side of the warehouse with lots of papers stacked on it. There was a man stood by the desk receiving papers but it wasn't him, not the one she was looking for. Then a tall figure emerged from behind some crates, he was speaking loudly and people were taking notice. She looked at his hands and sure enough he was wearing a large ring on his finger. This was Frederick, the Grand Master.

Dena headed carefully towards the stairs she didn't want him to see her. She had noticed there were lots of symbols written on the walls and some were in strings that made runes or spells. These she thought must be for him to use. They couldn't be for protection or limitation as these were in his time. They must be to help him in some way. She tried to read them but it was difficult with the type of letters used and some of the symbols she wasn't familiar with. There was one symbol she knew and it was used to signify "home." Dena had seen this in old texts supposedly for witches to mark a place to travel to quickly – like a short cut. She looked out for the symbol hoping that if she touched it then it would take her back to where she started.

She looked at Frederick and to her horror she could see he was staring right at her. She had let her attention wander and he started walking towards her. She ran as fast as she could up the stairs but she needed to be all the way to the top. Her heart was racing and she tried to calm herself down. She could hear him shouting for people to get out of his way as he was rushing towards the stairs. Dena was travelling up the stairs as fast as her legs would allow. He was a lot taller than her and when he reached the stairs, he could take them two at a time. He was gaining on her and she knew it. She had a decent head start but she doubted it would be enough for her to get to the top floor before he caught up with her. He was rushing up the flights of stairs in double quick time. She knew it was useless so she waited for him on one of the landings. In no time he was there looking right at her.

Dena shouted for him to stop and for a few moments he did. She walked backwards away from him on to one of the storage floors. She recognised it as one she had examined earlier. There were lots of white bales in rows. This must be the sixth floor she had done well to get so far up. She ran between the bales catching her breath and buying herself some thinking time. Frederick was following her slowly as she now had nowhere to go, there was only one way in an out of each floor. He asked what she was doing there and she shouted that she was going to stop him. He laughed loudly and said, "You have no idea." She said, "I know you need young boys." He stopped and frowned and said, "You know nothing!" Dena said she knew he had taken me but that I had escaped and she said she would prevent him from taking any more. Frederick returned to smiling and said Dena had no way of stopping him.

She was heading towards the back wall of the storage floor and he was following her stride for stride. She managed to distract him by throwing one of the nails she had put in her pocket. He didn't see what she had done but he did hear the noise. It put him off a little as he thought there was just the two of them present, now it sounded like someone else was there. While he looked, she dodged down below the height of the bales. She manoeuvred herself to the side wall as quietly as she could. She was trying to work herself around him as he was slowly walking forward but more cautiously now. She threw another nail as hard as she could at one of the windows. It smashed one and he ran forward so she ran towards the open doorway. He hadn't seen her so she ran quickly up the stairs which creaked. He ran after her but she had got her breath back by now and was at the top of the warehouse in no time. She ran to the point where she had started and she could hear Frederick running up the stairs. She drew the symbol for home on the floor with a nail and slapped it with her hand. Just as he came into the room she disappeared and was back with Eric.

Eric asked if everything was alright and she said they had to leave quickly. She was afraid Frederick might decide to follow so they quickly descended the warehouse stairs and went outside. Dena at last felt safe and took some deep breaths. She told Eric a little of what had happened. They knew they were both safe outside due to the grounding and protection spells. They were now beginning to understand more about why these had been inscribed all over the estate – to limit where Frederick could travel to.

Dena and Eric were back in their own time and once they were satisfied Frederick wasn't following them, they went back inside the warehouse and Dena spoke to the foreman. She asked them to look for a crate marked in red that said 'Fragile' and 'China' on the side and had a 'D' scratched into the top edge. He said they would look for it but it could take some time. She told them to try the first floor to start with. Dena knew it might not even be in the warehouse, it could be in the Chapel or it could have been sent elsewhere as cargo. It was only an educated guess on her part where it might show up.

Dena told the foreman they would be back in an hour to see if they had managed to find the crate. It was high time she had something to eat so she and Eric went to a nearby café to have some brunch complimented with a big mug of tea. Dena filled in the gaps for Eric including her interaction with Frederick. She mentioned the names of the ships and what she had done with one of the crates. He asked her what she was expecting to find but she was still being a little guarded about her theory in case she was wrong. They both enjoyed their brunch and took a slow walk back to the warehouse. On the way Dena took a good look at the mostly empty dock and explained to Eric the sights she had seen and of how busy it had been. She looked at the information boards and read some of what they had to say. The information fitted in well with what she had experienced. When she looked at the outside of the warehouse, she could see the pully system they used and the doors on each level so they could get heavy goods up and in without modern equipment. It was quite neat but hard work for the men involved.

She asked the foreman if he had found the crate she had described and he said no, this puzzled Dena as she was certain it would be there. He did say they had taken a lot of crates out of the warehouse and transported them to the Chapel for storage there. She asked him if he could check amongst the crates there and get back to her, the foreman agreed to get back to her as soon as he could.

Dena decided not to wait for the foreman and she and Eric went off to the Chapel to see if they could find the crate Dena had marked. There was a lot of crates there but the stamped-up markings should help them find it reasonably quickly. They arrived at the Chapel and workmen let them into the basement that was filling up with wooden crates. They decided it was best to split up and search for crates marked China. After her experience, Dena felt better about being away from the warehouse. The two of them walked up and down the storage basement searching, then double checking but nothing that had Dena's markings on. Dena decided to talk to the workmen and ask if they had brought any crates in recently or placed them somewhere differently. One of them said that they had come across one crate that had special instructions attached to it.

Dena asked what the instructions were and the workman said that a piece of paper had been tacked to the outside of the crate stating that, when moved out of the warehouse, it should be placed upstairs in the Chapel in a specific side room so that's what he had done. He didn't understand what the instructions were for but he had done what it said. She thanked him and both her and Eric went to find the room and hopefully the crate. They went upstairs and after a bit of searching, found the room. There inside was a crate marked Fragile, China. Dena went over to it and sure enough, scratched into the top edge was a D on all four sides. The special instructions were still attached to the crate. Eric went to fetch a couple of workmen with some tools to break open the crate. They were far from enthusiastic as they said they had felt something strange about this crate. It was large and would take some time to open, especially as they had to be careful with the contents marked as fragile.

After some considerable effort they managed to loosen the top but as they did, they suddenly began to feel unwell and wanted to stop. Eric told the two workmen that he would finish opening it and they could go back downstairs. They hurried out of the room and went back to the basement. Eric asked Dena if she felt okay and she said she could feel there was something attached to the crate that she hadn't felt downstairs. It was something dark and menacing. Eric decided to go about removing the top of the crate very slowly. If there was something in here, he wanted to be careful. The crate stood about four feet high and was of similar proportions all the way around. Eric finally prized off the lid. Inside was lots of packing material as they expected but on top was a large envelope. It had Dena's name on the outside. They both looked shocked, how could this be?

Dena paused and just looked at the open crate for a while, she was wary after what had happened in the warehouse. She decided, after some time, not to touch the envelope and searched in her pockets for a pair of gloves. She put them on and took out the envelope. It was clearly old in style. She looked inside and could see a piece of paper with black ink writing on it. She pulled it out of the envelope and began to read out loud so Eric could hear. The first page read, "Dearest Dena, it was interesting to see you in the warehouse today presumably following in the footsteps of the brat I had taken from the house attic. He tried to steal my ring but it returned to me. I should have kept a closer eye on him but no matter there are plenty more for me to use. I noticed you marked this crate, so that must mean you suspect me of something. Enjoy searching and wasting your time and I will see you very soon. Yours obligingly, Frederick. P.S. there is a special package at the top for you."

Eric and Dena looked at each other in disbelief. It confirmed in one way what Dena had suspected but to be confronted in such a way was still a shock. It meant Fredrick knew of her and noticed what she had done to the crate. He must have placed this in the crate after he had seen her escape the warehouse and marked up one of the crates. She pushed away some of the packing material and there was a sack. She pulled it out and turned it upside down. Out fell a modern young boy's full set of clothes, black jeans, blue tee-shirt, red briefs, white sport socks and trainers – these are what she knew Steve had been wearing when he was taken by Frederick from the attic and forced to change from in the ship's cabin. Dena picked up the pair of red briefs, she looked inside and sure enough they had Steve's name on a label sewn into the waistband. (This was standard practice for school so that clothes couldn't get mixed up in the changing room during sports lessons.) Frederick, was demonstrating that he could come and go relatively freely in some circumstances, even being able to take someone back to his time. This is powerful magick to allow him to do such a thing. This crate had stayed in the warehouse all this time and Frederick had presumably thought it amusing to leave a message for Dena using conventional methods of the time. It sent a shiver down both her and Eric's spine.

There was also a second envelope that had fallen out of the sack with the clothes. Dena now focussed on this and there were several documents inside with some drawings and what looked like specifications. She couldn't believe what she was reading. Frederick was clearly an opportunist with a sick sense of humour. He had taken the clothes I had left behind, realising they would be commercially desirable in the future, and taken out patent applications for each piece. This meant when the time was right and companies wanted to manufacture jeans etc. that they would have to pay Frederick royalties for each piece of clothing for many years. These patents would now be out of date but they would also have earned a vast amount of money due to the quantity of pairs of jeans, for example, that must have been manufactured during the term of the patent. Along with the license for the patent, Frederick had instructed any manufacturer to add a little tab with his logo on it to each item of clothing. When Dena double checked my clothes that had been in the crate, sure enough there was a little tab added with the triangle and all seeing eye logo stitched into it.

Both the money and the patents would have also helped clean up the Markle family name. Maybe this is when the name changed to Wilson, it would be an obvious opportunity for them to do so. Legitimate wealth would allow the establishment to ignore the name change and to bury any negative rumours associated with the old name. This would be the ultimate in whitewashing the family name as if it was brand new. This would also limit the negative influence Frederick could have on his descendants. A clever move that would allow them to invent the Wilson family as rich merchants and fashionable clothes manufacturers and nobody would think anything could possibly be wrong. When Dena thought more about the logo on my clothes, she knew this would play with her mind which presumably is what Frederick wanted. My clothes didn't originally have his logo but they travelled back in time with me, he supposedly had them manufactured at some point and now they had the logo. This was a circular problem that she decided to put to one side for now.

Dena removed more packing material to see what else was in the crate. There was a specially constructed supporting framework to protect some fine-looking pottery, which most people with very little knowledge could recognise as Chinese. They were large vases heavily decorated in the style of the time. Dena neatly put the clothes back in the sack along with the letter which she had placed back in the envelope. She wanted to do some controlled tests on the contents and the sack before she decided what to do next.

She told Eric she thought it best to head back to the team's base, the camper van. He was happy to be leaving the Chapel. They left the crate and rest of the contents in place. Off they went to meet with the rest of the team to discuss what they had found.

As soon as they got back to their base, Dena placed the sack and contents inside a large polythene bag. She didn't want anyone to touch the items in case it alerted Frederick somehow. She wondered if this was why he had left the clothes inside or was it just proof and him showing off what he could do? Dena thought at the very least she could probably use the items at a séance to get Frederick's attention.

Dena explained to the group what she thought Frederick was doing at least part of it. She said he was buying up goods, in his own time period, from all over the world using his own ships as transport. He was buying a range of goods so as to increase the chances of success for his scheme. Some would be bound to increase in value such as gold coins but other items that were relatively cheap in his time such as paintings and pottery, could be worth great sums of money if left untouched for long enough. They would become rare and collectable and so increase the family fortune many times over. His idea was simple, put these items in crates in a warehouse that had its future secured via a maintenance trust. Gradually fill up the warehouse with these crates and at some point, they could be opened and their contents sold, making a huge profit at the same time. He was being very philanthropic for his descendants, unless they were for him all the time so that he could travel to the future and have riches whenever he wanted.

The one thing she hadn't fully worked out was how he was managing to travel through time. She knew it had something to do with the ring. She also couldn't be sure, who was limiting his movements. It had to be one of his relatives that had found out what he was doing. Did they want his goods for themselves or did they just want to keep him under more control?

There was an obvious suspect for the one who was limiting where Frederick could go and it was Edith. The team had witnessed Edith instructing Frederick to leave during a séance and he had protested by throwing over a table but still he had gone. Edith was the one who had gone to great trouble to hide the ownership of the buildings from the public and the authorities. She had been the one who had moved the crates from the warehouse to the Chapel. Some things at least were falling into place.

If it was Edith who had managed to limit Frederick, why had she not decided to rid herself of him completely? She had the wealth and he was clearly a serious blot on her ancestry, that's why the family had changed their name so as to break the link with the horrendous things that had gone on in his name. Dena and the team thought this one through. They wondered if the simple reason was that she didn't know how to get rid of him. The Grand Master was certainly no push over with the amount of power he was demonstrating.

Dena began to wonder if it would take the help of someone else to keep Fredrick in his own time frame. He wasn't just a spirit he was a presence moving between times, distant times.

He was fully understanding where he was from and where and when he could go. He was a very dangerous individual to anyone who got in his way. Dena remembered that Marge's oldest son had some society regalia in his bedroom. Could this provide a link to where she needed to be? There was only one way to find out and that was to go and ask.

Chapter 14

Dena contacted Marge and asked if she could meet Philip, Marge's oldest son. Dena explained that I had mentioned about his regalia and that she wanted to talk to him about this society he belonged to. Marge explained that he wasn't very forthcoming about any of that but that she was free to ask him. The three of them met over a morning cup of tea at Marge's house. At first Philip denied all knowledge of a secret society and said even if he was a member of such a place that he wouldn't be able to say. Dena explained she understood about the oaths that were taken and that all she was really after was an introduction to one of the senior members. Dena explained it was to do with what had happened to me, the noises in the attic and the movement of the wardrobe doors. It was at this point that Philip became more amenable and started asking questions of his own about what she thought was going on. He admitted that he had gone into the attic to look at some things that were in there and that he recognised some small pieces of furniture that must have hidden compartments and that were probably made by the company he was working for. They boasted they had been in business for hundreds of years and had protected people's secrets for all that time.

Dena knew she was getting somewhere and told him a little about the Grand Master. Enough to suggest he was the one causing the noises in the attic and that the items of furniture, initially belonged to him. She didn't mention the rest of what had gone on as she didn't want Philip saying too much to the society, he was a member of as she knew very little about it so far.

Philip said he would have to speak to a member of the society before he could promise an introduction and Dena thought this was only fair. He claimed his role was mainly to play music for the group when they met. Although he did say he helped them with organisational things but that was as far as he was prepared to say. Philip assured Dena he would do his best and would get back to her if he was successful.

In the meantime, Dena and the team conducted some research into the likely home of the Society of the Eye. It wouldn't be easy as it was a secret underground movement. The one thing they did have was the family line of Markle and then Wilson. At the very least the head of the families would presumably see the title Grand Master pass to them as it was invented by Frederick as a vehicle for him to become rich and powerful and then pass it on to his descendants. It would be interesting to know at what point Frederick found out how to exist in multiple time frames. They started to realise there could be a conflict with the Wilson family line, when it came to a female being the head such as Edith. Most of these societies were exclusively male so how did that work?

From what Janet had said, Edith had the Grand Masters ring, so had she taken up the role? She couldn't pass it on to another member of the family as supposedly there was none. Did the society still exist, there was no way of knowing if it did. The most obvious society today with similar symbols was that of the Masons. Had the old society disappeared into one of the Mason's lodges? There were several not too far away. The Masons were a lot more open these days about what they do and their charitable fund raising. Dena thought the last thing they would want would be to be associated with a group with potential for terrible publicity if the history ever came out.

She would wait until Philip came back to her before she would try and find anything else out. If nothing came of that then she might have to resort to another séance with Edith to see if she would be more open to questions of her heritage. Where had Edith got the knowledge to restrict Frederick? Was she now wandering through time just as he was doing? Finally, she got a telephone call from Philip saying he could introduce Dena to a member of his group. He wouldn't say any more than that and wouldn't even say the name of the group this person was from, only that his name was Stefan. The three of them agreed to meet in a quiet friendly pub over a glass of wine. This was seen as neutral territory for all concerned. As soon as Philip introduced the two of them, he excused himself and left them to it.

Stefan was handsome and had an air of being in control, not stuffy or arrogant, just quietly confident and well mannered. He could clearly hold a conversation without any difficulty and moved from one subject to another with ease. He was making small talk and Dena wondered if she would ever be able to get to the questions she had waiting. She picked up the wine bottle and offered to fill his glass and as he was politely thanking her, she jumped in with her introduction. Dena told him that she realised what she was asking was not usually discussed but that she had some serious reasons for raising the issues. Stefan acknowledged by appearing to concentrate on what she was saying. Dena stated that she wasn't too interested in the Masons. Stefan looked a little quizzical but nodded and waited for Dena's next words. She told him she was interested in a particular group, probably a small but potentially powerful one. Stefan looked even more focussed. Dena said she wanted to discuss the Society of the Eye. Stefan smiled and said nothing.

Dena went on to explain that maybe they were nothing to do with Stefan and that if she had the wrong person that he should say so. Interestingly, Stefan didn't utter a word but continued a broad smile. This, Dena took to mean, that Stefan was aware of what she was talking about and that was quite a relief to her. She tested her theory by placing a question in a different way. Dena asked him to stay quiet if he was aware of the group and if it was still operating today. Stefan took a drink of wine and smiled at her, she was nearly dazzled by his shiny white teeth. So, she now thought he had confirmed but managed not to say anything. She had come across this approach before when dealing with so called secret societies. She was happy to play the game provided she was talking to the right person.

Stefan ordered another bottle as it looked likely they were going to be having quite a long one-way conversation and Stefan liked his wine so long as it was of the right quality. Dena decided she had nothing to lose and cut straight to the chase. She told Stefan that she was looking for an introduction to the current group Grand Master and that she had some vital information for him as well as needed his assistance. Stefan remained calm and smiling and enjoying his wine. Never have so many words been said by a man remaining silent. Dena said that if she was talking to the wrong person as far as being able to arrange a meeting with the Grand Master that he should say so. Again, no words were uttered. Dena thought if she was talking to the right person that he would surely know the distant family name and possibly some of the dark history that is attached to it.

Dena waited until Stefan was just about to take a drink of wine and then said she wanted to discuss the Markle family with the Grand Master. The reaction was hilarious and she knew she had the right group and hopefully one of the right people to discuss it. Stefan had nearly choked on his wine and spluttered into a handkerchief. Dena offered him some water but Stefan waved it away. He coughed some more then took a drink from his wine glass after filling it to the top. He did his best to remain silent until Dena threatened to say the name louder. Stefan was clearly very surprised that Dena would know that name and that it was associated with the group. Dena asked if he now realised, she was being serious and Stefan nodded. Dena further surprised Stefan by mentioning the name Frederick. This made him look quite shocked as he emptied another glass and ordered the third bottle of wine.

Finally, Stefan asked Dena what she thought she knew about Frederick and the name Markle. She told him she knew a lot and urgently needed to meet with the current Grand Master. Stefan said that he was a very busy person and couldn't meet with everybody who asked. Dena felt she needed to push things along so she was quite firm when she told him that unless she met the person she needed to, she would be forced to let some potentially damaging revelations into the public domain and that she was trying to give the group the opportunity for that not to happen. Stefan told her not to be hasty and that he could arrange a meeting as she had requested. He asked if he could have her assurances that she wouldn't discuss anything openly prior to meeting with the current Grand Master. Dena agreed as she really didn't have any intention of releasing what could be very damaging information to who she presumed to be totally innocent people. After all she thought, they shouldn't be held responsible for the historical deeds of an ancient ancestor they weren't even related to.

Stefan asked Dena for some contact details so that he could arrange a meeting. Dena asked if it could be in the lodge. At first Stefan said that was unlikely and that this pub was more to his liking. Dena insisted by saying what she had to discuss was not to be overheard and that the Grand Master would realise that. Reluctantly, Stefan agreed and said he would get in touch with her shortly with a mutually agreeable date and time. Dena thanked him and filled up his glass. Stefan smiled broadly.

Stefan was a fixer for his Grand Master, he would make things happen by using various means of persuasion, some more subtle than others but he was also the life and soul of the party and his heart was certainly in the right place. He could be relied on when really needed and that set him apart from a lot of others. Stefan was well aware of the history of the group and knew it could be explosive in the media for the group's reputation not to mention that of the individual members of the group. So, he was in damage limitation mode and needed to satisfy himself of Dena's credentials and how reliable she would be in keeping things quiet. He contacted Matthew, who was the current group Grand Master, to tell him of the meeting he had and advised that they should all meet again soon to find out what Dena knew and formulate a strategy for going forward.

Matthew agreed and asked Stefan to set things up and to meet in the Masonic Hall, as Dena had requested. Mathew was a very charismatic figure who could fit in with any gathering regardless of social background. He could play his part at expensive fund raisers with politicians, lawyers and businessmen but equally he could look at home at a small charity event for local children. His profession was hospital consultant and he had a physical presence when he entered a room. He was a good person but definitely not one to be crossed. He was very competitive in everything he did and was very happy to help people he thought needed or deserved it. He was more than capable of dealing with undesirable attributes in people and he was the perfect character for the group position he held. He kept them in line when he needed to and made sure that promises of mutual aid were kept. This was like a mutual aid group for its members but they also performed good deeds for those in need.

If he needed to, Mathew could more than look after himself in a physical altercation. He was tall strong and very fit and had plenty of money in his own right. Stefan was there to help him keep order, a bit like an enforcer, he would gather useful information on members of the group. Information they would rather stay out of the public domain and he would use it to gain leverage when needed. They could both play hardball when required but then the members of the group were no pushovers either. Some of them were very senior in their professions and didn't always appreciate being told what to do. At those times they were reminded, membership was a lifetime commitment and that they were in the positions due to help from other members and that help could easily be used against them. The group was considered separate from the Masonic lodge like a sub-group or side branch and you had to be invited to join. They were very secretive about membership but they insisted they were for good. It's just as well they were so secretive as conspiracy theorists would be in their element if they found out about them.

Those conspiracy theories would get much worse if they ever heard about Frederick and made the link between him and the current group. It would be easy for Matthew and Stefan to get paranoid about such news being leaked but they were stronger characters than that, they just dealt with any issues as they arose and kept calm and in control and that was the key to everything as they saw it. Of course, in a group like this there would always be someone keen to take over from the boss and that's where a lot of the friction came from. Most of the group had their own agendas but it was up to the most senior inner circle to make sure the wider group was kept on track as they saw it.

Dena didn't know about the composition of the modern group or its' intentions but she knew enough about these secret societies to be careful as they often had influential people at the helm and often hated the glare of publicity. She knew, of course, that she could use that part to her advantage and that would be her leverage if she needed it. She knew that's how the meeting had been arranged in the first place. That the current Grand Master wouldn't want the spotlight falling onto his group.

Dena kept the investigation team in the loop so they knew what was happening and it also gave her some protection as she made sure Eric knew everything she did, just in case something was to happen to her. That was her insurance against anyone wanting to do her harm. She also made sure she documented everything and kept multiple copies both paper and sound recording. Nobody, no matter how powerful, would be certain of obtaining all of the copies of her document. She told herself when she met with Matthew, she must tell him all of this just in case. After all she didn't know him but she sure had witnessed Frederick and his dark deeds.

The next Dena heard from Stefan he was trying to arrange a meeting between him Matthew and herself one evening in the Masonic Lodge. She agreed to meet that evening and Stefan said he would pick her up in his car. Dena insisted on Eric being with them, that at least would make it two on each side she thought. Reluctantly it was agreed, especially after she told Stefan that Eric knew everything she did.

They had arranged to meet in the middle of the night to try to make sure there was no prying eyes. It was 2.30 in the morning when they got to the lodge. Stefan ushered them in and closed the door behind them. He showed Dena and Eric into a small side room that looked like it was used as some sort of administrative support. The three of them waited and Stefan offered them both some tea or coffee to help keep them awake. They settled for tea from some beautiful bone-China cups, this was all very civilised but a little surreal considering the time.

After a short while, Matthew entered the room and introduced himself. He had a very strong handshake and was dressed quite elegantly but casually. He clearly knew how to dress for an occasion but at the same time not to overdo it. He asked Dena to give him some background as to what had happened to warrant her involvement in the first place. She slowly explained what had been going on and about the research that they had all done. She told him that it didn't really matter what he believed in as these things were happening regardless whether he believed in them or not. She told him what had happened to me which seemed to disturb Matthew but he kept on listening. Dena told him about the ring they had found and the items in Marge's attic.

Dena also told him about the buildings and tunnels and about the symbols. Matthew was very interested in what she had to say about those symbols. He wanted specifics and she had guessed he would and so she showed him a notebook she had used to write down some of the spells and symbols from Marge's attic and from the tunnels. Now Matthew was hanging on her every word. Dena knew she had finally got his attention and that he was taking her seriously.

When she had finished explaining her role and at least some of what had happened she asked Matthew what he intended to do. She was trying to get a feel for how he was taking the news of a rogue Grand Master. Matthew was used to keeping his cards close to his chest and not giving too much away. He sat back in his chair and smiled and thanked her for coming to him and for not going to the press. She explained she was not interested in creating publicity, negative or otherwise. Dena had kept certain facts to herself so she could use them later if she needed to.

Matthew suggested showing Dena and Eric around the lodge, so as to dispel any myths or misconceptions they may have but also to see some of the symbolism that was present on the walls and ceilings. Dena reminded Matthew that Frederick was a Grand Master of a separate smaller much darker and more malevolent group that bore little relation to the Masons. The only similarity was that they had adopted some of the same symbols presumably to make themselves appear more mainstream. Matthew acknowledged what Dena had said and he told her he was willing to let her and Eric into his confidence provided they both swore an oath never to repeat what he told them. They looked at each other and agreed. They knew they needed his help against Fredrick and that a lot of this wouldn't be fair on the modern membership if it got into the media. They would just scandalise everything and anyone remotely involved.

The Grand Master told them both that he was the current head of the modernised group that Frederick had founded. He also said he was well aware of a lot of the history of the group and that if they compared their research, they could probably fill in any gaps in the knowledge. He said he would make them officially honorary members of the group and in that way, they would be closer bound to keeping things quiet. They both agreed and Stefan said he would take care of the administration. In response Dena told Matthew everything she knew, including the taking of souls and the murder of ancient convicts and disposal of the bodies to the medical profession.

Matthew did his best not to appear shocked, he always wanted to appear to be in control, not to be phased by anything anyone could say to him, but she knew this must be difficult even for him. She explained about the change of name and he already knew about that. He knew Edith and had met with her on many occasions. He now admitted that on some of those occasions he had witnessed Frederick's presence in her house. This was a revelation to Dena but a relief at the same time as this must mean that Matthew couldn't deny any of what she had told him. He confirmed that it was Edith who had managed to limit Frederick's movements after she had carried out a lot of research and purchased some ancient books on the occult.

Apparently, Edith had told Frederick what sort of collectables he should place in the crates that were worth a lot of money today. She knew he had been selecting goods for decades before she found out about it but then decided she might as well tell him exactly what to put in the crates for maximum gain in today's market. Her plan was to gradually sell off some of the lesser items but then to create a museum to display the rest. Despite outward appearances, Edith was in fact extremely wealthy, courtesy mainly of Frederick's exploits. She had just played her wealth down so as not to cause too much attention to where it had come from.

Edith knew some of the items Frederick had purchased and placed in crates for his descendants, had now become priceless. Matthew told Dena that some of the discussions he had with Edith and Frederick, made it clear that what Frederick was really trying to do was to secure a fortune that he himself could use to live in the modern world. Neither Edith nor Matthew ever knew how Frederick had managed to make himself travel through time and even exist in modern time rather than just as an apparition. Dena suspected and she thought Edith had too by the fact that she had taken steps to limit his movement in the modern world. Fredrick had crated up a huge fortune in collectable antiques courtesy of the addition of time and the fact they were all in mint condition. Unlike his other activities it was all legitimate, paid for in prices of the time.

Dena finally confided in Matthew that she thought Frederick was using the souls of people as some sort of battery. One that would allow him to move through time and that she suspected that younger children in particular gave him greater energy. This would account for him wanting young male children – to use up their, very being for his own fiendish means. She also thought items like the decorative box found in Marge's attic could allow him to travel to those due to spells written on them.

There was of course another theory that Dena had kept to herself until now. Dena told Matthew that Frederick may be a devil worshipper and may have done some sort of deal with a demonic entity to exchange souls for the power to exist and travel through multiple times. This shouldn't be too much of a shock as he had demonstrated he was using murder as a means to rid himself of the evidence of taking souls from the convicted and the discarded of his time. He could get away with it easily due to his power and influence and the fact that the poorest in society, of the time, were seen as dispensable. No doubt some of his peers might even say he was performing a service by removing them from the streets.

Up until this point, Matthew had no idea Frederick was a murderous figure. Edith had only told Matthew part of the story one she was prepared to admit to. It was mainly about the crates of antiquities. He hadn't seen the original founding document for the group for which he was the current Grand Master. He had seen a much more sanitised and modern version and saw it as a mutual aid group for its members. He was happy to be associated with that and to help develop younger people in their professions. Dena's story had come as a revelation to him and he realised the damage that could be done if this knowledge were ever to get into the press.

Matthew agreed to help Dena in any way he could and he instructed Stefan to do the same. Dena wanted Matthew to see the tunnels and in particular the anti-room so he could see the symbols and spells, but also experience the feelings of despair and hopelessness and fingers crossed some of the apparitions that still lingered down there. Stefan wanted to throw the weight of their organisation against the problem but Matthew knew that potentially this could have dire consequences if too many people were involved. He wanted only the most senior of the inner group to know, the most trusted and powerful members. They would need a mystic, someone who knew about spells and runic symbols. This is old world majick that very few people understand but Matthew knew he could contact the perfect individual for the task. He told Dena he had someone in mind who could help and, in the meantime, he would join her in documenting some of the inscriptions.

Chapter 15

David was a scholar of ancient texts, ones that most people had never even heard of. He had devoted his life to collecting books, manuscripts and writings on every conceivable writing surface. He had metal scrolls, vellum documents written in the blood of the author and huge decorated volumes from many different religions and languages. David had gathered together a considerable library on the occult and dark majicks, he would insist, if questioned on the subject, that majick was only called dark because of the way it was used or as he would say misused. So long as it was for the right purpose he saw no problem with it, especially as the majority of people wouldn't believe in such outrageous beliefs. He had been quietly using his knowledge and skills to help with exorcisms and cleansing of evil spirits for many years. He had written many books on the more commercial aspect of old religions like Wicca and theories about ancient sites such as stone henge. This had provided him with the finance to pursue his true passion.

David had known Matthew for many years as they had gone to university together, although not in the same subjects. They had become good friends around the debating chamber, putting the world to rights and opposing many who would be quite happy to see the working class as something to be despised and used without a thought. They were a formidable team to come up against as they thoroughly researched their arguments and truly believed in the rights and abilities of the ordinary working person to join forces against the bosses through the organisation of such things as trade unions and other such collectives. It was this that had both attracted them at first to the Masons but then to go much further and to form a core group of their own to nurture talents in other people that were brought to their attention. As the group's net worth increased over time, so they pledged to provide funds to help others. They didn't care if someone had no money, so long as they demonstrated raw talent that could be developed and allowed to blossom. They in turn would be encouraged to add to the same funds that had helped them.

Several decades had passed and this core group had expanded considerably and the funds available to help others were also considerable and had been invested wisely over the years. The group had become quite geographically spread but still came together when needed. Matthew and David had jointly managed the group for several years but then Matthew had become the head of the group at the behest of David as he wanted to concentrate more on his research and Matthew had more enthusiasm to grow the membership. It's with this background that Matthew contacted David to ask for his assistance with the situation of Frederick. He didn't give too many details over the phone as he wanted to leave plenty of intrigue which would interest David. Matthew knew if he asked for help, David would be all too pleased to respond but he also knew that a little tempting intrigue wouldn't do any harm either. Who knows he might even be able to turn it into an idea for one of his more commercially successful books, he could even call it, 'Noises from the Attic.'

David arrived at the museum on a bright sunny but cool autumn day. The trees were turning their beautiful hues and he was in no rush to enter the building as he found the garden much more interesting. Horticulture was one of his hobbies and he loved Japanese Maples. There were several around the grounds and he would have been more than happy to hold a meeting outside and maybe even do some wild foraging amongst the extended grounds. Matthew, however, was expecting him and so he reluctantly entered the open front door. David was very punctual and hated being late for anything. As he entered and introduced himself to security, he was ushered in to the staff kitchen area so he could help himself to hot drinks and even cakes and hot sandwiches now. Janet had decided that the staff were constantly being stressed by the environment they worked in and the museum certainly had plenty of funds now, so she had taken the decision to have the visitor centre, at least for now, as a staff canteen with food and drink free of charge as a thank you and perk for staff and visitors. David plumped for a tea and a chocolate chip cookie.

Matthew, Janet and Dena entered shortly after. They let David enjoy his refreshments after his journey and they passed the time of day about the season and then a little background of the museum. This of course, added to his intrigue which is exactly what they wanted. Janet politely excused herself as she thought she might get in the way of their discussions and she wanted them to be able to discuss the whole situation without feeling the need to be careful of her thoughts or beliefs.

Matthew appraised David of the situation at least as far as the spells and symbols were concerned. There would be time later to give the full story and when nobody else was around to hear it. He also introduced Dena and said she had been working on paranormal activity around the site for a considerable time. David had brought several books with him to use as reference material, books that no library would be able to stock. They decided Edith's study would be a good place to reconvene while David went to his car to retrieve some of the books.

Once they were all in the study, they could talk freely without causing alarm to anyone else. There was also the chance of some spiritual activity that David would be able to experience first-hand. Dena had copied some of the symbols she had seen repeat themselves on the walls of the tunnels and in the anti-room. She showed them to David who reached for one of his books. He was very familiar with what was inside but even he had to refer to contents and particular likely chapters. He did some thumbing of the pages and then opened the book on a nearby table for them all to see. He compared the images with those from Dena and pointed out some similarities. There appeared to be a mixture of spells, runes and symbols from different times. David offered that maybe the people inscribing these had been developing their craft as time went on and so they added parts to existing carvings to make them stronger or more relevant.

David pointed to parts of the explanatory text in the book which said this group of symbols were associated with souls and some kind of demonic worship. A specific demon's name was mentioned – Lilith, who is an ancient and very powerful demon. Dena said she had heard of Lilith and the thought of her possible involvement terrified her. David agreed and said they should all be terrified if these symbols couldn't be countered. He reassured the two of them that there are possible ways to remove such symbolism but it wasn't just as simple as chipping out the engravings – they would simply reappear if they had been inscribed correctly. This was one of the misconceptions some people had, simply remove the spells by destroying the stonework, however, this was powerful majick that couldn't be removed so easily. The runes wouldn't be too much of an issue as they could be countered quite readily once you know what they are meant to do. Equally the symbols, most of the time these were either just name representations or something to scare the unwary into submission. This fitted perfectly with the anti-chamber which, was covered in them and the main aim seemed to be to intimidate the people entering.

It was the spells that would take more time and research to remove or counter. Some of these could be bound by some horrendous behaviour such as human sacrifice. This came as no surprise to Dena as she further clarified some of her experiences and visions, she had about what had gone on in the tunnel network and at the docks. David was particularly interested in the time Dena had found herself watching what was going on in the warehouse and being chased by Frederick. He was intrigued how Frederick was able to move through time and interact with people and objects. He was also keen to see the spells, presumably Edith, had used to restrict his movements.

David wondered if Edith had been a white witch or if she in turn had been more of a malevolent presence in her own right. After all, anyone who could get the better of Frederick couldn't be an enthusiastic amateur. David said they should be careful of her too as she could have left some traps behind her. She knew she was restricting Frederick so wouldn't she then try and stop anyone doing the same to her. Matthew announced with great satisfaction, this is why we wanted you here so you would think of things like this. David explained it was possible to have spells that aren't visible in normal light and would need either black light or even another spell to show them.

Edith might have even left invisible spells that are triggered if a spell is used to make them visible. In which case David would have to use some of the oldest and most obscure spells that even the practitioners like her would not have heard of or had access to. Thankfully David had brought some of the oldest texts in existence full of ancient spells and counter spells. They would need some very specialist ingredients and be fully prepared before they tried moving forward. Now the lights in the study started flickering and David said the spirits had been listening. Dena agreed and said they needed to be careful where they spoke of their intentions. She said she could feel a presence in the room as the curtains starting moving and the table was pushed over.

Dena assumed it was going to be Frederick as he seemed to like causing chaos in this room, but David wasn't so sure. He was more open minded having not had any supernatural experiences on the estate and he was thinking more widely about the family and the purpose of what they had left behind. He was expecting Edith as the temperature in her old study plummeted and the lights completely failed. There was a silence in the room, the three looked at each other and David signalled for them all to just stay quiet and wait for what was going to happen. David had them all join hands in a circle around a small table. They were all looking around the room expectantly, no more disturbance happened. The temperature had dropped so much they could see their breath in front of them. David whispered for them to stay quiet and to maintain the circle no matter what. At that moment there was a horrific, bone chilling scream that echoed around the room. They all jumped and could feel their hearts thumping. David held their hands tighter to reassure and to protect them.

Another scream from beyond the grave pierced their ears followed by the manifestation of a dark figure in one corner of the study. They all turned to look as it rushed forward towards them. They held their ground and instinctively closed their eyes for a second. When they opened them there was a menacing figure close to them, still manifesting out of a black form. David reached into his jacket pocket still maintaining the circle. He placed an object in the centre of the table and the entity backed away. David began reciting Latin and the spirit backed off even further. David broke the circle, picked up the object and pointed it at the dark figure. He continued to speak Latin, slowly and at a normal voice level. The entity began to flicker as if it was some sort of projection that was losing power. David got out of his chair and moved towards the apparition. He thrust out the object so it was at arms-length and slowly moved forward until he was directly in front of the figure. Another blood curdling scream rang out at huge volume but then the entity disappeared.

Matthew and Dena were both transfixed on David and what he had in his hand. For a second or two there was absolute silence and then they both wanted to know what he was holding and what was the entity. David smiled and said the object was a sacred holy relic he had been given for protection and that it was bound with ancient and very powerful majicks. He had come prepared for the worst type of paranormal encounter as it wasn't every day Matthew asked for his help in this way. David said that the spirit hadn't been able to fully manifest itself but it was a woman and he felt it was Edith, the former owner of the house. She had heard them talking in her old study and hadn't liked what she heard and was trying to scare them away.

David explained this was just the first encounter they could expect from her and that she was merely testing their resolve to be there. She was a powerful entity which was just confirming what David had thought, that if she could restrict Frederick's movements, that she would know a lot about ancient powers and spells. He warned them they would have to be careful from now on if they wanted to combat what she was doing. Matthew and Dena both expressed their gratitude for their protection and for the way David had handled the situation. In true form he was modest but appreciated their thanks and said that's what he had come to do – to make sure they and everyone else, for that matter, remained safe.

They would have to come up with a plan not only to counter Edith but also Frederick and then try and put the rest of the spirits to peace. This would be no small task, especially as they suspected Edith of leaving traps behind for them. They went to find Janet to inform her what had happened and she told them she had been in the library briefly, which was underneath the study. She told them several books had come off the shelves and were circling in mid-air and at that point she had left the library and guessed it was something to do with what was happening in the study. She had made sure none of the staff were nearby so they wouldn't experience what was happening.

David said they should take a walk in the garden but said it in such a way that there was no argument. They all went outside and he led them to a beautiful Sugar Maple that had leaves of scarlet thanks to the autumn colour. This was well away from any buildings and he explained to them that he felt it was important to be away from any structures associated with the hauntings. He told them that spirits as powerful as these often used, physical structures such as the house or tunnels to act as a conduit for them to move around. He said it was much more difficult for them to freely move around outside say in the garden as there was nothing for them to latch on to. David continued that due to this, it would be a good idea for them to discuss their plans outside or in places not associated with the estate and only in ones where he could place some protective warding to keep it secure and private. The Masonic Hall, for example, would be ideal as he could place protective spells around the perimeter. It would also help that Matthew could come and go as he pleased in there.

The obvious thing to do would be to force Edith to pass over to rest so that she couldn't affect anyone again. However, David explained this could backfire as she was the one restricting Frederick. For all they knew if Edith's presence was no longer there, then Frederick could be released to act in the very same way he was doing before Edith controlled his movements. The preferred option was to do to Edith what she had done to Fredrick and so maintain control of both powerful entities at the same time. It would be like keeping the gene in the bottle. They would just have to be very careful about what bottle they chose and how they kept it safe from prying eyes. David said he should be able to get his hands on a suitable containment vessel that had strong enough warding to keep both Edith and Frederick contained within.

Janet said she was very happy for them to proceed as they saw fit and that she was very grateful for all their help. She said she would just like regular updates as to how things were progressing but other than that they could come and go as they pleased and use whatever resources they needed. She made sure they each had executive security badges which meant no one would question what they were doing and that everyone would follow their instructions.

David asked for a small team of builders be sent to the Masonic Hall the next morning. He told Matthew that he wanted to get the warding up as a priority and that it would need some additions to the building. Matthew would just say it was some additional ornamentation being placed around the building if anyone asked. He offered to show Dena the inside and some of the historical texts while David would be instructing the building team. They all reconvened the next morning at the Hall. David had prepared some drawings he wanted the builders to replicate in stonework and add to the roof corners of the building. He added some ornamentation to disguise the true intent and the builders readily agreed and began forming the work in stone and preparing the building for the additions. They would carefully remove a little of the brickwork and replace the gap with the worked stone artefacts. In effect they would look similar to modern gargoyles and appear to add some character to the building. Once they were in place, the warding protection would be complete and the inside would be off limits to any supernatural entity.

The builders worked quickly and had planned to complete the job within a week. This gave David time to procure a suitable containment vessel and Dena and Matthew some more research and planning time. The vessel Matthew needed to use had to be older than Frederick and had to be some sort of sacred relic so as to be strong enough to take the spells he planned to use. The physical size wasn't important as it was to contain spirit entity not physical bodies. Such items weren't easy to come across but he was a collector not just of ancient texts but also of religious artefacts. He knew he would be able to use something from his collection. He would also have to be careful where it was placed longer term, away from anyone else's access.

David spent some time adding ancient majicks to the object. He was turning it into an impenetrable containment vessel that, if all worked well, he could transfer both Edith's and Frederick's essence into. Matthew also wanted to attend an online auction of a small privately owned specialist library. There were some books coming up for sale that he had wanted for a long time and they would be valuable to a collector in more ways than one. These were ancient texts, so called majick books and runic volumes that only a museum or one or two collectors would even know about. They may prove to be invaluable with his latest investigation which meant he was even more keen to secure them. He told Matthew about them in case they were going to be expensive and needed his financial help to pay for them.

When they both went on the telephone for the auction, they were mystified to find out some of the books were no longer listed and they were the very ones David wanted. They waited until the end of the auction and then asked the auctioneer what had happened to the other books. He told them that another collector had approached the seller's estate and paid a lot of money to have them withdrawn from the auction and paid an undisclosed amount to his descendants. The auction house was disappointed but had also been paid a compensatory fee for their inconvenience and loss of commission. As far as they were concerned that was an end to the matter and they couldn't furnish any contact details as that was part of the transaction – for it to be confidential. David was perplexed, nothing like this had ever happened at an auction before. Was it a museum that particularly wanted this collection? If it was a library maybe he could get access to the books but how would he find out which one? This was quite troubling and meant he couldn't use them to help Matthew, this was a blow he wasn't expecting. He would have to make the best use of the resources he already had. David desperately wanted to know who the purchaser had been, maybe with Matthew's help he could buy them, giving them a profit as an incentive. He had no idea how he could find out so he asked Stefan if he could find out. This is what Stefan was good at, digging into stories to find out facts.

Stefan had plenty of contacts he could ask to help and he always had traditional methods he could fall back on like buying the information from a member of staff at the auction house. The staff would be discouraged from divulging such information but weren't paid a great deal so, providing the price was right, most would be prepared to drop hints in the right direction. Stefan went straight to the source as time was a factor. He visited the auctioneer's shop and waited for one of the younger members of staff to appear. He enquired if they were familiar with the recent book sale and the member of staff proudly said that he was and that it had all happened very quickly as a serious collector wanted them and was prepared to pay a premium. Stefan asked for details of the individual but then the staff member sited confidentiality and smiled. Stefan bluntly said that if a suitable file was left unattended on a desk that provided the correct information, that when the staff member returned there would be a four-figure sum in cash in an envelope added to the file, for the same staff member to do with what he wanted.

The member of staff looked shocked at first and was about to be indignant but then thought of the cash envelope. He gestured two with his fingers to Stefan who nodded and tapped his inside coat pocket. The member of staff went to a filing cabinet and took out a file, opened it at a certain point and placed it on a small desk out of the way. He looked towards Stefan and walked away. Stefan quickly went to the file to see what was there. The file had a bill of sale listed as consultancy fees received and paid by an individual. That was all he needed and he took an envelope out of his pocket and placed it in the file and closed it. He looked briefly in the direction of the young man and said goodbye as he left the shop. The assistant went to the file and took out the envelope, carefully placing it in his pocket. He returned the file to its cabinet. When he had chance, he checked how much money had been left. To his surprise there was £3,000.

Stefan was prepared to pay the figure and just because the young man had agreed a lower amount, he had left the full payment with a little note saying not to mention this to anyone. It would be more than the assistant's job was worth so he wasn't about to say anything about it. Stefan in the meantime had a valuable insight now to the purchaser of these books David was so keen to get his hands on.

David wanted to meet with me as I was the only one who had been snatched by Frederick and had moved through time with him. He asked that I dress in clothes that I had similar to those I had on that day in the attic. He promised he would keep me safe and I went with Dena to the museum gardens to meet him. David asked me a lot about that day, both in the attic, and at the warehouse tunnel. Once I had finished giving every detail I could remember, David asked if I had noticed anything about my clothing. I said that I hadn't so he asked my permission to point something out. He reached over to my jeans to a tab that was inserted by the manufacturer. I hadn't noticed it before and when we looked it had a triangle with an eye inside embossed in the design. David asked if he could look at the label inside my tee-shirt and he smiled. There was the same design. When I had originally chosen them, I was fairly certain that motif wasn't present. Frederick had not only patented and licensed a clothing-line, he had insisted his label be added to the garments. As he had done this in his own time, he had effectively altered events going forward and so my clothes now had his label on them. This was quite tricky for me to get my head around. Dena said she had noticed when she looked at my clothes that were in the crate, they also had the same motif in the label but she thought nothing of it at the time. This could really play with your mind.

I had worn clothes and been snatched, he had taken them and created his own clothes range, technically before they had existed. When I had got back my similar clothes had now been manufactured after his time and so had the label. This could develop a circular argument or as David put it a paradox. Even more so when you looked at the clothing I was wearing on that day. Before I was snatched there was no label. Once I returned there was! I now didn't like the idea of wearing clothes that had Frederick's emblem on them but there wasn't a lot I could do. Both Dena and David recognised my discomfort and said they would happily buy me some new clothes for my co-operation. That made me feel a lot better as I didn't want anything I was wearing to be associated with him.

Chapter 16

David had been thinking about the problem of the books he had missed out on buying. He spoke with Dena and confirmed the thought that it was Edith who had managed to control the movements of Frederick. If that was the case then there must be old texts, presumably in the library, that she used as a source of the spells etc.. Nobody had thought about this before and if they could be used to control Frederick then they should be just as good at controlling her. The only trouble would be that Edith might have planned for that which is why David wanted to tread carefully so as not to make things worse.

If you knew what you were doing it was relatively straight forward to show any hidden runes or inscriptions but this could cause a chain reaction to complete other spells left behind for the unwary. So, the question was, how to proceed? David thought the most obvious route to take would be to try and deal with Frederick first. He was the one who seemed to be able to travel through time and materialise at any one of the buildings and tunnels.

Dena suggested that David speak to Marge as some items from the current museum had turned up in her attic. Maybe there was something else that hadn't been considered important at the time. David thought it was a long shot but had nothing to lose so asked to be introduced. Dena said she would arrange a meeting as soon as she could. She knew my mum was still very interested in what was going on at the museum and was keen to help if she could. Dena contacted my mum and arranged a meeting with David for the next day. They had arranged to meet at my mum's house rather than the museum as they felt that would be safer with less people to over hear them.

David told Marge what he was looking for and what had happened at the auction. This jogged a memory for mum. She remembered being offered some old books by the retiring antiques shop owner, Eileen. David was intrigued, if "old house" was Edith's, these books could be very interesting. Why would Edith want to give old books as a thank you to her staff? They seemed an odd gift unless they were something special, maybe worth a lot of money. He thought they maybe first editions of some important books which would mean they could be very valuable. David asked Marge if she was able to introduce him to Eileen so he could see what the books were. She readily agreed and said she would meet outside the shop the next morning. Dena offered to come along and David liked the idea of that so she could get a feel for anything happening in the shop from a spiritual point of view. All three agreed to be there for 9.00 hoping that Eileen would still be inside even if she hadn't planned on opening the shop.

When they arrived at the shop the next morning, there was a notice on the door saying the owner was only opening the shop now to appointments and there was a telephone number to ring. Marge rang the number from a telephone box and Eileen answered. At first, she was a little concerned that Marge was still having difficulties in the house but when Marge said that was now under control, Eileen became more talkative. Marge asked if she would open up the shop so the three of them could look at the old books they had once discussed. Eileen chuckled and said she was actually in the basement of the shop right now and that she would be happy to get rid of them if someone was interested. With that she put down the phone and slowly came up the stairs to the door of the shop and let the three visitors inside.

It still looked like a functioning shop with lots of items for sale. Eileen explained she was ideally looking for someone to take it on as a going concern and buy the stock so they could take over the business and be ready to trade from day one. My mum wondered if it was worth putting in a bid as the family had money to invest from the museum buying items from the attic. Eileen said she would let it go cheap, if Marge was serious. That gave her something to think about. It could provide an income and something all of the family could help with. Eileen even offered to be a sleeping partner and share in the profits in return for Marge running the place. This would help Eileen retire with an income and be less cost to buy. This was sounding like it could be a good deal and mum was thinking about it very seriously.

David asked if they could see the books that had been discussed and Eileen took them to the basement where she had moved them to in anticipation. When David looked at them, he recognised them as very special, very old in fact ancient texts. There weren't many copies of these in existence. When he asked where they had come from Eileen reiterated the tale she had shared on the telephone. He rephrased his question and wanted to know who the ultimate giver of the books was. At first Eileen made out as if she didn't know but David was having none of it. No way would she buy these for the shop unless she knew the provenance of the books. Reluctantly she admitted they had come from Edith as had the other things that had appeared in Marge's loft and some still in the shop. David had suspected this was the case but now he knew for sure. These were, the books Edith must have used for reference for the various spells and runes to restrict Frederick.

Why then had Edith wanted to give them away? Especially when she must have known they were valuable. The only thing that seemed to make any sense was if Edith wanted to get rid of the books by selling them on at a cheap price so they would be lost as a collection and couldn't possibly be used against her at some point in the future. Books like these can't just be put on the bonfire as there would be consequences for anyone trying to destroy them. Ancient texts like these have built in protections which is why they had survived down the ages. David had also heard about the symbols in Marge's attic and asked Eileen why they were there, after all it was Eileen's home first and he wanted to know if she had placed them there then for what reason? Eileen became very sheepish when she was asked about the symbols in the attic but both Marge and David saw an opportunity to put pressure on Eileen to tell them the full story. They said if Eileen wanted a deal on the shop, then everything better be out in the open.

Eileen relented and said she would tell them everything she knew. She said she had just been used by Fredrick and Edith. She had seen Frederick in the attic of the house when she lived there. When Eileen had spoken to Edith about it, she had told her to write certain symbols on the structure of the roof and this would prevent him from having free movement and would restrict him to the attic or anywhere else the objects were kept. That was the real reason she had left the objects behind she didn't want to have to deal with Frederick once she moved out of the house and she had hoped that Frederick wouldn't bother the new owners. That of course was very naive as he considered those items to be his property and part of the original estate of which he still considered himself to be in charge of.

Edith of course had made sure that wasn't the case and was doing her best to weaken Frederick's influence and to try and stop anyone doing the same to her. Edith had told Eileen to put the various items she had given her, in the antiques shop and sell them at a good price to get rid of them. Once Eileen had realised that Frederick was somehow attached to them, she had thought twice about selling them but when she sold the house, she had neglected to do anything about them and the rest they both knew. Marge wasn't pleased to hear this, especially after what had happened. Eileen apologised and said she never meant any harm to come to anyone.

David was prepared to pay a lot of money for the other books at the auction and maybe ask Matthew to part fund them. That being the case it would make sense to do the same with these and maybe more so, as these had proved their worth in practical terms. David wanted a private conversation with Marge and the two went back upstairs into the shop. He asked Marge if she was serious about the shop and if so, he might be able to help. David said he was prepared to offer Eileen a lot for money for the books and tie in a deal to get the shop for even less money than probably Eileen was thinking originally. Mum's face lit up at the prospect and said she loved the idea of running the shop. David liked the idea as they could get access to books through the trade using the auspices of the shop. Marge said she would do anything to help. David said that was enough for him and resolved to make a deal with Eileen. The two of them went back downstairs and David and Eileen went into negotiations about the value of the books and the shop together.

All three wanted this to work out and after some haggling, David had purchased the books and done a deal for the shop so that his name would be added as a minor partner. Eileen would keep a quarter interest in the shop and so have an income in retirement and Marge was going to be the proud owner of the rest of the business and able to open the shop the next day if she wanted. She was delighted and everyone considered they had got a good deal. They all shook hands and agreed to get it finalised with solicitors as soon as possible. Eileen said that because she felt so guilty about Frederick and the attic, she was happy for Marge not to have to wait until solicitors had finalised everything and that she could open and run the shop as soon as she wanted.

David phoned Matthew to tell him what had transpired and he too was thrilled at the prospect of the book purchase. He also asked the same question, why had Eileen dispersed some of her possessions like this? Not just any possessions but ones she knew were involved in controlling Frederick? For now, all they could do was speculate. It was becoming more like a jigsaw puzzle but they didn't have the full picture to guide them.

Eileen agreed to stay on for the next six months to help Marge gradually take over the business and to understand the suppliers. Marge was excited and couldn't wait to tell the family. She had already decided not to change anything in the shop including the name. That way existing customers would still visit and there would be no cost for changing things around. Eileen was delighted with that decision as she had owned and run the shop for many years and the thought of it continuing as it was made her feel very reassured. David could also now use a business card with the name of the shop on to legitimately have access to trade only sales.

Dena had been doing a lot of listening and thinking about the books and possessions Edith had given away. There was only one thing she could think of and the more she thought about the situation, it was the only thing that seemed to make any sense. She decided to let David in on her reasoning to see what he thought. If the books were the source of the inscriptions around the various buildings and tunnels, and they had proved to keep Frederick under some sort of control. Maybe Edith had dispersed them so that anyone like Dena or David coming along to try and achieve the same thing with her, would be unable to achieve that same control. This made perfect sense, she may have left spiritual traps behind, but without these critical texts, anyone wanting to prevent her from moving around, would ultimately fail as they wouldn't have the original texts to work from. If the books were given away, their true value would be lost. If they stayed in the library, they would be easy for any specialist to find and use against Edith. This was all sounding like a lot of premeditation from Edith and maybe she wasn't so innocent in the family goings on after all.

They decided they should update Janet on what they had been involved in but David suggested keeping the purchase of the books quiet for now. She could be told about everything else but for now at least, David wanted to have something up his sleeve. The others were a little puzzled but agreed as they were all trying to work together to rid the world of Frederick.

Once Janet was appraised of the situation, she asked what they could do without some old texts they could use to counter some of the spells. David said he would study the inscriptions and try and work out what they were doing and how they were working. From that he hoped to be able to go further and either capture Frederick properly, or even better have him move to the other side permanently. He knew that would be easier said than done as Frederick was clearly very powerful and possibly using demonic power to exist.

Janet said she would help in any way possible and was ready to do so if and when needed. The team thanked her and David set about trying to understand the carvings and inscriptions. Some would be easy to ignore as they were more about scaring the unwary than actually achieving anything.

Matthew was formulating a plan to try to reach out to Frederick as the current Grand Master and try and get him to curtail his activities. The main thing was to stop him taking souls. It was unlikely he was going to do this voluntarily as he would lose his immortality. If he wouldn't do it himself, how could he be forced? Matthew didn't like where his thoughts were taking him. Lilith had been mentioned in association with the power Frederick was wielding. This is one of the oldest and strongest demonic forces known. The thought of somehow trying to make a deal with an entity such as this, filled him with dread.

Demons are tricky things to try and make deals with as they will make sure loopholes exist in their bargain so they can get out of it or turn it back on the one trying to make the deal.

All they want is payment, usually in souls and they aren't too bothered as to whose souls they are.

Another possibility would be to send me back to try to bind Frederick to his own time. This would be risky for me but there would be no need for a deal with a demon. The ideal would be to turn Frederick's own majick back on himself. They had the right books to achieve it but again this would have to be done in his own time and it seemed I was the only one who might be able to pull it off as I had travelled with Frederick and was now familiar with that time frame. Matthew was wondering if I could be sent back to the same time that I was there before. Dena could help me by being there also in the same way she had before. This was starting to sound like a plan was forming.

Matthew approached Marge about the possibility of me returning to Fredrick's time. She was absolutely adamant that no way that was going to happen, it was far too dangerous. He asked if he could at least talk to me with her present and see what I thought of the idea. She really didn't like it but reluctantly agreed for the three of us to meet. He also wanted Dena to be there as she might be the deciding factor if this was going to happen.

The next I knew several of us were meeting in the basement of the antiques shop. I loved the place and it felt safe. The others thought it was away from the wrong people over hearing the conversation. Matthew put the proposal to me about going back to see Frederick in his own time. The very thought made me shiver and at first, I said no. Marge said that was it and that they should stop. Matthew asked for our indulgence and explained the situation and the possible alternatives. It sounded pretty grim the thought of Frederick constantly using souls to move around time and effectively to be immortal. Equally the thought of having to do a deal with one of the strongest demons to exist didn't seem like any option at all. Matthew was pleased with my reasoning and he could see I was coming around to the idea of helping. Mum could see what was happening and said no that she wouldn't allow it. I told her not to worry and what option did we have? She had the nice shop and good friends who had helped a lot and that we should do anything we could in return. I agreed even though at this point I had no real idea what I was supposed to be doing.

Matthew suggested using my original clothes that I went back in time with – they were still in the crate in the Chapel as they were going to be used in a séance. They could also use the Grand Master's ring that had been found in the hidden compartment box. I would have to do what I had before, when I returned home – concentrate on the destination. I could fix on the point I was in the tunnel with the others. I asked what Matthew was planning and he said he was thinking the best way of tackling Frederick was head on. The time I went back with him was ideal. If I was careful, I could get access to him and that would probably have the strongest effect. At least that was the theory. I said if I went back, they had to find me a way of helping the men and boys stuck underground when I left. That would need some additional thought but Matthew said he would work on it.

Matthew and David set to work on their preparations and I tried to get myself into the right state of mind for returning. I liked the idea of Dena being there, she was very supportive and she felt more of a grandmother figure to me these days. She promised to watch out for me and make sure I got back safely. They figured a good starting point for me would be the dockside near the warehouse. This seemed to have a lot of spiritual activity such as when Dena had been transported back. Dena would be where she started before, at the top floor of the warehouse. At first the others said they would give me support by the dock but I said no, it might draw Frederick to a place we didn't want. I said it should just be the two of us. David said he would make sure I had some strong protective amulets to wear just in case and he would make sure Dena had the same.

When all was ready, I made sure I was wearing all the same clothes I was wearing the day I got snatched by Frederick. The downside to this was that I wouldn't blend in so the idea was I got changed when I arrived, I took a sack with some ragged old clothes that should work better. They dropped Dena and me off, Matthew gave me the Grand Masters ring and David made sure we both had the amulets. I would love to say at this point, nothing was left to chance but the very nature of everything we were attempting to do was incredibly risky with lots of possible snags but it was the best anybody could do. I went up to the top floor in the warehouse to make sure Dena was settled. There were windows at that level so she would be able to make sure I was in position too.

I moved quickly to the side of the dock where the ships had been lined up. I looked to the top of the warehouse and waved to Dena. This was it, I took a deep breath and ran over everything in my mind. I took the ring out of my pocket and started to focus on where I wanted to be. Ideally that was back on board the ship in a quiet cabin. I concentrated on that thought and closed my mind to everything else. I pressed the centre of the ring hard. Nothing was happening, but I remembered it took a little time to work last time. I concentrated as hard as I could and kept the pressure on the ring. I began to feel everything go dark and any background noise began to disappear. Then it all changed, the noise was much higher, people shouting and lots of frantic activity. Thankfully it was muffled, I was back in the ship's cabin and was alone.

I quickly changed clothes and stowed the sack on a shelf hoping it wouldn't be noticed. I went to the hold so it wouldn't look too suspicious when I emerged on deck. There was a barrow stood doing nothing so I grabbed it and quickly went on deck, down the gang plank and towards the warehouse. I did my best to blend in, trying not to catch anyone's attention. Someone shouted in my direction and I looked up, one of the older men was beckoning me to help him with a crate. I tried to ignore him but he kept shouting and I knew that would draw attention to me so, I went over with the barrow. He grabbed it off me and started to load some small crates on to it. He told me to get it in the hold but when I tried to tip the barrow to move it, the load was too heavy. He looked at me and I put all my weight on the handles but it was still too heavy. He laughed and tipped it up and gestured for me to take it. I would have to be careful not to let it fall over. I wasn't used to this sort of work but that was fine as it made me look weak, just the sort of look I needed. I staggered to the ship but no way I could get it on board. Another boy saw me struggling at that point and just helped me push it up the plank. Then a burley guy took off the crates and told me to get more.

I was blending in well which was a relief. For now, I just needed to stay out of sight of Frederick. He must be around somewhere but I needed to get to the boys in the tunnel before I could do anything else. I quickly got back into the warehouse and avoided being called this time. As soon as I could I dodged behind the crates and made my way to the back of the warehouse. I waited for a minute to get my bearings then headed for the tunnel leading to the chamber where I hoped the unfortunate group of men and young boys would be. I couldn't hear any sounds coming from the tunnel so I decided to go for it. I ran as quietly as I could, it would be interesting to see when I had arrived. After what seemed a lot shorter distance this time, I came across the larger area and sure enough the people I had left previously were here. I saw one of the young lads I had spoken to and went to him. He smiled and I asked how long it was since I had left and he answered that it had only been a few minutes. I was relieved at that as hopefully nobody would be rushing to take them to wherever was next.

With that Dena arrived and I went over to her, she was a welcome sight. She brought with her one of the boxes of sovereigns. If we were going to free this group, they would need some money and the only valuable currency still readily available that we could use were the sovereigns. They would be worth a lot and that in itself would be an issue but we could worry about that later. She had taken a handful out so she could bribe one of the guards. We had rehearsed what was to happen next, and I called for everyone to listen. I told them Dena had the means to free them all but they had to follow exactly what she said. They all looked forlorn and beaten but we had to give them their hope back. I told them I had used the Grand Masters power and I showed them the ring. Some of them looked horrified at the sight of it, one of them said I had stolen it. I told them I had used it along with the symbols on the walls to summon Dena. She was in modern clothing and we hoped that would be enough along with the inscriptions to convince them we had occult powers.

She took over and said if people wanted to stay here and receive their fate that was up to them but if they wanted to be saved then they should follow what she said without question. I asked them what they had to lose and they started to come around. I had brought a sharp pen knife with me. Dena asked them if they wanted to be released and they all said yes. I took out my knife and started cutting the ropes they had been tied with. They were all grateful and Dena told them to keep calm and quiet, that was their first task. The fact they were now untied was enough to lift their spirits and listen carefully to what she was saying.

She asked them to swear a solemn oath to look after each other and to build a refuge with the money she was going to give them. A refuge specifically for unfortunates, who otherwise would end up in the workhouse. Those who couldn't support themselves and of any age, young or old. None of them answered, it was what we expected, they hadn't got a clue how they would be able to do that. She asked them to swear the oath and then she would provide the funds. They were very half hearted and so Dena put on her sternest face and slammed her hand on one of the runic inscriptions. It started to light up and that changed the dynamic, now they were hanging on her every word. David had given her a rune to use, in case it was needed, all it did was illuminate the inscription it was put up against for a short while.

Now she asked if they would swear the oath and they all said yes with much more enthusiasm. She told them along with the money, she would give them written instructions regarding the refuge and they promised to follow them. She told them she was going to persuade one of the guards to help them. Now she showed them the box of sovereigns but she made it look like she had made it appear by setting off some magician's smoke powder. Behind the flash she placed the box and then took out one of the coins. They couldn't believe their eyes this was a lot of money – a fortune in their time. She warned them that if they misused the money, she would come back for them but this time not in a nice way. She blessed them and they all crossed themselves, she was beginning to get a cult following. Hardly surprising really, a moment ago everyone here had no hope of anything good happening to them. Now they were told their lives would be changed forever in a very positive way.

Now the next part of the plan had to be achieved, ideally bribing the foreman from the warehouse. My job was to get his attention by going up to him and showing him one of the gold coins. Dena told everyone to stay put and that she would be back. We both went back to the warehouse and it was obvious to spot the foreman as he was doing most of the directing of the others. I went up to him when he was alone and said he should come to the back of the warehouse to look at a crate. He asked what was wrong and why wasn't I working but I just said I had found a problem and he should come and see. I showed him the coin briefly and ran, he shouted for me to come back but followed quickly as he knew the coin was worth a lot of money and he could soon take it off me. I managed to get to the back of the warehouse to where Dena was waiting, no one else would see or hear us as it was a long way back and lots of crates were in the way.

She held her hand up and recited an incantation and slapped her hand on the back wall. It was the same trick she used earlier, only this time she used a phrase that sounded impressive to someone who didn't have a clue. The wall lit up and the foreman didn't know what to do, he was in shock. He hadn't seen anything like it before. Dena asked if she had his attention, he nodded open mouthed. She put her hand in her pocket and brought out several of the gold coins. She told him she had a job for him to do and that he could have twice as many coins if he followed her orders. This was more money that he was likely to see in a lifetime. His eyes lit up and asked who he would have to kill to get paid, she told him no one but that there was some danger involved. She told him he had to get all of the men and boys in the tunnel out to the Chapel and above ground and then to a safe spot where they could stay for a few nights. First of all, he laughed and said no way would he go against the Grand Master. She reached into her other pocket and brought out more coins. His eyes were transfixed on the sovereigns. She said this was more than enough for him to get away and start a new life somewhere.

She asked him how she could trust him to do what she wanted. She told him to put his hand flat on the wall against one of the inscriptions. She slapped her hand on the same one and it lit up. She kept his in place by pressing on it and he was clearly scared. She asked if he swore an oath to follow her instructions, for which he was being well paid, and to harm no one. She said if he betrayed her that she would tell Frederick what he had done. He agreed and she gave him half the coins from her pockets. She said he could have the rest later. Dena nodded to me and I ran off to get the others ready. I told them to hide the coins and one of them took off their shirt to wrap up the box and disguise it. I told them not to mention the coins to the man who was coming. I said that he would help them but not to trust him and they all got my meaning.

Dena came into the chamber with the foreman and gave the other half of the coins she was carrying, one each to the strongest men and told them to pay the foreman when they were happy, he had got them to a safe place. She also gave one of the men her protective amulet and I gave mine to one of the boys. She said if the foreman gave them any trouble that they could use her powers by invoking the amulets. The foreman protested but she said that would ensure he wouldn't try anything. He nodded and said they should act, quickly, Dena agreed and reminded the men to follow the instructions in the note she had left. They all thanked her. We watched the foreman lead them off down one of the tunnels and then headed back to the warehouse.

Dena apologised that she had given away my protection but I said it was quick thinking and that all I wanted was for them to be safe. She smiled and said we would just have to be extra careful. She made me check I still had the ring and I showed her. She nodded and we looked for Frederick's work table. It was in the same place I had seen it before but I couldn't see the man himself. I instantly regretted that thought as he suddenly appeared from the back of one of the stacks of crates. He had wondered where the foreman had got to and started to look around. Instead of finding him he had found us. He instantly recognised both of us and smiled a wide grin. He grabbed the pair of us and demanded to know what we were doing in his warehouse. I wriggled and protested as I thought he would expect me to. Dena switched to plan B and told him to remove his filthy hands from her. She said she had a message from Edith. He instantly released his grip on both of us. I ran off but Frederick was more interested in what Dena had to say. He asked how she knew Edith and she replied that she knew a lot about what he had been doing and his plans and what Edith intended.

Fredrick told her she knew nothing else she wouldn't be here like this bluffing. She pressed her hand on the runes on the backwall and they lit up. He smiled and said, "Nice party trick." He wasn't as impressed as she hoped he would be. He snarled and reminded Dena he had been travelling through time using this power and that if she wasn't careful, she would end up just like the others he already had in the tunnel awaiting their fate. She threatened to ruin him by exposing what he was doing but Frederick just laughed and said others had tried but had mysteriously disappeared just like the convicts. She changed tack and asked how he felt that a female descendent was restricting his movements and controlling his actions. She could tell this hit a sore spot as he went quiet for a minute, clearly thinking. He said she had no right to get in the way of his plans and that he would find a way to break free of her.

While Frederick was still considering what Dena had said, she slapped her hand flat on his forehead and he was instantly transported back to the house. She knew it wouldn't keep him there but it would buy them some time. I had been watching from a distance and waved at her, she gave me a thumbs up and I went to Frederick's desk while things were quiet. I quickly looked in the drawer where I had found his ring before, there it was so I swapped it with the one I had and put his in my pocket. At that moment one of the barrowmen came up and shouted at me, wanting to know what I was doing. I said Frederick had told me to put some papers in his desk. I was beginning to learn any mention of his name soon made people change their approach. He told me to hurry up and that there was more work to be done. I looked towards Dena, who was hiding behind a crate and she smiled, I had done what I needed to and now all I had to do was to get back home. She could go back to the top of the warehouse and watch out for me and then go back herself.

I picked up a barrow and put one of the smaller crates that was waiting to be loaded and headed to the cargo hold. I wasn't about to hang around. I took my crate to the hold and unloaded and sneaked off into the ship heading for the captain's cabin. I knew where to find it now but I would still have to be careful so as not to come across any of the sailors. I got to the cabin and listened at the door, thankfully I couldn't hear anything so I tried the handle and it opened – nobody else was there. I just had to hope the sack with my clothes in was there and when I looked on the shelf, I breathed a sigh of relief as there was the sack. I changed as quickly as I could but now, I could hear voices and they were heading in my direction. This was the largest cabin but it still wasn't huge. I was starting to panic I could feel my heart thumping. I looked around and there were two doors I could see at a glance that led from this cabin. I tried one and it was locked. I tried the second and it opened. I just managed to close the door behind me as two sailors came into the cabin.

They were looking for Frederick or the foreman. I could hear them saying that they couldn't find either of them and how was they supposed to know what to do next? They found a bottle of brandy and some glasses and decided if nobody was around to give orders that they would have a good time. They didn't waste any time downing half a bottle of brandy each and I heard one say there was plenty more where that came from. He was heading to the part of the cabin I was in. He opened the door and looked around and grabbed another bottle from the shelf. He shouted to his mate that Frederick would never be any the wiser. He closed the door and I was just about ready to explode with terror. I had just in time managed to hide under a pile of clothes that was lying there. It was just as well he didn't want to sleep as this looked like it was Frederick's bunk. If he had jumped on top, he would have soon discovered me one second later. Thankfully the sailors were more interested in getting drunk.

If I wanted to be back in the same spot, I had arrived I would have to wait a while for the two of them to finish another bottle. They certainly got rowdy enough, I never knew two sailors could make so much noise. After a while the noise died down and the inevitable snoring started. This was my chance as these two would need to sleep the brandy off for a few hours. I quietly opened the door and went into the main part of the cabin. I wanted to be in the far corner where I had been twice before.

To my horror one of the sailors woke up and saw me. He was having difficulty with who I was and shouted for me to come over so he could see me better. I went over to where he was sat and he grabbed hold of my waist. He pulled me close to him and asked who I was. I just said I was with Frederick. He said that I must be as I was wearing posh clothes he hadn't seen before. He offered me some brandy and said he knew where there was another bottle. I said I didn't want any but he insisted. I made it look like I was sipping some and he was in no shape to be able to tell the difference. He pulled me onto his knee and then I got to smell his breath. I was nearly overpowered by a mix of bad breath and alcohol. He still had his hand on my waist and I could tell he was strong. His mate was still fast asleep.

He pulled at my jeans and said how fancy they looked. I poured him a full glass of brandy and encouraged him to drink it. He loosened his grip from my waist and his hand fell onto my lap. He was still awake but only just. I needed to play along for a little longer and hopefully he would be unconscious. I stood up and he asked where I was going, I told him not to worry just got to sleep and I eased him back into his seat. He pulled me back in tight towards him and told me not to go far. I said that I wouldn't and eased his hand off me. It fell away and he was asleep.

Now was my chance and I couldn't wait. I went to the corner, put the ring in my hand and pressed hard, nothing happened because I needed to concentrate on where I was going. I took some deep breaths, calmed down and focussed my mind's eye on the dockside that was in my time – the one with no ships and lots of history boards. I pressed hard on the ring and I could feel myself getting lighter. I concentrated as hard as I could but then I felt a hand on my shoulder. I nearly cried out I thought it was one of the sailors who had woken up again. I was all ready to fight him off when I heard a friendly voice welcome me back. I opened my eyes and it was Dena, she had been waiting for me. She asked why I smelled of cheap brandy and I laughed and told her not to ask. She smiled and gave me a hug. That was so reassuring and I gave her a big hug back.

Now all we had to do was wait for Frederick to rush back to the warehouse, where he would bound to go looking for his ring. That was the last part of plan as far as he was concerned. It didn't take long for him to return to the warehouse using a horse. He figured if we were around, we might be wanting his ring so as soon as he got back, he rushed into the warehouse and straight to his desk. He pulled out the drawer and there was the ring, he smiled. What we were doing was secondary so long as he still had his ring. He placed it on his finger admiringly but as he did so it started to glow a strange colour. This had never happened before and he tried removing it but the ring wouldn't budge. He sensed himself being pulled and the next he knew he was in Edith's study looking out, while two men were looking back at him. David and Matthew could now tell the plan we had hatched had worked. They were in the study looking at The Grand Master contained in an ancient mirror. When they looked at the mirror, instead of seeing their reflections, they saw Frederick who could equally see outside the mirror but only in the direction it was pointed. They knew this wouldn't be the end for Fredrick but it would fully control him for now and that's what they wanted.

Matthew had some news for Dena and me when we next met. His face was beaming at us which made us feel very good but we wondered what was causing it, surely it wasn't just Frederick's capture. He told us he wanted to take us for a meal and one that we would remember for a long time. We both smiled at that and we asked when. He said that there was no time like the present and that we could have a brunch where we were going. We were intrigued but liked what we were hearing. He drove us in the direction of the Masonic lodge so we figured he must be wanting to pick something up along the way. When we got close, he parked up and asked us to go with him. We thought maybe he wanted us to help carry something from the hall.

He walked us to the lodge and asked if we had noticed anything. We both looked at each other and shook our heads. This was the usual Hall, yes it had those additional carvings on and we wondered if we should mention something else, we started complimenting the stone carvings that had been added. Matthew started laughing loudly and we both just looked quizzical. He asked us to look past the Hall, where they had previously been a piece of spare ground. It was owned by the Hall but hadn't been developed. They had bought it to stop anyone putting a building they didn't like too close to the Hall.

This time we looked the land wasn't vacant, there was a sizeable building there and we both looked open mouthed. No way could this have been built so quickly unless it had been a temporary setup. Matthew was smiling at our reaction and he said that's where we would be having breakfast. We didn't utter a word, just followed him. There were some people outside looking in our direction and they started clapping. We both looked at him and asked what was going on. He just smiled and said we would find out. The closer we got the more people came out to clap. They were all smiling and cheering so we looked around to see who was behind us, this welcome couldn't be for us. When we got close to the front of the building Matthew told us to look up above the entrance. This was an impressive building with a stone and brick frontage. Inscribed in large letters in the top stonework was the words, 'Welcome this is a Refuge for Anybody who needs it'. Dena and me looked at each other in disbelief as we were ushered inside like some sort of VIP's. As we entered, we passed an inscription on the inside of the doorway. It read, 'This place is only possible thanks to the efforts of Dena and Steve'.

Dena and me were bursting with pride. Neither of us had seen the instructions that were on the note to the people they had given the sovereigns to. Matthew explained that part of it was to build a long-lasting refuge centre and for the founders to make sure funds were invested and maintenance kept up so that many more people could benefit from what had happened. Matthew had tipped off the people who were currently running the centre and they had arranged for lots of people to come and show their appreciation and to provide the best breakfast we ever had. Thankfully they didn't want us to make a speech just to enjoy the food and their welcome. I have never felt so at home in all my life as that moment and that was the idea. It wasn't just us that were made to feel like that but anyone who felt in need of the refuge. This was such an amazing positive to have come out of what Frederick had been doing and had helped transform the lives of everyone who had stepped across its threshold in need of support.

Chapter 17

Once Dena and me had recovered from our amazing thank you, we all got back together to consider what to do about Edith. So far, she hadn't demonstrated being too bad to us but we knew she had the power to limit Frederick. We had then to presume we would need to do something to stop her acting in a similar way. Especially when she realised, as she was bound to at some point, that he was no longer roaming around as he did. This might empower her to unleash what she had learned from the books. There was also the question of Lilith that mustn't be forgotten but things would have to be taken care of in a certain order and next would be, Edith.

Janet said that Edith's ghost had been seen roaming the museum and the Chapel and even in the tunnels as if she was looking for something. So far, she hadn't caused any problems but had scared a lot of people as she always seemed to appear semi-transparent when anyone saw her. This was thought to be due to the fact she didn't have as much energy to call on as Frederick had. Presumably she was looking for Frederick, but what would she do when she realised, he had effectively been captured? Janet said she had told the staff to report any sightings of Edith to her. Trying to do the same to Edith as they had managed with Frederick, wasn't going to be easy. She wasn't relying on the likes of a ring to move around. She wasn't travelling through time in the same way. Janet even raised the question did they need to control Edith or could they just leave her to roam as she wished if she was doing no harm? This was definitely a consideration and Matthew said it was one worth mulling over while David poured over the books, he now had access to that might shed some light on how best to deal with Edith if it became clear they needed to.

If they wanted to know about the deal with Lilith, there was only one person who would know for sure and that was Frederick. Now he was fixed to one place it would be easy to communicate with him but why should he co-operate? After all they had captured him and prevented him doing the very thing, he had been at great pains to achieve. Maybe there was a deal to be had but they would have to be very careful doing a deal with someone like him. What could they possibly offer him that might motivate his agreement? The one possibility might be to offer Frederick to live out his life in the modern day but to limit his movement and powers and to stop him taking any more souls.

David and Matthew thought it was worth a try and they would have to make a judgement call about Frederick later. The first thing was to know what the deal had been. So, they went to talk to Frederick who, understandably, was in no mood to co-operate. One of the alternatives was to encase the mirror he was captured in, with concrete or similar material which meant Frederick would spend the rest of his existence in perpetual darkness and with no stimulation which would be worse than being in solitary confinement. The thought of this made him very angry but he soon calmed down when the two of them threatened to carry out the action. Another was to do a deal with Lilith directly and have her take care of Frederick in a way that was guaranteed not to be pleasant. Frederick was getting the message that his options were limited and that maybe it was a good idea to listen to what they had to say.

The deal was for Frederick to live out his days on the estate, move around the tunnels, the Chapel and to even act as a guide to visitors of the museum if he wanted to, so long as his murderous activity ceased and he bring to an end the deal with Lilith. The latter part wouldn't be easy as she would expect him to live up to his side of the bargain. Frederick admitted that he had done a deal to capture willing souls and give them to Lilith in return for him being able to roam through time. He said that Edith had found out and managed to limit the places he could move to by binding him to certain objects or places. He had given Lilith hundreds of souls and there was only one thing she would take as payment if he was to be allowed to exist in the modern day. That would be his soul once he died. David reminded Frederick of the very awful alternatives that could be done to him. Frederick said he wanted more than just to exist on the estate. He wanted free movement to come and go as he pleased. Matthew started to shake his head at the thought. Frederick said that was the only way he was prepared to give up his soul in the afterlife, for a good life now.

Matthew asked Frederick how they could trust him not to carry on his despicable deeds? He volunteered they could place a tracking spell on him so they could see where he had been and tell if he had been involved in any unlawful activity. This, they thought, was a definite possibility. Apart from anything else they needed to know Lilith was out of the picture. They didn't want any demonic activity or involvement as the books they had access to were certainly not capable of matching anything she could do. This was starting to sound like both sides were coming to an agreement, knowing there was little alternative if they both wanted a positive and workable outcome.

Frederick also wanted Edith's spirit putting to rest. She had done no demonic deals, just used his old books to restrict his movements. He knew of spells in the books in the library that could be used to force her to pass over and be at peace. Matthew and David both thought this was a good idea. It would take a possible future problem out of the picture and wouldn't be needed if the deal could be made with Frederick.

The first thing to be done would be for Frederick to meet with Lilith and this would have to be in a suitable place. Frederick said the best place was the underground anti-room where the tunnels meet. This is where he had done the deal in the first place. The various inscriptions allowed for them to meet but gave a level of protection to him also. This would mean releasing him from the mirror and that was the most difficult thing to consider. Frederick said they could fill the anti-room with restrictive runes and spells so that he would effectively be captured in that spot instead of the mirror. The books David had, were certainly capable of that so long as it was done carefully. There was a complication David was aware of, there would only be one person who could remove the ring from Frederick and it was the one who had planted it in the first place, me!

They had come to an agreement almost by default, because of what they wanted. The main issue of course, was trust from David and Matthew. The prize, if this worked, was to rid the estate of Frederick's evil deeds. Remove the involvement of one of the strongest demons in existence and put Edith to rest so she couldn't follow her ancestor's dark path. This would need to be a very strong binding agreement on all parties. David suggested drafting a solemn written agreement with runic and blood bindings with built in consequences to anyone not fulfilling the agreement. Frederick was familiar with this sort of an agreement as he was the one who had drawn up the original founding document for the secret society.

It was agreed that David would do this and that he would also instruct masons to etch into the stone within the anti-room, restrictive runes and spells to act as a cage for any entity entering that place. This would mean the mirror could be taken down there prior to Frederick being released and he would be transported once I removed his ring. They also insisted they be present but at a distance when Frederick met with Lilith. They were also hoping Dena would agree to be there. Frederick didn't have much choice to agree.

All this was done with Janet's agreement also, she had asked to be kept informed of progress and she agreed this seemed like a positive plan going forward. Dena reluctantly agreed to be there to help give warning about any spirit entities present. As for me, needless to say, my mum wanted me to have nothing to do with it. I had travelled back once to trick Frederick into receiving the ring and now they wanted me to meet him face to face again to remove it. She hated the idea and I have to say, I wasn't exactly thrilled at the thought either. Both of us knew the present situation wasn't a permanent solution and this seemed to be one that would work. In the end mum left the decision to me. The thing that made it easy in the end was the thought of the refuge and what had been achieved with that. So, I added a condition of my own, much to everyone's amazement. I said that 10% of the value of all of the goods in the estate had to be transferred to the refuge to boost its financial security and to allow it to create new centres. Frederick agreed as did Janet. This would be a huge amount of money and help a lot of people find refuge. I thought this was very fitting as recompense for Frederick's actions. Matthew had a huge smile on his face when he heard my condition. He was a good man and knew that money would make a difference to people's lives – ones who needed it the most.

David studiously worked on the agreement, building in default clauses if it wasn't adhered to by the signatories. He attached runes and spells and built those into a huge wax seal attached to the document. The activation of the majick would be the addition of a drop of each parties' blood. This was to include me as I had become linked to Frederick by our various interactions. The others to sign would be David and Matthew, Dena and of course Frederick. We would all add our blood and then I had to take it to Frederick to do the same. If he refused, he would still be held in the anti-room. This was key to stop him backing out at last minute.

As each of us added our blood to the seal it glowed and lit up the piece of parchment. Thankfully it only needed one drop so a pin prick was all I needed to do. The next part wasn't so easy for me. I was to be sent into the mirror to meet with Frederick. The others would be able to see our interaction but wouldn't be able to do much if something went wrong. David did what he could and placed some warding on me as protection. Matthew gave me his ring and I concentrated on where Frederick was. David made an incantation and there was Frederick. I was in what looked like Edith's study in the house. There was a mirror on the wall and this is what the rest could look through to see us. It was quite surreal from my point of view. Frederick of course had got used to it and knew he could move around the substantial room but couldn't go any further.

Frederick greeted me like an old friend, something I knew was false and I had no intention of playing along. He asked why I wasn't wearing the clothes with the 'triangle' tag on them and I just looked at him without saying a word. He just laughed loudly. He said I had allowed him to make a lot of money from those clothes but also caused him a lot of heartache as it was my fault he was stuck in this virtual room. I didn't trust him one inch and I was on alert for whatever he might do. Of course, physically I wouldn't be able to do much if he decided to hurt me in some way but right now, he needed my help and I had that to focus on. I would have to get closer to him than I wanted as I had to remove the ring from his finger. He did seem to be making a bit of an effort to be nice but I figured that was because the others could witness what was going on.

I showed him I had the agreement and told him he needed to add a drop of his blood to the seal. He beckoned for me to remove the ring and as far as I was concerned, the sooner I did that the sooner it was over. I slowly approached him and he held out his arms as if he wanted to hug me. I told him to put his arms to his sides and just hold out his ring hand so I could do what was needed. He kept his arms close to his body but held out the one with the ring. I reached to remove the ring which sort of tingled at my touch. I slowly began to move it from side to side to free it from his finger. I pulled gently and it came away from him. At that moment he smiled and grabbed me, holding me close to his body. We were both transported to the anti-room to where the others were waiting. I struggled to get free but he was a strong man and had a firm grip of me. Matthew ordered Frederick to let me go. This was the first time the two Grand Masters had met and it wasn't going quite to plan. David reminded Frederick that he was now bound to this anti-room and there was nowhere else he could go so he might as well let me go.

I told them he hadn't added his blood to the seal. At that point Frederick became angry and I felt the most, strange sensation. It was a bit like when I had travelled back in time, it was very surreal and I felt very light as if I was floating somehow. I could still see everyone but now they looked shocked and Dena was holding her hands over her mouth in disbelief. Matthew ran forward and grabbed Frederick by his lapels and began hitting him hard. David ran towards me but it was now I could see what the strange feeling was. It was that out of body experience you can occasionally feel as if you are looking on at the scene from a few feet away. I could see I was falling to the ground and being picked up and held by David, just as Dena had got to me and was doing the same.

It began to dawn on me what had happened. Frederick hadn't liked the fact I had warned the others, he hadn't activated the seal with his blood. At that point in one movement, he had snapped my head back, breaking my neck and killing me instantly. He had released me when he saw Matthew running for him and I had collapsed on the floor only to be picked up, but very limp, first by David and then by Dena. I was now viewing the scene as a spirit. Thankfully I hadn't felt any pain, just a very strange sensation. I guessed what Matthew was trying to achieve, Frederick had been holding the agreement which was now on the floor. Matthew wanted to transfer some of Frederick's blood to the seal. It didn't have to be voluntary. Matthew was a strong fighter and it wasn't long before Frederick was regretting his actions. His blood was splattering on the stone wall. David saw what was happening and took the document. He took some of the fresh blood off the wall and placed it on the seal which glowed instantly. This was the sign it had been activated and Frederick knew it. He stopped putting up a fight and held up his hands to Matthew telling him to stop.

Matthew looked at Frederick, who now looked quite pathetic, and he launched a final punch to his face which knocked him unconscious. Matthew paused to make sure Frederick was out cold and then looked in my direction. He walked over to where Dena was holding me in her arms. He put his hand on my head and stroked my hair, tears were running down his face. We had been through quite a lot together in a relatively short time and Matthew had become like a second father to me. He of course felt he had let me down by not keeping me safe but it was always going to be a risk with someone like Frederick.

I wanted to let them all know that I could see them and wasn't upset with any of them but I couldn't think of a way to do so. Once they had taken a few minutes to gather their thoughts, they realised someone would have to tell Marge. That wasn't going to be easy and Matthew said he should be the one to do it. Dena said she would stay with me if Matthew went to deliver the bad news and David took care of the agreement and arrange for some workmen to take me to the Chapel so Marge didn't have to see me lying here. David also told Janet what had happened and she arranged for the Chapel to be cleared of workmen and for a room to be set aside for me to be laid in.

The worst of it for me was seeing my mum in floods of tears. I knew I had to find a way of showing myself to make it easier on the people who had been left behind.

Frederick had been left in the anti-room for now to think about his actions especially now his blood had sealed the agreement. Any further transgressions would lead to him in the hands of entities he would rather not contemplate.

Dena suggested a safer way to witness what Frederick would say to Lilith. She could visit the anti-room as she had the warehouse and Frederick before. Matthew and David thought this was an excellent idea as neither of them wanted to come face to face with one of the most powerful demons every to roam the earth.

The three of them went to talk to Frederick who tried to make an apology, but they all told him not to waste his breath. They told him to make the pact with Lilith at a certain time and they would witness what was being said through Dena using her out of body technique. He would have to swear to Lilith to stick by the agreement or be taken straight to purgatory where he would spend the rest of time. They all knew he wouldn't be able to double cross a demon and it would finally prevent him from causing further harm to anyone.

Under the circumstances the three of them thought the best place to be was the Masonic Hall, it had warding protection, they wouldn't be interrupted and they could look after Dena during her out of body time. Frederick had the incantations he had used before to summon Lilith, the tunnels and even the connected buildings had been cleared of everyone for safety. Dena explained to David and Matthew that it was very unlikely she would see Lilith as an entity. Frederick would summon her for the deal but usually you only knew the deal had been accepted because you had gained the ability you bargained for. She may show as something else but rarely in her bodily form.

All was set as the time got near, Dena settled down into a comfortable position, Matthew and David sat attentive but quietly close by. Dena relaxed and concentrated on the anti-room. She had been there many times before so it was easy to visualise. She started to hear Frederick; he had begun earlier than agreed but he was still making incantations so Dena wasn't too concerned. I was still in the Chapel and could sense what was going on. This was my chance to make myself known to Dena. If I was right, she would be able to see me while she was in this alternative plain. I concentrated on the anti-room and I guess I began to appear there in a similar way to what Dena was using. I could hear Frederick uttering strange words and he was concentrating so much he didn't notice me appear. To my delight, one person who did notice me was Dena. She had a wonderful smile on her face with tears running down her face and she outstretched her arms for me to have a huge hug. I rushed up to her and flung my arms around her. For a few moments we didn't say a word just hugged and snivelled.

I was so pleased Dena could see me, I could now tell her I was fine and asked her to tell my mum not to worry and I would find a way to make my presence known to more people. Dena said she might be able to help with that as might the books David had. She said we could both witness Frederick speaking to Lilith. It sounded like Frederick was getting to a crucial part of the summoning majick. The strings of lights in the anti-room began to flicker and the candle flames waved as if affected by air currents. Frederick made his pact; he swore to uphold what was written in the blood agreement if Lilith would grant him time to live in the present day. He offered his soul in payment after a long life or in payment sooner if he broke the deal. He asked for a sign this was acceptable and a sudden rush of air came through the room, blowing out the candles and the lights went out as if the power had been turned off. I couldn't make it out but something definitely materialised. It was very dark but Frederick reached and lit a candle. In that moment it looked like a huge winged female demon had appeared. It made Frederick fall to his knees in terror and the candle blew out. There was a pause with no sound then, in an instant, all the candles were lit and again I got a glimpse of something ancient, all powerful and dark. Moments later the lights came back on and Frederick stumbled to his feet. If the deal had been sealed, he would be able to leave the anti-room. He slowly walked over to Dena, presumably not able to see me. He handed her the agreement and tried walking to various tunnel entrances. He was no longer bound to the anti-room; the bargain had been made. Now he would want to see Janet and come to some financial arrangement.

Dena wanted me to return to the Masonic Hall with her so she could try and have me manifest so Matthew and David could see me. They couldn't at first but David managed to find a spell that showed up hidden entities and it worked with me. Now there were three people who could see me and they were very happy to be able to do so. As I got used to my new state, I found there was a way at least for a time to show myself to people. This made me feel so much better and was at least some sort of comfort for my mum. She of course had been devastated about what had happened to me but at the very least she could still interact with me.

Frederick made his deal with Janet, who was only too pleased to see the back of him. There was one final shock. Janet had been carrying out her own research ever since she had been made curator of the museum. She had followed it though the various buildings trusts and it turns out at the auction where it had been she, that bought the ancient books David had wanted. All the time she had been moving closer to proving something that she had only felt but hoped was true. Frederick, as part of his financial deal with her, had provided the piece of proof she needed. Janet was in fact a lost arm of the family and could now lay claim to the entire estate, all the buildings and artefacts contained within. She was in fact a distant relative of Edith.

Janet presented her findings to the trustees who had the proof verified legally. Once that was done, she disbanded the trustees and took over sole running of everything. She would make sure no scandal came out about the workhouse trap door or about Frederick or the ancestors by opening a very sanitised museum at the Chapel. The museum at the house was put on hold permanently.

She was now an extremely rich individual with all the power that brought and the worry for us was how she might use it. Afterall, she had kept this research quiet from everybody and that doesn't always bode well for the future. Especially as she refused to make Edith pass over peacefully. She said she liked her company; was that it or did she have something else in mind for their relationship?

Only time will tell.

www.ingramcontent.com/pod-product-compliance
Lightning Source LLC
LaVergne TN
LVHW012023060526
838201LV00061B/4432